BEYOND AFRAID…

It was an experiment ir.

Eight people, each chosen because they lived through a terrifying experience. Survivors. They don't scare easily. They know how to fight back.

BEYOND TRAPPED…

Each is paid a million dollars to spend one night in a house. The old Butler House, where those grisly murders occurred so many years ago. A house that is supposedly haunted.

BEYOND ENDURANCE…

They can take whatever they want with them. Religious items. Survival gear. Weapons. All they need to do is last the night.

But there is something evil in this house. Something very evil, and very real. And when the dying starts, it comes with horrifying violence and brutal finality.

There are scarier things than ghosts.

Things that torment you slowly and delight in your screams.

Things that won't let you get out alive.

HAUNTED HOUSE

People are just dying to leave.

Jack Kilborn, author of AFRAID, TRAPPED, AND ENDURANCE, brings back some favorite characters from those earlier novels and puts them through his own unique brand of hell. One that hurts real bad. One that will scare you to death.

Are you brave enough?

HAUNTED HOUSE

May 2013

HAUNTED HOUSE

A novel of terror

JACK KILBORN

Are you brave enough?

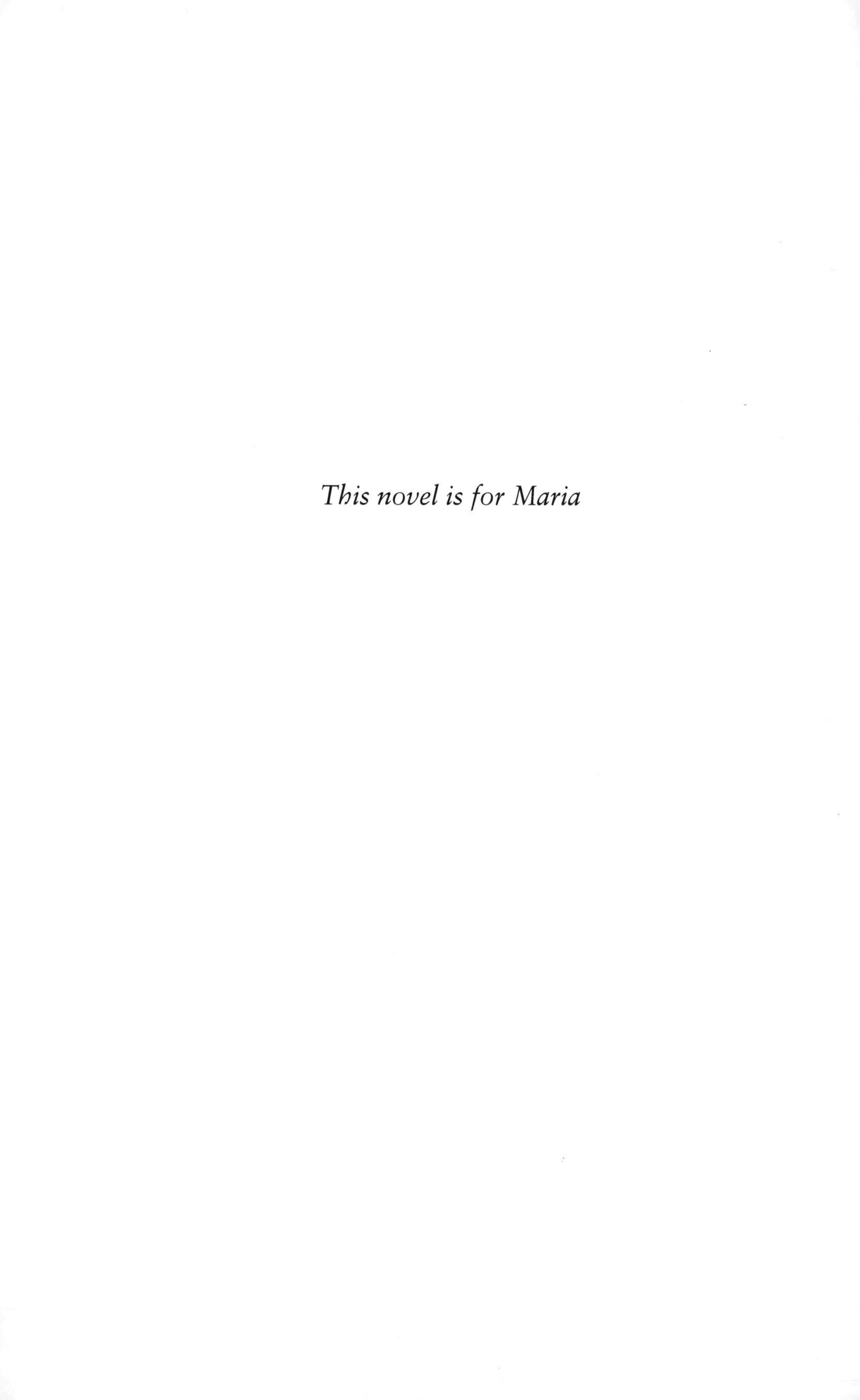

This novel is for Maria

HAUNTED HOUSE

Prologue

Roy Lewis cleared the doorway, then spun as something in the darkness lunged at him.

He fired, a double-tap at the approaching center mass, but it kept coming. Before he could flinch away the thing hit him in his outstretched Glock.

It took Roy milliseconds to process what it was, and then revulsion coursed through him.

A body bag.

Black plastic with a silver zipper. Hanging from a chain.

But something was wrong with it. The weight was… off.

Roy aimed his flashlight up at the ceiling, the tactical beam cutting through the ever-present dark of the house, and saw the rail system that had swung the bag into him. Pulleys and springs and a steel track, all automatic. Probably triggered by a motion sensor.

He reached out and gave the bag a tentative squeeze.

Foam rubber.

Not a real body. Just a goddamn Halloween prop.

Roy chewed his inner cheek, heart hammering, realizing he'd wasted two valuable bullets on a dime store scare.

Only one bullet left. Then he was out of ammo.

Roy checked his watch. Not even 4 A.M. yet. Hours to go before dawn. Might as well be days.

Breathe. Remember to breathe.

He took in air through his nostrils, tried to let it out slowly. His hands were shaking, and sweat was stinging his eyes despite the cool temperature. Roy holstered his sidearm, and drew his KA-BAR knife from his belt sheath, clutching it to his chest.

Okay, stay calm. Find a place to hole up. Someplace you can defend. Where they can't sneak up behind you.

A snort escaped his nose before Roy could stop it. All damn night he'd been searching for a safe place in this hell-on-earth. But there were no safe places. Every room, every corridor, in this damned house was lethal. Maybe, if the others were still alive, they could have protected each other. But that hadn't worked out, and Roy was pretty sure he was the only one left.

He thought back to his military days, before he became a cop. The Q course for Special Forces, the hardest training in the world. Desert Storm in Iraq. Then over a decade on the street, working his way up from beat cop to homicide detective. He was good, and his past had prepared him for a lot.

But not for this.

Nothing could have prepared him for this.

Roy sucked in another breath through clenched teeth. The air was musty, foul, like old running shoes mixed with…

Body odor.

Strong, noxious body odor that wasn't coming from Roy.

He flinched.

Roy knew that smell. Knew where it came from.

That's when he heard it.

Giggling.

High-pitched. Almost childlike.

But that's not a child.

"Oh, no," Roy whispered. "Not this again."

Roy waited, hoping, praying, it had been his imagination.

The darkness remained silent.

You're freaking out, man. Imagining shit. You need to keep it together if you want to—

"Hee hee hee hee."

Not imagination. This was real.

Real, and coming somewhere in the unlit room.

Somewhere close.

Roy stumbled backward, his bladder constricting, and then fell as his foot stepped into a hole in the floor.

He landed on his ass, strained to get his foot free, and the pain came hard and fast.

Sharp points. Stabbing through his pants, into the flesh of his calf.

A punji trap.

The hole contained spikes, pointed at a downward angle, trapping his foot there. The harder he tried to pull away, the deeper the spikes dug into his leg.

"Hee hee hee."

Roy swung his flashlight beam, locking onto the sound.

The giggling man who had been stalking Roy through the house for the last two hours was standing only a few meters away. Roy could see him clearly now, for the first time. He was tall, over six feet, wearing a black rubber gas mask that obscured his face. His chest was bare, covered in dried blood. All he wore was stained white underwear, and combat boots, their laces untied.

In the man's hand was a meat cleaver.

Roy reacted viscerally, immediately trying to scramble away, the spikes digging further into his calf. He cried out in pain, then stared at his stalker.

"Hee hee hee."

The Giggler didn't move closer. He simply stood there, swaying slowly from side to side. The BO coming off him coated Roy's tongue.

Roy pawed for his sidearm, drawing it and pointing the weapon at the man.

"Get the fuck away from me! I swear I'll kill you!"

The man stared.

"I said get away!"

He continued swaying. Staring.

"Hee hee hee."

Roy hadn't signed on for this. It was supposed to be simple. A way to get ahead, provide for his daughter. But the nightmare of the last few hours, the horrors he'd been through, was almost beyond comprehension.

"Someone help me!" he shouted to the house.

The house didn't answer. But the Giggler did.

"Hee hee."

Roy reached up, grabbed the sticky electrode on his temple, and tore it off out of defiance. Did the same with the one on his chest.

The giggling man watched, his expression hidden behind his gas mask.

"What the hell do you want?" Roy pleaded.

The man raised the cleaver—

—and placed it against his own chest.

What the hell is this guy going to...?

He drew the cleaver downward, splitting his skin open. The blood flowed, fast and red, soon drenching the man's soiled underwear.

"Hee hee hee."

Roy watched, slack-jawed, as the man continued to cut himself, making Xs on his abdomen. Over his nipples. Across his belly button. It wasn't long before his upper body looked like a dropped plate of spaghetti.

Pain be damned, Roy pulled his attention away from the freak and began to tug on his trapped leg, trying to free himself. His heart was beating so quickly it felt like it was going to break his ribs, and the man's giggling got louder the more he mutilated himself. But try as he might, Roy couldn't get his leg out of the hole.

Then the giggling stopped. Replaced by wheezing.

Fast, wet wheezing.

Not wanting to look, but unable to stop himself, Roy once again directed his flashlight at the man.

He'd stopped cutting. And instead, the giggling man had a hand inside his underwear, using the blood as a lubricant while he stroked himself.

Roy shook his head, like a dog after a walk in the rain.

No. Oh no no no no. This is not happening. This is NOT happening.

But it *was* happening. This wasn't some elaborate prank. Some gag where a TV crew was going to jump out and shake his hand for being a trooper. It wasn't a dream. It wasn't a hallucination.

He'd watched people die tonight. Die horribly. And he was going to be next.

Roy adjusted his flashlight, staring into the hole that refused to release him. He saw five metal rods, digging into his leg from various angles. With a trembling hand, he lowered the KA-BAR knife and tried to cut the first rod free.

The steel was too thick.

Roy took a breath and held it.

Then he gouged the knife into his leg, trying to pry out the bar.

Soon Roy's screams drowned out the moans coming from his stalker, but even after slicing his calf almost to the bone, the rod continued to hold him.

"Hee hee hee."

Roy looked up at the Giggler, who had moved several steps closer. He'd apparently finished playing with himself, and was now rubbing his hand across his chest, digging his finger into the cuts and following their lengths, over and over. Like a child finger painting.

Roy aimed the Glock at him, trying to steady his shaking hand.

One bullet. Make it count...

He squeezed the trigger, deadeye on the man's center mass—

Felt the gun kick—

Got him! I got him! I—

But the giggling man didn't even flinch. It was as if the bullet passed right through him.

Like he's a ghost.

He giggled again, "hee hee hee", and Roy giggled as well. He thought of all the other rounds he'd fired that night, sure he'd hit targets, and now finally understood what had happened.

Bullets can't kill ghosts.

He raised the KA-BAR like it was a crucifix warding off vampires.

"You want me! Come get me!"

But the giggling man—or whatever it was—just stood there. Watching.

"You gonna just stand there?"

"Hee hee hee hee hee."

"DO SOMETHING!"

It stopped swaying, and through the damper of its gas mask said, in a deep, wet voice,

"Iiiiiiiii wiiiilllll."

The throb in Roy's leg began to abide, replaced by a tingling numbness. His head began to cloud.

Blood loss? Exhaustion?

Roy closed his eyes. He knew if he passed out, things would only get worse. Being at the mercy of that *thing* was unthinkable, and there were others in the house even worse.

Roy closed his eyes.

He thought about his ex-wife. Their daughter. She only saw her daddy twice a month, due to his wife's overzealous lawyer.

Now she'd never see him again.

The image in Roy's head was fuzzy, growing fuzzier.

"I'm sorry," he told his child, his eyes brimming with tears.

Then the Giggler pounced.

FOUR DAYS LATER

Cleveland, Ohio

Mal

Mallory Dieter knew by his wife's breathing that she was also awake.

He thought about reaching for her, holding her close, but she didn't like being touched while trying to sleep. It startled her, even made her yell sometimes. At three in the morning, even a whisper from Mal could make Deb jump.

Mal understood this. Intimately.

Because he felt exactly the same way.

The bed was the best money could buy. The kind where each side could be adjusted for maximum comfort. No bed-frame, so nothing could hide under it. Expensive pillows, some with goose down, some with memory foam. Sheets with a 400 thread count. A ceiling fan that provided a gentle breeze, and calming white noise.

But all that wasn't nearly enough.

Mal shifted, slowly so he didn't scare her, letting Deb know they were both in the same boat.

"Need another Xanax?" Deb whispered. "I'll be up. I can watch you."

Often the only way either got to sleep was when one offered to watch over the other.

"Gotta work early. But you can take one, and I'll watch you."

Deb turned, rolling against him, the weight of her body both reassuring and confining. She trusted him enough to hook her thigh over him—a thigh missing the calf below the knee. Years ago, a fall while mountain climbing had taken Deb's legs.

But that wasn't the fear that kept her awake.

Mal knew it was something far worse.

A fear he also shared.

The Rushmore Inn.

He resisted her touch, wanting to push her away, hating himself for the feeling. During the daytime, he couldn't get enough of touching her, holding her, caressing her.

But nights were different. At night he didn't want to be touched, held, or otherwise confined. He couldn't even use heavy blankets. It made him feel trapped, helpless. As if he were still tied to that table and...

Mal shuddered.

Nights were a bitch.

"You up for something else?" Deb asked, trailing her fingernails down his belly, to his boxer shorts. Mal closed his eyes, tried to live in the moment, tried to push away the past. But the only part of him the alprazolam seemed to relax was the part Deb was rubbing.

"Sorry, hon. The pill."

Deb pulled her hand back.

"I could do you," he said, reaching for her. "Maybe my body will get the hint."

Mal moved his left hand down, stroked her. Deb didn't respond.

"Damn Xanax," Deb breathed. "Turns us into a couple of eunuchs."

Mal stopped his efforts. Stared at the ceiling fan.

He sighed. "Our lives would be perfect if we didn't have to sleep."

"I hear someone is working on a pill for that."

"I'm sick of pills, but sign me up for that one."

He thought about having the nightlight discussion again. Mal found it damn near impossible to fall asleep with the four nightlights Deb had in the bedroom. There were practically bright enough to read a book by.

The problem was Deb had panic attacks in the dark.

Or maybe that was just a way to blame Deb for his insomnia, because Mal hated the dark, too.

"We can get up," Deb said. "Play some rummy."

They'd done that the previous two nights. But Mal knew Deb was as exhausted as he was. And with exhaustion came crankiness, frustration, misery. Yesterday, they'd both gone to separate parts of the house because of some stupid fight over how to best shuffle cards.

"We need sleep, hon. You take another pill. At least one of us should get some rest."

"It's not rest with the pills. It's more like a coma. I hate them."

"So do I. But..."

Mal didn't need to finish the sentence. They both knew how it ended.

But I hate the nightmares more.

They'd been to doctors. Specialists. Shrinks. Mal knew his wife shared his condition.

PTSD. Posttraumatic stress disorder.

The newest research revealed brain chemistry actually changed in response to traumatic experience. And at the Rushmore Inn, Deb and Mal survived the most traumatic experience imaginable.

"We got a little sleep on Saturday," Deb said.

Mal grunted *mmm-hmm*. He didn't mention that during one of her night terrors, Deb's moans and cries kept waking him up, even though he'd taken several pills because of the weekend off.

"Maybe we're doing this wrong," Mal said. "Maybe we need to take speed instead."

His wife laughed, breaking some of the tension. "Speed?"

"Or some coke. Instead of sleeping, we party all night."

"I tried speed once when I was training, to boost endurance. I finished a marathon, then cleaned the house top to bottom. It was awful."

Mal smiled. "Awful? We should both take some, clean out that basement."

"Do you even know where to get amphetamines?"

"I work for a newspaper. We newsies know all the lowlifes."

"So we should embrace our insomnia. That's your solution."

"It isn't a solution, hon. Just a silly idea."

Deb didn't respond right away. And when she did, her voice was so sad it made Mal ache.

"There are no solutions."

They laid there, in silence, Mal unable to come up with a solution. Deb was correct. They were broken, both their bodies and their minds, and there didn't seem any way to fix them.

That's when someone pounded on the door.

The sound paralyzed Mal, adrenaline ripping through his body making his heart seem ready to pop. But his arms and legs locked as surely as if they'd been bound there.

He couldn't move.

Couldn't breathe.

After the initial startle, his mind went haywire with possibilities. Who would be at the door at 3 A.M.? Had those terrible people from the Rushmore Inn finally found him? Had they come to finish the job?

Unable to suck in any air, unable to turn his head, Mal's eyes flicked over to Deb and saw she was similarly frightened stiff.

A second ticked by.

Another.

I've got to get up. I've got to—

The pounding sound came again, even louder, a white hot spike of adrenaline snapping Mal out of his catatonia. He immediately jerked upright in bed, reaching for his nightstand, for the 9mm inside the drawer. But in his fear and haste he reached with the wrong hand, the one missing above the wrist. He quickly switched, pulling out the gun, as Deb clambered for her artificial legs, propped next to the wall.

She squeaked out, “Do you think it’s—”

“Shh.”

Holding his breath, Mal strained to hear more sounds. He wondered, fleetingly, if this was one of his frequent nightmares. But they always revolved around him being strapped to the table, watching those horrid videos. He was always at the Rushmore in his bad dreams. He’d never had a nightmare that took place in his house.

This wasn’t a dream.

This was really happening.

He quickly switched his thoughts to other, safer possibilities. A drunk neighbor, mistaking their house for his. Local teenagers, pranking people by knocking on the door then running away. A relative, maybe his brother from Florida, dropping by unannounced. Police, coming over to tell Mal he’d left the headlights on in the car parked in the driveway.

Anything other than *them*…

Deb was trembling so badly she couldn’t get her legs on.

“Mal… help me…”

But for Mal to help, he had to drop the 9mm—he only had one hand. And he didn’t think he’d be able to let go of it, even if he tried.

“Mal…”

“Deb, I…”

Then the phone rang.

Deb screamed at the sound, and Mal felt his bladder clench. He looked at the gun, clutched in his trembling fist.

If it is them, I know what to do.

Deb first. One in the temple while she's looking away.

Then me.

Because there is no way in hell they're taking us back there.

Grand Haven, Michigan

Sara

Something awoke Sara Randhurst from deep, intoxicated sleep.

She peeked an eye open, confused, her bleary eyes focusing on the clock radio next to the bed.

3:15 A.M.

Without thinking, she grabbed the glass next to it, raising her head and gulping down the melted ice, savoring the faint flavor of Southern Comfort.

Okay. Focus, Sara. Why am I awake?

She had no idea. In fact, she had no memory of how she'd gotten into bed. The very last thing she remembered was...

Was what?

FedEx. The damned letter from the bank. Then opening up the bottle and crawling inside.

She snorted.

Sure. Blame the bank. As if I need another excuse to drink.

A banging sound startled Sara, making her yelp.

The door.

Who could be at the door?

She thought, fleetingly, about the letter. Could they be kicking her out now? In the middle of the night? Weren't there laws against that?

Sara immediately dismissed the idea. Tipsy as she still was, she knew banks didn't foreclose at three in the morning.

That left... who?

Sara had no family that would be visiting. The only people who still cared about her, Tyrone and Cindy, had moved to LA years ago. The last contact she'd had with them had been a Christmas card this past year. Or maybe the year before. The holidays all blended together.

Another knock. Loud and urgent.

Sara flipped on the bedroom light. Her eyes were automatically drawn to Jack's empty crib in the corner of the bedroom, a blanket draped over the top because she couldn't bear to look at it. At the same time couldn't bear to throw it away. The blanket looked like a shroud.

Then she searched around for the bottle of SoCo, hoping she'd brought it into the bedroom with her. Sara found it, on the floor.

Empty.

Shit. That was the last one.

One more bang on the door. The big bad wolf, trying to blow the house down. Or in this case, the trailer.

Fuck him. There were scarier things than wolves.

Much scarier things.

Sara pawed at the nightstand drawer, pulling it open, digging through magazines for the snub nosed .38 she kept there. A gift from Tyrone. Not registered, but it wasn't like she could get into any more trouble than she already was in.

But the gun wasn't there. Sara had a fleeting recollection of being at the kitchen table, crying and drunk, the gun in her mouth.

Shit. I left it in the kitchenette.

Funny, how she routinely contemplated suicide, yet now that her life might actually be threatened she wanted the gun for protection.

Maybe she had some fight in her after all.

Sara gripped the bottle by the neck, holding it like a club, and eased her feet out of bed. She stood up, wobbly, but a pro at walking under the influence. Two steps and she was to the bedroom door. Two more and she was next to the bathroom.

Movement, to her right, and Sara screamed and swung, the bottle connecting with the mirror hanging on the bathroom door.

It spiderwebbed with a tinkling crunch, and Sara saw herself in a dozen different triangles, hair wild, eyes red, wearing a dirty sweatshirt crusted with old shrimp chow mien that she's apparently eaten while drunk. Once upon a time, she'd been clean and pretty. Looking at herself now, Sara guessed homeless shelters would turn her away for being too gross.

Another knock, so close it felt like a full-body blow. The SoCo bottle had survived the impact with the mirror, and she clutched the neck even tighter as she made her decision.

There is no way in hell I'm answering that door.

Instead she backed away, turning in the other direction, heading for the phone on the wall. Right before she snatched up the receiver, it rang.

Sara stared, the lump in her throat making it impossible to draw a breath. She remembered the fear she'd felt on the island, and the same sick, familiar feeling spread over her.

Terror.

Pure, paralyzing terror.

Hand shaking so badly it looked like a palsy, Sara's finger hovered over the speakerphone button.

The phone rang again, making her whimper.

Do I press it?

Do I?

She jabbed at it, hitting the wrong key. Then she tried again.

The speakerphone hissed at her, and a deep male voice barked, "*Open the door, Sara.*"

Sara wet her sweatpants.

Mililani, Hawaii

Josh

Josh VanCamp gasped, drawing air through his mouth because a tiny hand was pinching his nose closed.

He opened his eyes, staring at the capuchin monkey sitting on his chest. Josh brushed the primate's paw away from his face.

"Mathison, what are—"

The monkey put a finger over Josh's mouth, telling him to be quiet. A moment later, Woof began to bark.

His warning bark. Strangers were near.

"Someone's here," Josh said.

The monkey nodded. Josh glanced at his wife, lying next to him. "Fran?"

"I'm up."

She was already swinging her legs out of the bed, pressing the intercom button on the wall.

"Duncan," she said, "panic room. Grab Woof."

Her son responded instantly. "Meet you there."

Josh placed Mathison on his shoulder, and the monkey pulled Josh's hoodie around him. He was frightened.

Josh wasn't. He had too much to do.

He slipped on the boat shoes he kept next to the bed—thick leather and tough rubber soles—and reached for the closet door.

"Hon?" he asked.

"Ready."

Josh reached inside, grabbing one of the Browning Maxus autoloader shotguns, tossing it over his shoulder like they'd practiced so many times, not bothering to see if his wife caught it as he reached for its companion.

They walked the hallway in standard two-by-two cover formation, Josh favoring the left, Fran the right. The air conditioning kicked on, normal for nighttime in Hawaii. Other than that the house was quiet. Still.

Josh passed one of the burglar alarm panels, not bothering to punch in and access surveillance, confident the animals' senses were good reason enough to get into the panic room. Since they'd moved here five years previous, the monkey and dog had had far fewer false alarms than the ten thousand dollar system they'd installed. If this turned out to be another, no harm in it. They were due for a late night drill later in the week anyway.

Depending on your past, one man's paranoia was another man's common sense. And after what the trio had lived through in Safe Haven, Wisconsin, Josh couldn't think of a single thing they'd done to keep themselves safe that qualified as paranoia.

They reached the door, and Josh stared at the fake light switch. In the up position, meaning Duncan was already inside. He swiveled the switch to the right and punched in the numeric code on the revealed keypad. The door latch snicked opened, and Fran went down the stairs first, Josh locking and sealing the door behind him, tight as a bank vault.

Basements were rare on the Big Island. Blasting through the solid rock was difficult, and deemed foolhardy in light of the constant threat of storms. But Josh's basement had its own industrial sump pump that protected against flooding, run by its own generator that worked separate from the main grid.

Josh followed Fran into the equipment room. Duncan was standing at the ready, a Glock 13 in his hand and pointed downward. He had the same angular features as Fran, same eyes, but he was growing into his masculinity and had been letting the peach fuzz on his upper lip accumulate even though they'd given him a Norelco for Christmas. Like his mother, his expression was hard, but without fear. Even though Josh was only a father by marriage, he beamed with pride at Duncan's resolve. The kid had gone through hell, and had come out the other side stronger.

Woof, their fat beagle, looked up at them, tongue out, tail wagging. Mathison hopped off of Josh's shoulder and sprang onto the dog's back, like a miniature jockey.

Duncan already had the monitors live, and the perimeter sensors had switched on Camera 2. The front porch. They watched as two men in suits knocked on the door. Caucasian, mid-thirties, ties and sport coats too formal for the humidity.

"They're holding," Fran said, touching the screen, tapping the weapon bulges in their jackets.

Josh studied their footwear. Combat boots, incongruous to the tailored suits.

"Military?" Duncan asked.

The haircuts certainly were, which wasn't a good omen.

"Smart guess. Or maybe they're private. Or…"

Josh almost added, *"something else"* but he knew there was no need. His family was already thinking it.

He hit the camera's microphone switch. The equipment room filled with the loud mating call of the coqui tree frog, which sounded a lot like digital beeping. Beneath that cacophony, katydids and crickets, and the far off screech and hoot of a barn owl.

"What next?" Duncan asked.

A fair question. In all their drills, they'd never prepared for someone knocking at the door at 3 A.M.

"Now I press a button," Josh said, "open up the trap door that sends them into the alligator pit."

Duncan stared at Josh, his teenaged face confused. He rolled his eyes when he realized his stepfather was kidding. Again, Josh felt a stab of pride. Duncan could have been freaking out, but he understood how safe they were in the panic room. If needed, they could stay down there for a week. They had food and water, bunk beds, a toilet, a TV, and a computer. When they'd first built the room they'd slept down there as a family for several nights, making a party out of it so Duncan got used to the space. Popcorn and staying up late, watching movies and playing videogames. A safe area, not a scary one.

But his son's question was on the money. If they'd been under attack—a highly conceivable possibility considering their past—the next step would be to call the police, followed by the Feds. If that didn't produce the desired results, the media was next.

So far, the VanCamps had lived up to their part of the deal and kept silent. If threatened, Josh had memorized all the numbers for all the major news outlets on the Big Island. He could burn several key people if forced to.

Josh didn't want it to come to that. He and Fran had talked long and hard about bringing down those responsible for the genocide at Safe Haven, but in the end they opted to stay quiet for Duncan's sake. If they told the press what they knew, there would be reprisals.

He stared at the two men on the monitor. Is that what this was? A team sent to silence them? If so, why were they knocking on the front door? Why not an entire commando team? Or an airstrike to take out the whole house?

None of the other monitors were live, meaning the proximity cameras hadn't been tripped. Josh fired them up anyway to take a look.

No armed killers on the property.

No one at all.

Just the two guys on the front porch.

"I guess we ask them what they want," Fran said.

Josh looked at his wife, saw that strength in her eyes he admired so much. Someone else might have been hysterical at this point. Crying or catatonic or ranting in fear. And he wouldn't have blamed her if she reacted that way. But Fran was a rock, in many ways stronger than he was, and the love he felt for her right then gave him strength as well.

Josh hit the intercom button.

Pittsburgh, Pennsylvania
Frank

Dr. Frank Belgium yawned, needing sleep. He was grading an assignment, trying to figure out how this student had gotten into advanced biology. The paper had something to do with the ozone layer and photosynthesis. But the experiment made no sense, and the conclusions were unfounded and in several cases outright fabrication.

Belgium took one of the student's paragraphs and typed it verbatim into Google. After checking the results, he tried several more times with other sections.

"Dumb dumb dumb."

The student had plagiarized published experiments. And to disguise his cheating, he'd mixed and matched several different papers, without any apparent logic or reason.

Belgium printed the Google file, stapled the pages to the paper, and wrote F on the top, along with, *Scientists cite their sources. They also try to make sense.*

He was about to move onto the next paper, but stopped himself and added, *How did you get into advanced biology?*

It was a fair question. But as he stared at his handwritten words, Belgium wondered, *And how did I wind up teaching advanced biology?*

A combination of bad decisions and bad luck. But it was better than many alternatives—

something Frank knew all about. And being a biology professor at a state college still allowed him to do some genetic research. Not nearly on the same level as he used to, but enough to keep his mind active and hands nimble.

He frowned at the title of the next paper, *Plants' Reactions to Household Chemicals*, and was ready to delve in when someone knocked at the door.

Oh, Jesus. He's found me.

Belgium thought about the gun he'd always meant to buy, the one he'd use to shoot himself if the past ever came calling. But he'd been afraid to buy the gun. Just as well, because as frightened as he was right now, he'd be just as afraid to use it on himself.

It had been a while since he'd had to confront this particular fear. There had been nightmares, of course. Plenty of them since leaving Samhain. He hadn't spoken with his friends, Sun and Andy, since their wedding last March, and those were the only people he could talk to about their shared, terrifying experience. Because if he did mention it to anyone else, he'd be shot for treason.

Maybe that was the solution. If evil was at the door, Belgium could call the newspapers, spill everything, and then the US government would kill him. But the government was inefficient, bordering on inept, and would probably take days or weeks to get the job done. In the meantime, he'd be going through all sorts of unimaginable hell. Which made Belgium wonder, for the umpteenth time, why he hadn't ever manned up and just bought a damned gun.

"Dr. Belgium! Dr. Frank Belgium! It's the Secret Service."

Belgium's fear of demons vanished. But another fear climbed into its place. If this was the Secret Service, there could be only one reason they would call on him.

"The doctor isn't here," he called, trying to disguise his voice and make it sound lower. Which, in hindsight, was silly, because they didn't know what he sounded like in the first place. "I am his his his... lover." Belgium's eyes cast around his desk, looking for a suitable name. He found it on his computer monitor, the logo. "His lover, Vizio. Why are you bothering me at such an hour?"

"If you don't open the door, Doctor, we will break in."

Belgium shuddered. He didn't want to go anywhere with the Secret Service, because it wouldn't be anywhere pleasant.

And how could he be sure it was the Secret Service at all? The evil that Belgium had confronted in the past was wily.

"I am Vizio," he said, lamely. "The Doctor is out of the country at a biology symposium. I I I am staying here to water his plants."

The door busted inward.

Belgium gasped.

He was right.

It wasn't the Secret Service.

Chicago, Illinois

Tom

Tom Mankowski squinted at his Kindle Fire, determined to read the screen without making the font size larger. The author, some guy with a bunch of letters after his name who supposedly was on Dr. Phil a few times, was writing about the importance of intimacy in a romantic relationship.

No shit. I didn't need to spend $14.99 to figure that out.

The ebook was called *Twenty Tips For Keeping Long Distance Relationships Fresh*, and was the first self-help book Tom had ever bought. The price surprised him—he thought ebooks should be much cheaper than that—but the topic was important enough to warrant the purchase.

Unfortunately, the content so far had been less than revelatory.

Call and text often? Check.

Send gifts? Check.

Phone sex? They'd actually taken it once step further, and used video chat on Skype.

Visit when possible?

Tom looked to the right, to the empty side of the bed. Joan hadn't been over in two weeks. And it had been two months since he's visited her in LA. In the past hundred days he'd seen her only eight.

Tom smiled every time he got a text from her. It warmed his heart when Joan FedExed a screener DVD of some film she'd produced. And the site of her in a skimpy negligee, doing her best to talk dirty to him on his computer screen but constantly breaking character and giggling—well, it beat the hell out of Internet porn.

But it didn't beat being with her. Nothing beat being with her.

Tom was lonely. And the loneliness was made worse because he had someone who could fill that void. But she wouldn't quit her job to move to Chicago, and he wouldn't quit his to move to L.A.

He flipped the electronic page and read, *Plan a surprise visit.*

Tom had some vacation days he needed to burn or else he'd lose them. But Joan was in the middle of a shoot, and that meant 80 hour work weeks for her. Still, he could fly to California and be there for her at the end of her day, if only to sleep next to her for a few nights. It was better than lying in bed alone, reading an overpriced book by some PhD with a startling grasp of the obvious.

He blinked, yawned, and damned his pride, pressing the *Aa* setting on the screen to enlarge the font to a size 8. It beat getting eyeglasses. Then he adjusted his pillow and settled in to read about playing online games together.

Yeah. That's what Joan would be into. Us fragging each other in an Xbox Halo death match. How the hell did this guy get on Dr. Phil?

But curiosity got the best of Tom, and he exited the book and began to surf the net, seeing if there were any online games about fifteenth century France, which Joan did have an interest in. He was flipping through Google pages when there was a knock at his door.

Tom's first thought was the gun on his nightstand. As a Homicide cop, Tom had made enemies. And some of them were real doozies.

His second thought was, *Maybe Joan is reading this same stupid book and is surprising me with a visit.*

She'd called earlier that day, but it had been hours ago. Had she phoned from the airport, just before hopping on the red-eye?

Tom swung his legs out of bed, grabbed the terrycloth bathrobe on the floor (a gift from Joan) and stuck the Sig Saur in his pocket, first making sure there was one in the chamber. He walked out of the bedroom softly, on the balls of his feet, and traversed the short hallway to his apartment door. After an altercation with a very bad and very powerful man several years ago, Tom had improved his home security. The door was bulletproof, with a reinforced security bar. It was the same setup he'd installed at Joan's house, and nothing short of a charging rhino could get through it.

Tom took a peek through the peephole, and saw two men in dark suits standing in the hallway. Caucasian, thirties, blank expressions. He noted how their jackets bulged, indicating they were carrying.

He palmed his Sig and said, "Yeah?"

The man on the right said, "FBI."

They both held up badges and ID cards. Tom had seen a few in his day, and they looked legitimate enough. But you could buy anything online these days.

"What do you want?"

"It's about your partner. Roy Lewis."

Tom hadn't expected that.

"What about him?"

"We believe he's in trouble, Detective Mankowski. Can we come in?"

Tom didn't like it. It was 2 A.M., a highly abnormal time for the Feebies to drop in. But they both shared the classic, bored expression of government drones, and Roy was like a brother to Tom. Keeping his gun at his side, he went through the complicated process of unlatching the door and letting them in.

"The gun is hardly necessary, Detective," said the same one, eying Tom's piece.

"I'm a nervous type."

They didn't reply. Tom stepped aside and allowed them into his apartment. He noticed two things immediately.

First was their footwear. Rather than the expected Florsheims or equivalent, these men had heavy boots on, with thick rubber soles, suitable for combat. The second was their scent. It was odd, sort of a musk combined with something medicinal. Nothing that came from a bottle, and unlike any body odor Tom had ever smelled. Neither offensive or appealing, but certainly unusual.

He followed the men into the living room, where they turned to face him. No one made any move to sit on the sofa or easy chair, and Tom didn't offer them any of the cold coffee still in the pot on the kitchen counter. He waited for them to speak first, an old cop trick. After a few seconds of silence, they did.

"We understand you and Detective Lewis were invited to an unusual gathering last weekend."

Tom remembered the invitation, which had arrived via FedEx at work.

"Some sort of gameshow thing," Tom said. "Win a million dollars or something like that."

"Did you discuss it with your partner?"

Tom hadn't. At least, not in depth. He and Roy had each gotten identical invitations, but they'd been working a gang hit, interrogating seven members of the Latin Kings over a period of four days, and he'd forgotten about the FedEx ten seconds after it arrived. After making the arrest, Roy had taken leave, mentioning he might check the invite out.

As far as Tom could recall, it was for some stupid reality show contest. Tom didn't need the money, and he certainly didn't want the fame. He preferred to keep to himself. One of the things he hated most about Joan's work was the parties he was forced to attend when he visited her. All those Hollywood phonies, each trying to shine brighter than the next. Joan never acted that way, but it seemed almost every single one of her friends did.

"We spoke about it for less than a minute. Roy wondered if it was a scam. I had no interest. Didn't even read the whole thing."

"Do you have the invitation here?"

Tom had it on the desk in his bedroom, but something made him withhold that info.

"Not sure where it is."

"Can you find it?"

"Why?"

The Feebies exchanged a glance, then focused back on Tom. "Because it's evidence in a possible homicide investigation."

Tom gripped the butt of his Sig tighter. "What are you saying?"

"We have reason to believe that Roy Lewis, your partner, has been murdered."

It had been a long time since anyone had punched Tom in the face.

This was a whole lot worse.

Cleveland, Ohio

Deb

Deb Dieter stared at the ringing phone.

Her mouth was dry, and she could feel her heart fluttering in her chest like a hummingbird was trapped in her ribcage.

She began reaching for her husband to grip his arm, and then hesitated. Her walking legs—made of carbon and fitted with a microprocessor—were harder to get on than her other prosthetics, and she was torn between the need to be comforted by Mal and the need to get dressed and flee.

Flee from what? The phone? The door?

Is this what my life has come to? Letting fear dictate my every move?

Deb forced herself to look at the phone. She flinched when it rang again.

Just answer it.

Do it.

Now.

But Deb couldn't do it. She couldn't even reach for it. She'd run marathons, fought mountain lions, and survived the Rushmore Inn. She'd even been taking a karate course, and had just advanced to 3rd Mon Kyu; Purple Belt with Red Stripe. But she couldn't get herself to answer a telephone.

Mal seemed equally paralyzed. In many ways, his ordeal had been even worse than hers. On the rare nights she was able to fall asleep, Mal often woke her up, in the throes of a night terror, whimpering in a way that never failed to raise the hair on her arms.

The phone rang again.

And again.

Then the answering machine picked up.

"You've reached the Dieters, please leave a message."

"It's the FBI. Open the door."

Deb managed to look over at Mal, whose expression was somewhere between terrified and confused.

"This is about West Virginia."

The Rushmore. Most of those responsible for the atrocities committed there had died.

But there was one man, who was currently in prison.

Could he have escaped?

Deb couldn't imagine anything worse. Her mind went into overdrive, conjuring scenarios so fast they became one big blur in her head. He got out... he's coming for her and Mal... he's been seen in the vicinity... he's...

He's the one on the phone right now, impersonating the FBI.

More pounding on the door. Deb didn't know what to do. She felt glued to the bed. Mal was shaking so badly he wouldn't be able to hit anything with the gun he held.

"This is extremely important," said the voice on the answering machine. *"open the door. We know you're in there. We can see you."*

Deb jerked her head from left to right, searching the bedroom, not understanding how someone could be watching her. There was no one there, nothing at all but—

The window.

The window, over the headboard of the bed.

Mal and Deb looked up, at the small, rectangular window directly above them. The venetian blinds were closed, but there were gaps and cracks. And they were on the first floor.

Someone could be standing right there.

"Open the blinds," the voice said. *"I'm holding up my badge."*

But what if he wasn't holding a badge? What if it was the escaped psycho, and he was holding a brick, or a crowbar, or a—

Someone rapped lightly on the window.

Deb screamed.

A flashlight appeared behind the blinds.

"Put down the gun, Mr. Dieter. We're not going to harm you or your wife."

Sweat had broken out over Mal's forehead, dripping down the sides of his face. He stared at his wife, and she sensed him fighting to be brave. Gun still in his hand, Mal slowly reached for the cord to the blinds—

—and yanked them open.

Standing there was a man. Not the psycho they remembered. But a tall man in a suit, holding a cell phone in one hand, the flashlight in the other, pointing at his own face.

"I'm going to take out my badge," he said, and his words on the machine weren't quite synced to his lips, due to the satellite delay. *"We're here to help you."*

Deb watched, transfixed, as he slowly reached into his pocket and took out an official-looking FBI badge and ID.

Trembling, she reached for the phone and picked it up.

"Help us wi...wi... with what?" she managed, teeth chattering.

The man smiled, but it was hollow and emotionless.

"Open the door and let us in. And we'll tell you."

Grand Haven, Michigan

Sara

"What do you want?" she said into the phone, her voice so soft she could barely hear it.

"It's the FBI. We're here to help you get your son back."

Sara blinked, then shook the cobwebs from her head. The fear she'd been feeling was replaced with something else. Something she hadn't experienced in so long she'd forgotten what it felt like.

Hope.

"Jack?" she croaked.

"Yes, Jack. Open the door, and we can talk about it."

"I... uh... gimme a minute."

The fear came back, and her mind twisted in two. To have her child again would be a miracle. It would, quite literally, save her life.

But there was also a chance this was a trick. Sara knew there were bad people in the world. She'd had to endure some of the worst that humanity had to offer. This call could be connected to all the bad things from her past. Or it could be some new predator, looking for an opportunity.

As she considered her options, Sara quickly changed out of her soiled sweatpants, tossing them into the shower and shimmying into some jeans. Then she went into her kitchenette, seeking the gun. She found it on the floor, next to an old pizza box, and peeked through the curtains at the entrance to her trailer.

Two men in suits. They stared right at Sara, as if they'd anticipated her looking at them. Both held gold badges. Sara wondered if the shields were real or not, then realized it didn't matter. They could kick in her flimsy trailer door with less energy than it took to sneeze. If these men wanted to get in, they easily could. But so far, they'd opted for the polite approach.

So maybe they were FBI and telling the truth. Or maybe they'd try to kill her. In either case, there wasn't anything she could do to stop them. The gun she held only had one bullet in it. Sara hadn't ever expected to use it for self-defense.

She placed her hand on the front door knob, feeling as if she were inviting trouble inside. But the reality was, no matter what they could do to her, it couldn't be worse than what had already been done.

Sara unlocked it and opened the door.

"Can we come in?"

Sara nodded, stepping aside. She gestured to her cheap dinette set, one of the chairs wobbly. The cool, fresh air from outside made her realize how sour the smell was in her trailer, and she caught an acrid stench similar to spoiled milk. The men came in and stood there, seemingly oblivious to the mess around them. And a mess it was. Dishes piled high in the sink. Fast food wrappers strewn about. A garbage can filled to overflowing. A single strip of fly paper hanging from the overhead light, speckled with dozens of the dead.

But Sara didn't care what they thought of the mess, or if they judged her. She just wanted to know if they were speaking the truth about Jack.

Neither man made a move to sit down. They were taller than they seemed to be when standing outside. Beefier, too. More like pro wrestlers than FBI guys.

"So, you're in," she forced herself to talk slowly, deliberately. "What do you want?"

"We know what happened on Rock Island."

Sara may have flinched at that, but she still had enough liquor in her system to mask her reaction. Rock Island—which she thought of as Plincer's Island—was the cause for her current situation.

"You went through a lot," he continued. His eyes, and expression were blank. "But you survived. It must have been quite an ordeal."

Sara wasn't going to get into a conversation about the past, especially about what happened on that island. "What about Jack?"

"The government has a proposition for you. We want to help."

The sneer formed on her lips before she could stop it. "The government? They're the ones who took my baby."

The agent continued. So far his partner hadn't spoken. "Child Protective Services took Jack. You were caught doing sixty miles an hour in a thirty mile zone, and he wasn't in a car seat."

"I... I'd left the car seat in the house."

"You blew a one point eight."

Sara considered responding, but the fight had long been beaten out of her.

Yes, she was a drunk. After Plincer's Island, alcohol was the only thing that drowned out the nightmares. She came away from it scared and broke, and the DUI had been the final nail in her coffin of failure. Sara had to sell the house to pay for her legal fees, and still spent six months in jail for wreckless endangerment. When she got out, and was unable to get Jack back from the foster home the state had stuck him in. She was a single parent with a criminal record, no means of employment, and many—including the judge—were dubious of her role in the Rock Island Massacre. Without money for a good lawyer, Sara went back to drinking, winding up in this shit hole trailer park, trying to find the guts to eat that single bullet.

"How can you help?" she whispered.

"There's an experimental program, going on this weekend. If you volunteer for it, you'll be given one million dollars, and we'll work with CPS to get your son back."

Sara snorted. "A million bucks, and Jack? This is a joke, right?"

"It's for real, Sara." He reached into his jacket, took out some folded papers. "The details are in here."

"What's the program? Some sort of rehab?" As she said it Sara found herself looking around the kitchenette for any alcohol that might be left over.

The silent one finally spoke. "It's about fear."

Sara stared at him, and his smile was chilling.

"Fear?"

The other one continued. "You understand fear better than most people. The government wants to study how you react to fear."

"Why?"

"Understanding fear can lead to controlling it. Certainly you can see the advantages to that."

Sara's brow crinkled. "So this is a fear study? Do they hook me up to some machine, then make me watch scary movies?"

The quiet one let out a chuckle. "Oh, it's a bit more complicated than that..."

Pittsburgh, Pennsylvania
Frank

"You're not the Secret Service," Dr. Frank Belgium said, scrutinizing the proffered badges that quite distinctly spelled out FBI.

"Our friends in the Secret Service told us where to find you," said the agent on the right. His breath smelled medicinal. "We're all Feds, so does it really matter?"

"Yes yes yes, in fact it does."

Belgium inadvertently flashed back to the last time the Secret Service came calling, which is how he wound up at Samhain. Two men in black suits, with the proposition of a lifetime.

"We have a proposition for you," the same agent said.

"No, thank you. I'm quite done done done with government work. Have a good night."

Belgium moved to close the door, but the Fed stuck his foot in it.

"We're well aware of your role in Project Samhain, Doctor. And how it turned out."

Belgium again thought back to how that particular part of his life came to a close. About the evil loose in the world, which was partly his fault. He braced himself for the bad news.

Instead, he was surprised by bad news of a completely different kind.

"Instead of being a researcher, your government would like you to volunteer to be a test subject," the agent said. "On a topic you know intimately well."

"Molecular biology?"

"Fear," said the other one.

Belgium wasn't sure, but when the man spoke he flashed teeth that looked...

Well, they looked *pointy*.

"You're invited to spend the weekend taking part in a unique experiment. You'll be closely monitored to see how you react to fear. As you might guess, you have more experience in this area than most."

That's the understatement of the century, Belgium thought.

"For one day of your time, you'll be given one million dollars. Plus your old job back at Biologen."

Belgium raised an eyebrow. "Excuse me?"

He'd been justifiably fired from Biologen years ago, due to negligence. Since then, they'd merged with the pharmaceutical company DruTech and had become the premiere biotech firm in the world.

"A million, and a job as head of the molecular biology department."

Head of the department? That meant pure research, the thing in life Frank loved more than anything else.

He allowed himself a few seconds of fantasy. His own lab. Access to the best equipment. The most competent staff in the world. And no more grading ridiculous papers about plants' reactions to household chemicals.

Then reality kicked in again, reinforced with some well-earned skepticism.

"So this has nothing to do do do with Samhain?"

"No."

"Have you," he chose his words carefully, "spoken with anyone else?"

"Several people. But no one you know."

Which meant his friends from Samhain, Sun and Andy, hadn't been approached.

But working for the government again? Could he possibly trust that?

The answer came swiftly and with finality.

Absolutely fucking not.

"It's a tempting offer, gentlemen, but but but I'm going to decline."

The lead agent stared deep into Belgium, his eyes emotionless. "If you don't accept this offer, you'll be executed for treason."

"Treason?" Belgium squeaked. "I've never breathed a word of what happened, to anyone."

"You know exactly what you did," the agent said. "You know what you're responsible for."

The Fed spoke the truth. And Belgium had waited years for the evil he'd unleashed upon the world to appear again. He spent hours every week monitoring the world news, looking for evidence.

But so far, the evil had remained dormant. Belgium had even begun to hope it had disappeared completely.

"Your choice is to submit to the experiment and get a large cash settlement, along with your dream job. Or be taken to a secret prison and executed without a trial. And that threat extends to your associates."

"Andrew and Sunshine Dennison," the other said, giving Belgium another quick glimpse of his sharp teeth.

"I understand they're expecting a child. Do you want to be responsible for destroying their family?"

Belgium did not want them to die. Nor did he want to die. Death was one of many, many things Frank feared.

"Then apparently I don't don't don't have a choice. Where is this experiment supposed to take place?"

"Have you heard of Butler House?"

Belgium had. And as the blood drained from his face, he seriously wondered if being executed for treason was the better option.

Chicago, Illinois
Tom

"You think my partner was murdered, and it is somehow connected with this game show thing?"

The Feebies looked at each other.

"We've been investigating a man named Dr. Emil Forenzi. He may be involved in the disappearance of over a dozen ex-military personnel. From what we've been able to find out, he's doing some sort of scientific research on the physical characteristics of fear."

"He's the one who sent the invitations?"

"We believe so."

"And you think he may have killed Roy?"

"We're not sure."

"You guys don't know much, do you?"

"Detective Mankowski, we believe Dr. Forenzi may in fact be funded by the US military. So certain avenues have been closed to us."

Tom could understand that. The army, much like the government, tended to keep hush-hush about things above your pay grade. "Do you have any actual evidence?"

"Just circumstantial. We've been trying to get a man on the inside of Forenzi's operation, but security is tight. However, we do know he has been inviting people to participate in his experiments. People who have undergone a particularly frightening experiences. We've done a background check on you and your partner, and you both certainly qualify."

No shit, Tom thought.

"We'd really like to know what's going on, Detective."

"And you want me to find out."

"We've gotten permission from your boss, Captain Bains, to work with you on this."

That seemed odd to Tom, as Bains didn't like working with the Feebies. And justifiably so. They were territorial, smug, and often looked down on city cops. But Bains also had an almost paternal sense of responsibility toward his men. If Roy was missing, the captain would want him found.

"And you can't do this yourselves because...?" Tom asked.

"We weren't invited. You were. You could poke around, talk to Forenzi, try to get some evidence. We've tried to interview him, but he lawyered up. And we've found obtaining a warrant to be challenging. He apparently has friends in high places."

"Where is Forenzi?"

They exchanged another glance. "He's set up his laboratory in the Butler House."

"*The* Butler House?"

"You've heard of it?"

Next to the house made famous in the *Amityville Horror,* Butler House was probably the most famous paranormal site in America. Tom even remembered streaming a low budget Netflix movie about it. Located in South Carolina, an insane doctor—the brother of a plantation owner—built a laboratory-slash-dungeon underneath the estate, where he performed horrible experiments on the slaves they owned. Tom watched ten minutes before turning it off. Even though it was poorly acted, and the special effects were shoddy, the ghosts in the movie were hideously deformed and reminded Tom of a real night he spent in the real basement of a real mansion, and he didn't need to be reminded of that.

"Supposed to be haunted," Tom said.

"Forenzi is apparently convinced it actually *is* haunted. And he believes the fear of the supernatural induces the purest terror response in his volunteers."

"Have you talked to any of these volunteers?"

"No. We've tried to track down those we know of, but they've... disappeared."

Tom almost laughed at that. Almost. It was ridiculous enough to be the punchline for a campfire ghost story. But neither Feebie looked amused.

"How many people are we talking about here?" he asked.

"Two or three dozen."

"Including the missing military men?"

"In addition to them."

"So you're saying there have been… how many?… maybe fifty people who have disappeared in Butler House since Forenzi moved in?"

"That number might be low."

"And no one has done anything?"

"We're trying to do something, Detective. Which is why we're at your apartment at three in the morning."

Tom rubbed his eyes. "I need to think about this. Do you have a number I can reach you at?"

One of the agents produced a card and held it out.

"We really would like to see that invitation," he said, pinching the card so Tom couldn't take it.

"When I find it, I'll show it to you."

The Fed released the card. Special Agent John Smith. Go figure.

"We've heard that Forenzi is conducting another experiment this weekend. Our informant says guests are being picked right now."

"Who is this informant?"

Neither agent answered. Obviously the Bureau had their *need-to-know* info just like the military did.

"Goodnight, gentlemen," Tom said. "You can find your way out."

They left without so much as a nod. As soon as the door closed, Tom went to his cell phone and called Roy.

It went straight to voice mail.

"Roy, it's Tom. Call me back as soon as you get this."

It was too early in the morning to call Gladys, Roy's ex-wife, so instead Tom went into the bedroom and found the FedExed invitation. He snapped on a pair of vinyl gloves he kept in his drawer, and pulled the invite out of the blue and orange cardboard mailer. It was a standard 8.5" x 11" sheet of paper, off white and a heavy stock. The writing on it appeared to be calligraphy.

Survive the night in a haunted house and receive $1,000,000.
Call 843-555-2918 to confirm.
Invitation 3345

Tom turned the paper over, finding nothing, then looked for a nonexistent water mark. Next, he sniffed it, and it smelled like paper. Finally he took out a magnifying glass and studied the script. It was inkjet, not handwritten.

It said nothing about this being a gameshow or a reality show, but those were the possibilities he and Roy had brought up during the fifteen seconds they'd discussed it. But this seemed more likely to be a joke, hoax, or scam.

And yet the Feebies were extremely interested in this invitation, and they didn't think this was a put on.

Tom switched on his computer monitor, saw he was still on the Skype program he used to talk to Joan. She was offline. He frowned, then Googled *Dr. Emil Forenzi*, spelling it like it sounded.

He found him on the Linkedin social network. Born in Brazil fifty-six years ago, his father Italian and mother a native. Moved to the US when he was a child. Full scholarship to Brown. Doctorate at MIT. Then he went to work for the DoD, and apparently still did. Specialties included a bunch of technical and science skills that Tom had to scroll down to read completely.

So why does a genius scientist believe in something as ridiculous as the supernatural?

Tom squelched the thought. If he described some of the very real things that had happened to him, the majority of the world would think they were ridiculous as well. Trying to keep his mind open, he searched for *Butler House* on Google and found a website dedicated to it.

Tom settled back in his desk chair and began to read.

<u>BUILDING HISTORY</u>

Butler House was built in 1837 by wealthy landowner Jebediah James Butler on a cotton plantation in Solidarity, South Carolina, fifty miles outside of Charleston. Boasting more than one hundred and fifty rooms in the neoclassical antebellum style, it was home to Jebediah, his wife Annabelle, and his younger brother, Colton, until their deaths in 1851.

Construction began in 1835 and faced many setbacks, including a severe storm, a fire, and the deaths of three workers. One died when a pallet of bricks crushed him. Another was scalded to death by hot tar. A third fell into the concrete foundation when it was being poured, and drown there. A generally accepted rumor is his body wasn't discovered until the concrete had cured, and it was unable to be removed, so Butler indicated more concrete be poured on top of him.

Many point to this lack of a proper burial as the beginning of the rumors that the property was haunted. Others contend that the source of the problems was the land itself. In the late 1700s it was a thriving village of Cusabo Native Americans numbering over two hundred. The village was burned, its people massacred, by white settlers desiring the fertile land.

During the lengthy and troublesome construction, Annabelle had been heard to say, “Maybe the Lord doesn’t want us building this house.”

The slow completion time is also attributed to the architectural demands Butler made. He hired three different architects, each to design a different part of the building, so no one but Butler knew the exact layout. This was especially important because the manor was outfitted with many secret rooms and passageways, false walls, staircases that lead nowhere, a labyrinthine basement with several kilometers worth of tunnels, and a torture chamber.

SLAVERY

At its peak in 1841, the plantation boasted dozens of slaves, the majority working several hundred acres of cotton and tobacco. Butler was known to openly boast that he was breeding his own workforce, and many of the slaves born on the property were fathered by Butler or his brother. On several recorded occasions, if a child born on the property was too light skinned, Butler would feed it alive to the passel of hogs he kept on the property.

Butler soon became one of the largest slave buyers in the South, which caused one of his contemporaries to remark, *“[Butler] has purchased so damned many he could farm the entire state.”* But at any given time, Butler never seemed to have more than fifty slaves working for him, even though records have shown he had bought more than four hundred.

Known to be unusually cruel masters, the Butler brothers seemed to have delighted in inflicting punishment on their slaves, for slights real or imagined. They made full use of the house’s torture chamber, where slaves were skinned, boiled, crucified, scourged, whipped, mutilated, and burned.

Colton Butler, a self-professed physician who demanded to be addressed as "Doctor" even though he held no known medical degree, conducted many surgical experiments on slaves, without anesthesia, with the apparent goal of joining them together.

"I believe I have the ability and necessary determination," Butler wrote, *"to fuse the parts of two Negroes together into a single being. Consider a slave with four strong arms, which would double his work output, or with six breasts to suckle young..."*

REBELLION

The Butlers hired ten armed men to guard them and their property, and they were known to be as cruel as their employers. Daily beatings, corporal punishments, and public executions (even though the killing of slaves was against the slave code) were commonplace. A one-eyed man named Jonathan "Blackjack" Reedy, worked as taskmaster in the fields, and once said, "Spilled blood is good for the soil, makes the cotton stronger."

On October 31, 1847, near the end of the annual cotton harvest, Blackjack was whipping a young boy whose only infraction was said to have been stopping for a moment to wipe the sweat from his brow. This appeared to have been the final straw for the mistreated slaves, and they revolted, beating Blackjack so severely the only way the authorities could identify his corpse was by his black leather eyepatch.

The rebellion spread throughout the fields, the guards either being surprised or running out of ammunition, and after the last was killed the angry slaves converged on Butler House.

Jebediah Butler, and his wife Annabelle, were hung naked by their ankles from the rafters in Butler House's great room and beaten to death with whips and scourges. Colton was chased into the bowels of the basement, and dragged to the torture chamber where he was placed upon the rack and stretched until his arms and legs were broken in several places each. Then he was set ablaze.

The majority of the slaves escaped to nearby states, some making their way to the North and freedom.

AFTERMATH

The deaths of the Butlers was headline news for weeks after the incident, and bounties were put on the runaway slaves' heads. But there weren't many takers. There were rumors of a "slave curse" which claimed any who tried to capture the Butler slaves would meet the same fate as the Butler family.

The house, and plantation, went unoccupied for five years, until a man claiming to be a distant cousin of the Butlers, Sturgis Butler, petitioned the court for ownership and moved in during the summer of 1852.

Sturgis tried, unsuccessfully, to hire workers to fix up the house, which had fallen into disrepair and still bore the damage incurred during the rebellion. But laborers always quit in terror after a few days, claiming to have witnessed strange ghostly figures, or disembodied screams.

Sturgis resorted to repairing the house on his own, but he didn't try to recapture the farm, and the land soon became a dense marsh.

Though Sturgis never married, he entertained a wide variety of women at Butler House, many of them prostitutes. At least a dozen were never heard of again.

CIVIL WAR YEARS

When the War Between the States broke out in 1861, Butler House was commandeered by the Confederate Army as a garrison. Between 1861 and 1865, at least six soldiers committed suicide on the grounds, and sixteen more were remanded to a local insane asylum, ranting about supernatural phenomenon. While under psychiatric care, four killed themselves, eight died of unexplained causes, and one man plucked out his own eyes with a fork.

Sturgis, exempt from the draft because he worked as a druggist, remained at the house during its occupation by troops, though he kept to himself in a closed off wing of the basement. Rumors abounded of him being "in league with the devil" and a proponent of "black magick." Milledge Luke Bonham, governor of South Carolina and Brigadier General in the army, said of Sturgis, "There is something dark and twisted about that man. He is certainly no Christian."

RECONSTRUCTION YEARS

During the four decades after the war ended, little was heard from Sturgis Butler. Prostitutes from the county continued to disappear, and the locals paid little mind to it. But in in 1902, Mia Lockwood, the only child of Southern poultry magnate Earl Lockwood, vanished the night before her debutante ball in Charleston.

Gossip and rumor led to the formation of a posse/lynch mob who raided the Butler House on May 1, the pagan holiday known as Walpurgis Night. Upon breaking into the house, the group discovered Sturgis presiding over a Black Mass replete with occult paraphernalia including black candles, severed animal heads, sacrilegious objects, and a seventeenth century binding of the *Compendium Maleficarum*, a notorious text on witches. Sturgis had hung a naked and violated Mia upside-down on a cross, and was lapping at the blood streaming from her slashed throat when the mob arrived.

Sturgis was immediately dragged outside, lashed to a black oak tree, and set ablaze. He allegedly laughed as he burned.

Inspection of the property over the succeeding weeks discovered three mass graves, some going back over seventy years (determined to be the bones of slaves) and some more recent (the corpses of missing prostitutes) making Sturgis one of America's first, and most prolific, serial killers.

<u>1910-1945</u>

Butler House remained unoccupied for a few years after Sturgis Butler's death, until the county acquired it, making the mansion a home for the blind, and for invalid veterans of the First World War . At the height of its use, it housed over a hundred. During its thirty-five years of operation, there were many fatal illnesses that infected patients.

1911 – Tuberculosis killed 35.

1918 – The Spanish Flu killed 63.

1920 – Diphtheria killed 9.

1924 – Botulism killed 40.

1931 – Cholera killed 5.

1940 – Measles killed 5.

In 1945, a fire broke out in the great room, and all of the 86 residents died of smoke inhalation or third degree burns. It is unknown why they were unable to escape, as the doors were all in working order.

AFTER WWII

Butler House remained abandoned until 1956, when it was acquired by a land development company intent on tearing it down and building a housing development. The day before demolition occurred, the owner of the company, J.J. Hossenport, was struck by lightning and killed while getting into his car.

During his funeral, lightning struck and killed his widow, Myrtle Hossenport.

Their heirs, believing the property to be cursed, put it up for sale. It remained on the market and vacant for twenty-nine years, though six different realtors showed the house dozens of times.

It was finally acquired by eccentric millionaire Augustus Torble, the lone heir of a restaurant mogul, who spent over a million dollars restoring the house to its former shape. In 1985, he moved into Butler House with his young bride, Maria.

In 1992, Maria was discovered by hunters, wandering naked in the woods six miles from Butler House. She was malnourished and incoherent, scars covering eighty percent of her body.

In the hospital, she told the police a tale of captivity and severe abuse by her husband, who kept her locked in Butler House's torture chamber and committed unspeakable acts upon her for several years. She also told of being forced to participate in the torture and murder of eleven women, whose remains were found in one of the underground tunnels.

Torble was arrested, tried, and sentenced to life in prison. Shortly after the trial, Maria committed suicide. To this day, the women Torble killed remain unidentified. Torble refused to cooperate with authorities, and it is unknown where he found them or how he lured them to the house. He remains incarcerated at the Fetzer Correctional Institution in Charleston, SC.

CURRENT OWNER

The house remained vacant until 2002, when it was purchased by Unified Systems Association, which built an electrified perimeter fence around Butler House. Since then it has been off limits to ghost hunters, thrill seekers, and the curious. Those caught trespassing on private property are promptly arrested.

HAUNTINGS

During its 176 year history, dozens of strange happenings and unexplainable phenomenon have been linked to Butler House. Some highlights include:

1848 – A string of arsons in Charleston, including six churches that burned to the ground, were attributed to a shadowy figure with an eye patch. Several witnesses swore it was the ghost of slave driver Blackjack Reedy.

1863 – Eight Confederate soldiers staying at Butler House reported a floating ball of light that roamed the lower tunnels at night. It had the ability to go through walls and locked doors, and if it touched a person, that person died of fright.

1908 – There were seven verified attacks and sexual assaults on women in the Charleston area, by an assailant whom they claimed to be Sturgis Butler... six years after his death.

1915 – Returning WWI veterans, many of whom were victims of chlorine, phosgene, and mustard chemical weapons, claim to have been tormented by a giggling spirit in a gas mask.

1918 – During the Spanish Flu epidemic, over a dozen patients reported being assaulted, molested, and in some cases raped, by an unknown entity. The spirit supposedly smelled like burned flesh, and paralyzed its victims so they couldn't move or cry out while the attacks were taking place.

1958 – Since the deaths of J.J. and Myrtle Hossenport, descendants have suffered a streak of bad luck many attribute to supernatural phenomenon. Six car accidents, two fires, a drowning, a stroke, and a dog attack, have killed sixteen Hossenport family members. The last remaining Hossenport in the lineage, Mary Kate, was murdered by serial killer Charles Kork in 1993.

1965 – Reknowned psychic medium Mdme. Francesca Sillero gathered with a group of wealthy benefactors at Butler House to hold a séance on Halloween night. During the proceedings, she claimed to have channeled the spirit of Colton Butler. While Butler's spirit was inside her, he allegedly forced her to pluck out both of her eyes and chew off her tongue.

1982 – A group of Charleston teenagers broke into Butler House to have a late-night party. Shortly after arriving, one of teen's gums began to bleed for no explainable reason. By the time her friends got her to the hospital, every one of her teeth had fallen out. No medical explanation has ever been given.

1998 – A TV crew from the paranormal investigation show *Ghost Smashers* spent Halloween night in Butler House. Unconfirmed reports indicate a tragedy occurred. No one knows what happened, but the host, Richard Reiser, immediately retired from television without the program ever airing.

Tom clicked on the PHOTOS section of the website. The first picture looked a lot like the White House, but no columns and a darker color. The second was of three people, the Butler brothers and Annabelle.

Jebediah Butler was a bespectacled man with white hair and a Van Dyke beard. He looked a lot like a fatter Col. Sanders, minus the mirth. His wife was also plump, and either there was a spot on the photo or her left eye was severely crossed. Colton was the tallest, and rail thin. He leaned on his cane, hunched over as if his back was hurting him, and had one of those walrus mustaches with the ends curled up and waxed.

The next photo looked like a hole in the dirt filled with rocks, and Tom had to read the inscription to understand what he was seeing.

Over four thousand human bones found buried on the property.

Creeped out, he made the mistake of clicking on the next photo, which was a shirtless African American man who had so many scars on his body he no longer looked human. As Tom hurried to hit the ESC button, something in the image stopped him.

Something hanging on the man's mangled shoulder.

A third arm.

It was small, withered, hanging over his chest like a wrinkled leather belt. But there were clearly five fingers on the end of it, and they were—

Holy shit. The fingers are holding a tin drinking cup .

Tom zoomed in, trying to spot if the photo had been altered, but it looked real enough.

What the hell was wrong with some people? Assuming even some of the facts on the website were true, what could make someone treat his fellow man like that?

Tom went to the next picture, partly out of morbid curiosity, partly because he wanted to see the Butlers get what was coming to them. He was rewarded by a photo that looked like two bloody, skinned deer carcasses.

Wrong again. The caption read *The bodies of Jebediah and Annabelle Butler*. They'd had every inch of skin on their body whipped off.

Thankfully, there were no pictures of the tortured Colton. But there was a portrait of Sturgis Butler, and Tom was shocked at how much he looked like Vlad the Impaler. Same dark, bulging eyes. Same pointy black beard. Tom found himself staring into those eyes, revulsion wiggling in his stomach.

Next came a picture of the house after the fire in '45. The structure remained intact, but there was telltale soot and fire damage surrounding the windows and front doors. Tom was going to move onto the next page, but something in the photo caught his eye.

He made the jpg the size of his monitor. In one of the blackened windows was a speck of white.

Tom zoomed in further.

The white speck looked like the ghostly face of a man screaming.

There was a sound and movement to Tom's right, and he immediately glanced over his shoulder, adrenaline kicking in, and watched as his bedroom door—

—closed by itself.

As his fight-or-flight response kicked in, Tom remembered his window was open a crack. The draft sometimes blew the door open and closed; something that happened often enough that Tom actually looked it up and discovered it had to do with air pressure in the room.

Still, it was disconcerting after reading the history of Butler House. Tom's mouth was dry. His heart was doing a fox trot. And he both felt, and saw, all the tiny hairs on the backs of his hands stick straight up.

He was afraid.

And the Feebies were right. Tom knew, more than most, what it was like to be afraid.

He didn't like it. Not one bit.

Tom stared at the phone, wanting to call Joan. Hearing her voice would reassure him, calm him down.

Instead he visited YouTube and played an upbeat rock performance by Bob Walkenhorst.

He also turned on the bedroom light.

In the bright room, with the music playing, Tom felt less frightened.

But he couldn't relax enough to sleep. Every time he closed his eyes, he saw that poor, scarred, three-armed slave. And thought of his partner, Roy.

Mililani, Hawaii

Fran

Fran stood in the safe room with her family, watching the porch monitor. The two men who stood at their front door looked around when Josh hit the intercom button and spoke.

"Who are you and what do you want?"

"Mr. VanCamp?" They still couldn't find the camera. *"We're from the FBI. We want to talk to you and your wife."*

Josh glanced at her, and Fran gave her head a small shake.

"We're not interested," Josh answered. "Go away."

"It's an opportunity for you to each earn a million dollars."

"Two million bucks?" Duncan said. "Mom, that's a crapload of money."

"And probably a crapload of trouble," Josh added. "Hon?"

"No way," Fran said.

"If you'd let us in," the man on the porch continued, *"we could explain in detail. It will only require a day of your time. It's a government-sponsored experiment."*

Josh snorted. Fran saw the incredulity in his eyes. She felt exactly the same way. She'd jump off a cliff onto a bed of nails before trusting the government.

"You have ten seconds to get off of our property," she said into the intercom. "Or we're going to shoot you."

One of the men on the monitor reached into his pocket, and produced some folded papers. *"We have all the information right here."*

"Five seconds," Josh said.

"We'll, um, leave it here for you."

Fran watched the man stick the papers in the door jamb, and then they left. She followed them, monitor to monitor, until they walked off the grounds.

Duncan stared over at her, his eyes wide. "Would you really have shot them, Mom?"

Fran didn't answer. But her thoughts went back to Safe Haven. To all the friends she'd lost. To all the horror she and her family had endured.

Would she have shot them? Hell yeah.

No one will ever have a chance to harm her, or her family, again.

Not as long as Fran still had the strength to rack a shotgun and pull a trigger.

Cleveland, Ohio

Mal

"It's just for twenty-four hours," said the FBI agent in the doorway. "You'll arrive, have a meal, get examined by a doctor, then be locked in the Butler House overnight, and closely monitored to study how you react to fear."

"So they'll be purposely trying to frighten us?" Deb asked.

Mal had tucked the gun into his bathrobe pocket, and his wife was holding his hand so hard she was cutting off his circulation.

"It's a fear study," the agent said. "You both have had unique experiences that make you ideal candidates."

"And we live with those experiences, every day," Mal said. His apprehension had been fading since they answered the door, and was slowly being replaced by anger. "You have no right to come here and make this offer."

After all he and Deb had survived, why would they willingly expose themselves to even more horrors, real or convoluted? To even ask that of his wife made Mal's blood pressure skyrocket, and there was no way in hell he'd ever allow—

"Can we think it over?" Deb said.

Mal stared at her, unable to hide his surprise.

"Deb?"

"I didn't say we'll do it, hon. But I think we should talk about it."

Mal didn't understand. Sure, two million dollars was a lot, but they were doing fine financially. Why would Deb even consider this?

The agent who'd done all the talking reached into his jacket and handed Deb some folded papers. Mal detected the tiniest smirk in the corner of the man's mouth.

"The experiment begins this weekend. Good evening to you both."

The Feds left, and his wife closed the door, locking the various latches and deadbolts.

"Debbie, you're not serious." He searched her pretty face. "Are you?"

"I think we should at least discuss it, before you make a decision for the both of us."

"I don't understand." Which was as true a statement he'd ever made. "I thought—"

"That's the problem, Mal," she snapped. "*You* thought, but didn't ask me."

"Is it the money?"

"I wasn't even thinking about the money."

"So what's there to discuss? We can't sleep as it is. You want to go someplace where they're purposely trying to terrify you?"

"It's a *fear* study, Mal. Something you and I suffer from, every single day."

"Exactly, so—"

"So maybe a doctor who studies fear could somehow teach us how to deal with ours."

Mal was about to object, but caught himself. They'd both had psychiatric treatment since the Rushmore Inn. Hypnotherapy. Exposure Therapy. Cognitive Behavioral Therapy. Interpersonal. Group. Eye Movement Desensitization and Reprocessing. And a pharmacy's worth of drugs, from sleep agents to SSRIs to beta-blockers to anti-psychotics.

Nothing seemed to work. In fact, some of the treatments worsened their condition.

"You remember exposure therapy," Mal said.

"Of course."

They'd been subjected to shocking images of mutilations and congenital malformations in order to desensitize them. Deb had freaked out during a session, crying so uncontrollably they'd had to quit, and later that night Mal had gone to the

ER, unable to stop hyperventilating, convinced he was having a heart attack.

"This seems even worse, Deb. They're not just going to show us pictures. They're going to try to scare us."

"We'll get through it," Deb said, reaching for him again. "Just like we got through the Rushmore. But maybe we'll learn something this time."

Mal chewed his lower lip. The worst part about fear wasn't the dread, it was the helplessness. The FBI agents said they'd be able to bring any items they wanted to with them for the weekend, including weapons. But the gun in Mal's robe didn't make him feel any safer. Quite the opposite. The very fact he owned a gun was a constant reminder of what he was so afraid of.

"I don't know, Deb..."

"Can we discuss it, at least?" She moved a step closer to him, the hydraulic cylinders in her prosthetics whirring softly.

Mal didn't want to discuss it. He wanted to run away, someplace where it never got dark. Where nightmares didn't exist, both the ones in his head and the real ones.

But the longing in his wife's eyes made his heart hurt.

"Of course, Deb. If this is something you want."

"It is."

Deb moved in for the hug, and he reluctantly embraced her, a thought bouncing through his mind and forcing out all others.

Be careful what you wish for, because it may come true.

Solidarity, South Carolina

Forenzi

Dr. Emil Forenzi could barely hear the phone ring above all the screaming.

"It's okay," Forenzi told his patient, giving him an affectionate pat on the cheek. "It's all going to be okay."

The screaming didn't abate. Forenzi gave him a dose of traumesterone and the noise went down to a hoarse wheeze.

Forenzi answered the phone, located on the wall next to the EKG machine.

"I'm with a patient," he said into the receiver. Which was unnecessary, because he was always with a patient. Even at ungodly hours like this. Who could sleep when there was so much to do?

"We have a head count for this weekend."

"Go on."

"Three confirmed."

"And the others?"

"Still deciding."

Forenzi frowned. He'd been hoping for better results.

"Which three?"

"Sara Randhurst. Moni Draper. Frank Belgium."

Forenzi rubbed the stubble on his chin, and his eyes drifted across his laboratory. Besides his patient, and the various pieces of equipment, there was a large, glass apparatus on a stainless steel table, which looked like something out of a mad scientist movie. It was currently distilling a batch of Serum 3.

That serum, Forenzi knew, was going to win him a Nobel Prize.

Some believed that most of humanity's conflicts, be it person-to-person or country-to-country, were based upon one possessing something the other one wanted. Land. Oil. Water. Food. Religious and political differences were used as excuses to dehumanize the enemy and grab their resources.

But Forenzi knew that this greed was bolstered by another, even more base and powerful emotion.

Fear.

Mankind reeked of fear.

This fear led to distrust, and ultimately to hate.

Being able to conquer fear meant a fresh start for the world.

"Let me know if the situation changes," he said, then hung up.

Of the three who signed on, Dr. Belgium interested him most. A molecular biologist, he would recognize what Forenzi was doing here. It would be refreshing to talk to someone who could grasp the magnitude of this invention. Who would understand it.

He turned back to his patient, whose eyelids had drooped in sleep. Forenzi yawned sympathetically.

"You're exhausted, my friend. So am I. We can continue the therapy tomorrow. Sleep well."

Forenzi left the lab, walking into a hallway that looked more like a tunnel in a coal mine than the basement of a mansion. The floors were crumbling concrete, the walls lined with stacked railroad ties. There were wood ceiling braces every five meters, and Forenzi wouldn't have doubted the bare 60w bulbs hanging from them were older than he was. As he passed beneath one, it buzzed and flickered.

One of the many ghosts of Butler House, demanding attention.

Forenzi paid it no mind. Instead, he took the hall to a fork, went right, and headed for the veterinary clinic. As he approached, he heard some lone trilling, and recognized it as Gunter's.

Forenzi's spirits dipped, and his pace quickened. He entered the clinic through the metal push door and beelined for Gunter's habitat, which was situated to the right. It was several cubic meters in size, with a window of clear, unbreakable Plexiglas, the interior foliage meant to mimic a Columbian forest, with twisted, dead tree branches and fake plants.

The Panamanian Night Monkey watched his approach while upside down, hanging from a limb. Gunter was large for an *A. zolalis*, nearly three pounds in weight. His bushy brown fur was mottled with blood, and his enormous red eyes stared at Forenzi dispassionately.

"Gunter... Gunter... what have you done?"

Of course, Forenzi already had the answer to that. Gunter's two cagemates, capuchins named Laurel and Hardy, were dead on the fake grass in the habitat. They'd been dismembered and eviscerated, their insides strewn across the bathing pond and staining the water pink.

"You just can't play well with others, can you?" Forenzi shook his head and tsked.

Gunter stared, unmoving.

Aphobic.

Forenzi picked up the clipboard next to the habitat, recorded the event, and then flipped through the previous five months to get an accurate count.

"This makes twenty-eight," he said. "You're a regular little monkey serial killer."

Gunter grunted, as if agreeing.

Forenzi left a note for the morning help to clean the cage, and order more monkeys. Serum 3, for all of its potential, still had some kinks to work out. There was undoubtedly a broad line between fearless and homicidal, but Forenzi hadn't found it yet.

"I think we'll lower your dosage," Gunter said. "Maybe then you'll be able to make friends."

Gunter continued to stare, and Forenzi wondered how much the night monkey actually understood. Besides the expected changes to Gunter's amygdala, the primate's frontal lobe had also enlarged, increasing his intelligence. Forenzi wondered, half-joking, if one day Gunter would become so smart he'd solve the dosage problem himself.

Gunter dropped from his upside-down perch, startling Forenzi with the sudden movement. Without taking his big eyes off the doctor, he reached for a dismembered capuchin leg and began to gnaw on it.

"Apparently I don't need to feed you, either," Forenzi said.

Gunter grunted.

There was a great crash from above, and a small plume of dust drifted downward. Both Gunter and Forenzi stared at the ceiling.

Directly above them was Butler House. At this time of night, it should have been quiet.

But it rarely was.

"I wonder if monkeys have ghosts," Forenzi mused. "Perhaps your friends Laurel and Hardy will visit you tonight, Gunter. And they probably won't be pleased with the whole murder-dismemberment-cannibalism debacle. But then, that wouldn't scare you, would it, Gunter? Nothing scares you at all."

Forenzi wondered if he should mention Gunter during his Nobel Prize acceptance speech, since the animal had been essential to his research.

If so, perhaps the multiple killings should be downplayed. Or left unsaid.

"Goodnight, my friend. And don't eat so quickly. You'll choke."

Forenzi left the lab, turning off the overhead florescent lights so his experiment could dine in the dark.

Chicago, Illinois

Tom

After four hours of troubled sleep, Tom reached for his cell phone next to the bed and hit redial.

It went straight to Roy's voicemail.

Peering at the nightstand clock, he judged 8 A.M. to be late enough to call Roy's ex-wife. Tom located the number in his address book, and she picked up on the second ring.

"Hi, Gladys. It's Tom Mankowski."

"Is Roy with y'all? Fool missed his visitation time with his daughter."

Hell. Tom went into cop mode. "Does he do that often?"

"Not without calling he don't. And he didn't call. She was really upset, Tom. I was, too. I had plans. Tell him we're both extremely disappointed in him. He hook up with some hoochie mama and lose track of time? Now he's playing you to smooth things over?"

Hoochie mama? "I don't know where he is, Gladys."

"Really? This isn't a game?" Glady's voice had shed its ghetto attitude, and Tom sensed the concern.

"Apparently he's been missing since last week."

"A week? Oh, Jesus, Tom. I… what do we do?"

"I'm going to look for him, Gladys."

"Thank you. Please keep me posted, okay?"

"Sure thing. And if you hear from him, please call."

"I will. What should I tell Rhonda?"

Double hell. Rhonda just turned five. Old enough to wonder where her daddy was.

"I don't know, Gladys."

"You think it's one of his old cases? Or a new one?"

"I don't know. Did he mention going anywhere to you?"

"No. Nothing. He usually calls the day before he picks up Rhonda, which was supposed to be Wednesday. But he didn't. His phone goes straight to voicemail."

"Did he say anything about a haunted house? Or a reality show? Or getting some money?"

"I haven't heard from him since he took Rhonda to a Cubs game, over two weeks ago. Do you think… do you think he might be…"

Then he heard it. A sniffle.

Gladys was crying.

"You know, Tom, that son of a bitch makes me angrier than anyone I've ever met. But if anything has happened to him..."

"I'll find him, Gladys."

"Rhonda needs her father."

"I'll find him. My love to Rhonda."

Tom hung up. Listening to women cry was almost as bad as informing next of kin that someone close to them had died. And Tom had to wonder if that's what he just did with Gladys.

He found the FedEx invitation and dialed the number, using his land line. A machine picked up, the voice synthetic. One of those text-to-speech generators that just missed sounding human. Futurists called it *the uncanny valley*. A sense of revulsion that people felt when they experienced something that was *almost* human, but not quite. It was thought of as a survival mechanism, to help people avoid those who looked or sounded strange. Tom could understand how that worked, on a genetics level, because procreating with those who had some sort of defect meant potentially defective children, and avoiding someone who was odd decreased the chance of getting whatever disease they had. At least that's how the futurists explained it.

But listening to the voice, Tom realized it could help humans survive in another kind of way. By helping them avoid things that almost looked human, but weren't.

Things like ghosts.

"Please say or punch in your reservation number, followed by the pound sign."

Tom used his phone keypad.

"Hello, Tom Mankowski," the creepy robotic voice said. *"You are invited to spend the night at the haunted Butler House in Solidarity, South Carolina, where you will participate in a fear experiment. The house is located on 683 Auburn Road. You are expected to arrive on Saturday, before noon. You can bring whatever items you'd like, including weapons,*

religious paraphernalia, and ghost detecting equipment. If you take any prescription medication, please bring it along. The experiment will end Sunday at 4 P.M. Informing others about this experiment will disqualify you from your million dollar participation fee. Polygraphs will be administered to ensure compliance. Have a nice day. We'll see you soon."

Tom held the phone, trying to understand the weird feeling that had come over him. The instructions were straightforward and polite, but the call hadn't left him with warm, fuzzy feelings.

Quite the opposite, he was experiencing something that only happened rarely. like when a perp ducked down an alley, and Tom had to follow. Or the second just before he had to kick in a suspect's door.

Fear of the unexpected. Also known as dread.

He shook his head, trying to brush off the feeling. But the dread clung there like cobwebs.

Tom startled when the off-hook tone began to beep from the handset.

"If you'd like to make a call, please hang up and dial again. If you need help—"

He hung up.

Tom considered calling Joan, but the two hour time zone difference would have meant waking her up. Instead, he padded over to the shower and turned it on, hot as he could stand it. Then he stared into his bathroom mirror and began to scrape the stubble off his face. His beard, like the hair on his head, was turning prematurely gray. He also needed a haircut.

The mirror began to steam up, and Tom raised his hand to wipe it off, but stopped before his fingers touched the glass.

The fogging had revealed words, handwritten on the mirror.

I'M WATCHING YOU

THE NEXT DAY

Mililani, Hawaii

Josh

Fran was in a bikini, sitting on their porch, stripping and cleaning one of their AR-15 semi-automatic rifles. She had a look of intense concentration on her face as she ran a cleaning rod through the bore. If there was anything sexier than a woman in a bathing suit with a firearm, Josh didn't know what it was.

He set the lemonade he'd brought for her down on the table, and took a sip of the one he'd kept for himself. It was a perfect Hawaiian day, sunny and hot and smelling like paradise, and the lemonade was cold and sweetened just enough to take the edge off the pucker.

Mathison was perched on the seatback of Fran's chair watching damselflies. Though Josh had never seen him do it, he had a suspicion that the monkey liked to catch the bugs and eat them.

Mathison chittered when he saw Josh. He hopped down, ran into the house through the dog door, and returned a moment later with his plastic infant cup. He held it out to Josh, who poured in some lemonade. Mathison chirped a thank you, took a drink, then made a face and stuck out his tongue.

"I like it tart," Josh said.

Mathison set down his cup, ran inside again, and came out with a packet of sugar and a spoon. As the monkey mixed his drink to taste, Fran spoke.

"Are you sure about this?"

"Didn't we discuss it? I thought we agreed."

"Can it hurt to discuss it some more?"

"No," he admitted.

"So are you sure?"

Josh took another sip of lemonade. Mathison did as well, then made a sound like he was throwing up. He put his tiny hands on his own throat to emphasize his displeasure.

"So get more sugar," Josh told him.

The monkey ran off. He came back a moment later with five more packets.

"You're going to get diabetes," Josh said.

Mathison gave him the finger.

"Did Duncan teach him that?" Josh asked his wife.

"What?" She was absorbed in her cleaning.

"Mathison flipped me the bird."

"No. I think it was South Park."

"The TV show?"

"Yeah. He has a few DVD box sets." Fran squirted more solvent on the patch holder.

"You bought South Park DVDs?"

"No. He grabbed them in the store while I was shopping, put them in the cart, and paid me. He also bought *The Untouchables*. He's watched it seven times. I think he wants to be Sean Connery."

Mathison nodded at Josh, then added more sugar.

"And how did the monkey get money?"

"He was doing tricks in front of Walmart with his cup."

"Huh." Maybe the monkey had an organ grinder heritage. "How much did you make?"

The capuchin held up three fingers on his right hand, five on his left.

"Thirty-five dollars? Seriously? How long did it take?"

One finger, and five fingers.

"Only fifteen minutes? Fran, that's a hundred and forty bucks an hour."

"Josh, can you get back on topic? I asked you if you're sure."

Josh sipped more lemonade, then thought about the invitation to Butler House. The whole concept of it, from the way they were approached in the wee morning hours, to the dial-in number with the weird voice, failed to pass the sniff test.

"It's bullshit," Josh said. "The military is trying to hoodwink us. Those weren't feds."

"I agree."

Josh settled back in his chair, putting a foot up on the table. Mathison added a fifth sugar packet, took a sip, and gave Josh a thumbs up.

"Brush your teeth when you finish," Josh said.

The monkey replied in sign language. *"Woof ate my toothbrush."*

"The dog ate it? When?"

"A week ago."

"I watched you brush your teeth last night."

"That was Fran's toothbrush."

Josh frowned. He'd just kissed Fran less than an hour ago.

"What did he say?" Fran asked, looking up from her bore cleaning.

"We need to buy everyone in the house a new toothbrush. Maybe I'll let Duncan drive. He's getting his permit next week."

"And Butler House?"

Josh swirled some tart lemonade around his tongue, then swallowed.

"Fuck Butler House."

Chicago, IL
Tom

There weren't any homicides in Tom's jurisdiction in the last few days—unusual for Chicago—so it gave him time to work on Roy's disappearance. After arriving at the office and getting his cup of burned coffee, Tom went to his partner's desk and fired up his computer. While it booted he snooped around, finding nothing of interest.

As expected, Roy didn't have a computer password. Detectives preferred that, so if anything happened to them in the line of duty, their last actions could be easily traced.

Tom checked Roy's email, finding a confirmation for a rental car at the Charleston airport dated last week. He dialed the number and pretended to be Roy, reading off the confirmation number.

"What can we help you with, Mr. Lewis?"

An odd thing to say if the car hadn't been returned.

"Can you email me all the details from my rental, for tax purposes?"

"Certainly." The woman repeated Roy's email addy.

"Also, can you remind me when I returned the car?"

"You returned it last Sunday, at 11:35 A.M. Anything else I can help you with?"

Tom declined and disconnected. Next he called the airline Roy used and said he lost his return flight ticket. Did someone else possibly use it?

"No, Mr. Lewis. That ticket hasn't been used. Would you like us to book a return flight?"

Again Tom declined, and hung up.

Either Roy had returned the car at the airport, and something happened to him to prevent him from boarding his flight. Or something happened to him earlier, and someone returned his rental car for him to tie up a loose end.

Tom got on the Internet and began calling hospitals in the Charleston area, asking if Roy or any African American John Does fitting his description had been admitted. He also checked the morgues, and Charleston PD.

No luck.

Next he checked Roy's browsing history, and saw he'd been on the same Butler House site Tom had been on. Roy also had been on the *Ghost Smashers* website. Tom recalled reading that they'd shot an episode of their TV show at Butler House, but it never aired and the host quit TV immediately afterward. Tom went back to Roy's email, checking the Sent folder.

Roy had several exchanges with Richard Reiser, the host of the show. The last one ended with Roy asking if they could Skype. Skype was a VoiP—a voice over internet protocol. It allowed two people to talk to one another using computer webcams and headsets. Tom accessed Roy's Skype account, and sure enough Richard Reiser was listed as a contact. Tom found Roy's headphones in his top drawer and plugged them into a USB port. Then he video called Reiser.

As it rang, Tom accessed the National Crime Information Center and searched for Dr. Emil Forenzi. He didn't find any info. Apparently Forenzi didn't have a criminal record.

"You're not Roy."

Tom looked at the Skype window. He saw the profile of a man's head, obscured by shadows. Richard Reiser was Skyping without any lights on.

"I'm Roy's partner, Detective Tom Mankowski." Tom raised up his badge, holding it to the webcam embedded in the monitor. "When was the last time you spoke with Roy?"

"Is Roy missing?

"Do you know something about that, Mr. Reiser?"

"Rich. Call me Rich. I told him not to go to the Butler House. But he went, didn't he?"

Rich's voice was slurred, and Tom wondered if the man was drunk.

"No one has heard from him in seven days," Tom said.

"I warned him. I practically begged him not to go."

"When did you last speak with Roy?"

"Eight days ago. It was Thursday. He said he got some sort of invitation to Butler House."

"Why did he get in touch with you?"

"He wanted to know what happened on my show, Ghost Smashers. Why I quit show business."

"Did you tell him?"

Rich paused for a moment before continuing. *"The network did a good job of covering it up. They paid me off not to talk about it. I signed some non-disclosure agreements."*

"So you didn't tell Roy?"

"No. I did. I did so he wouldn't go. But I guess he went anyway."

"Can you tell me as well?"

"He didn't listen to me."

Tom lowered his voice. "Mr. Reiser, please tell me what you told my partner."

Another pause, and Tom began to wonder if Rich was going to balk. But then he began.

"It was nearing midnight. I was doing my intro in Butler House's great room—this huge space in the front of the house when you walk in. Two story roof, curved staircase, weird tapestries on the walls. It looked like the set of a Roger Corman Poe flick from the sixties. We'd gotten there in the daytime, did some establishing shots, set up our equipment. EMF, IR, EVP, full spectrum motion cameras."

Tom didn't know what any of those abbreviations were, but he didn't want to interrupt the story to ask.

"During set-up, one of the camera guys caught an RSPK on tape. That's recurrent spontaneous psychokinesis. *Poltergeist activity. A painting fell off the wall, right in front of us. Portrait of that serial killer, Augustus Torble. We checked the nail it was hanging on—a big, thick, six inch nail. Bent right in half.*

We'd never gotten footage like that before. In hindsight, we should have left right then."

Rich grabbed something and lifted it to his face. A bottle. Beer? Whiskey? He tilted it and swallowed, and then began to gag and cough. More evidence of being drunk.

"At midnight, I'm set to do my first piece of the night. Explore the basement of Butler House. We were using the dual head cam. Have you seen the show?"

"No."

"It's a two way camera, mounted on my head. One lens is pointed ahead of me, where I'm looking. One is pointing at my face, so the viewers can see my reactions. It's mounted on a helmet, and with the batteries… it's pretty heavy. So… we had a… a… thick strap around… my chin… to keep the rig steady. Right after I started my segment… the batteries…"

Rich's voice trailed off.

"What happened to the batteries, Rich?"

He didn't answer.

"Rich?"

"They… exploded."

He reached off to the side, and then the lights in his room came on.

Rich's face looked like it had strips of half-cooked bacon glued to it. Eyebrows burned off. No nostrils, just a gaping hole for his nose. Part of his upper lip missing, showing his teeth, which explained his slurring. He wasn't drunk. He was Frankenstein's goddamn monster.

"Lead batteries contain sulfuric acid. So my helmet was both on fire, and leaking acid down my face. And because of the chin strap, I couldn't… I couldn't get it off. I couldn't get it off…"

"I'm sorry," Tom said. It took everything he had in him to not turn away from the screen.

Rich lifted the bottle—a water bottle—to his face and took a sip, gagging again, some of the water running down his ruined chin.

"The network sued the company that made the camera. But when they took the rig in for testing, no one could find anything wrong with it. No faulty wiring. No bad parts. It's like it exploded for no reason at all."

Tom felt terrible for the guy, and he didn't like making him talk about it. But for Roy's sake, he had to ask. "But you think there was a reason."

"Something in Butler House did this to me. I'm sure of it. Something evil. That's why I begged Roy to stay away. And you should stay away, too."

Tom pursed his lips.

"Look, your partner, your friend, Roy. He's dead, man. Butler House got him. And if you go looking for him, you're going to die."

"Thanks for your time and insights, Rich. I've got to get going."

Tom disconnected, guilty about his lie. He didn't have to leave. He just couldn't stand looking at Rich's disfigured face anymore, and the conversation had greatly disturbed him.

Tom's hair on the back of his neck suddenly stood at attention, and he had a very strong feeling he was being watched. By who? Eavesdropping co-workers?

Or was someone else watching? Someone, or...

Some thing.

Tom swiveled around, seeking the staring eyes he knew were on him.

But no one was there.

At least, no one he could see.

Realizing he was letting his imagination mess with him, Tom called Joan's cell phone. Thankfully, his girlfriend picked up on the third ring.

"Tom? I'm in the middle of something. Director wants a rewrite on set, writer is throwing a hissy fit. Is this important?"

"I just wanted to hear your voice, babe."

"That's sweet. Can I call you back?"

"Yeah, sure. And hey, wait... Joan... you still there?

"Yes?"

"Did you write anything on my mirror?"

"What?"

"My bathroom mirror. Someone wrote *I'm watching you* on it."

"Wasn't me. Gotta go, lover. Call you soon."

His long distance romance hung up, and Tom's creepy feeling got a whole lot creepier.

THE NEXT DAY

Charleston International Airport

Frank

Dr. Frank Belgium walked out of the baggage claim area and onto the sidewalk, the warm blast of summer air welcome against his overly air-conditioned body. The plane had been chilled to meat-locker temperature, so cold he'd had to ask an attendant for a blanket. The airport had been similarly refrigerated.

He closed his eyes and took a deep breath, letting the temperate heat warm him. But he couldn't feel the sun's rays.

Belgium squinted up at the overcast sky. The clouds were an ugly swirl of gray and black, but the air didn't feel humid or sticky. It didn't look like rain. It just looked ominous.

A man of science, Belgium publicly scoffed at the paranormal. Omens. Superstition. The afterlife. These didn't hold up to the scientific method, and had no empirical evidence to support them.

But privately, he feared the supernatural. Because he had, in a way, experienced it. To Belgium, the sky looked like a warning meant specifically for him. Like a big sign that said GO BACK WHILE YOU STILL CAN.

Something reddish brown darted toward Belgium, swooping into his peripheral vision, and he dropped his carryon bag and ducked down, emitting a less-than-masculine yelp as he did. Covering his head with his hands, he prepared himself for another attack.

"It's a finch," a female voice said from behind him.

Belgium turned, squinting through his fingers. "What?"

"A house finch. They won't hurt you."

Belgium stared at the woman. She was maybe in her late thirties, short hair, baggy sweater, no make-up. He could guess, on a good day, she'd be cute. But it didn't look to Belgium if she'd had any good days in a while.

He tried to swallow, but his mouth had gone dry.

"Oh. Thanks. I I I thought it was a..." he let his voice drift off, and then picked up his bag and stood up, warily searching the area for more dive-bombing finches.

"You thought it was what?" the woman asked.

"Hmm? Oh. A bat."

"A red bat?"

Belgium frowned. "You'd be surprised."

The woman shrugged. Belgium glanced around, trying to get his heart rate under control, wondering why there weren't any cabs. Shouldn't an airport have cabs?

He watched a traveler cross the street, where he was met by a blue Honda. A woman got out, they had a quick but poignant hug, and then he loaded his suitcase and got into the car and they drove off.

"Where are the taxis?" the finch lady asked.

"I don't know. I'm waiting for one one one myself."

Another minute passed. Belgium considered renting a car. But he didn't want to go back into that freezer of an airport. In fact, he didn't want to be in South Carolina at all. The thought of being arrested for treason began to hold some appeal. At least, in that case, he knew what to expect. Knew who his enemy was.

There was security in knowing. But the unknown, however…

"Do you have a cell phone?" the finch lady asked him.

"Hmm?"

"To call a taxi."

"No. Don't carry one. You?"

"Me neither. We're probably the last two people in the world who don't."

Finally, a lone yellow cab pulled onto the throughway. Belgium held up his hand and at the same time noticed his companion did as well. He'd gotten there first. And at the rate cabs arrived at this airport, this could be the last one of the day. But even though Belgium was rattled, and hadn't been with a woman for a very long time, he still had a streak of chivalry in him.

"You can take it," he summoned the courage to say.

"Are you sure? You were here first."

The cab pulled up. Belgium took a quick look at the sky again, which was getting even uglier.

"It's okay. I'm sure sure sure another one will come along."

The lady smiled, and it took ten years off her face. "I didn't know there were any gentlemen left. We could share it."

"I'm heading west. Solidarity."

Her brow crinkled. "Really? So am I."

Belgium did a quick mental calculation on how coincidental that was, and considering Solidarity had a population of less than a thousand, he found the odds to be extremely high. Unless…

"The Butler House?" he asked.

The woman nodded, eyes wide.

He remembered his manners and offered his hand. "Frank Belgium."

"Sara Randhurst," she said. Her touch was soft and warm, her grip strong.

Belgium opened the door for her, then helped the cabbie put their bags in the trunk. When everyone was seated, he gave the driver the address.

"I don't go there," was the gruff reply.

"Pardon me?"

"The Butler House. No hacks go there. Bad news, that place."

Belgium considered asking how close he'd take them, but then realized they'd have the same problem once they got there. Renting a car was still an option, but that would be a hassle.

Plus, he had the paranoid delusion that if he left the cab, the sky would open up and lightning would fry him.

"I'll double your fare," Belgium said.

"No way."

"Triple it."

The cabbie turned around in the driver's seat to face him. "You serious?"

Belgium nodded.

The cabbie let out a noise that was part sigh, part shrug, and said, "It's your funeral buddy."

They pulled out of the airport parking lot and headed west, into the woods. Belgium kept his eyes out the window, trying to look casual instead of nervous. He was aware that the side of Sara's foot touched his, and he was hoping she'd keep it there. That small measure of human contact was keeping him grounded.

"So," she said, "you're doing this to win a million dollars?"

"Hmm? Me? No. I'm… well, being coerced into this."

"By whom?"

"I'm not not not at liberty to say. Sorry."

Sara nudged him with her thigh, and when he looked she was smiling again.

It dazzled him. She looked so pretty, so real, so near. Like a safe port in a terrible storm.

"Real secret stuff, huh?" she asked.

He smelled something on her breath. Whiskey. Belgium rarely drank these days, but he really wished he had something to take the edge off.

"I was involved in a government project that I'm not allowed to talk about."

"What do you do, Frank?"

"I'm a a a molecular biologist."

She seemed to appraise him, and Belgium lapsed into self-consciousness. Had he combed his hair? Were there crumbs on his face from breakfast? Did he have any stains on his shirt?

"This is a fear study," she said. "I take it something bad happened with that government project."

"Yes. That's... well, it's actually understating it a bit."

The horrors of Samhain all came rushing back at him like they were still happening. The deaths. The blood. The certainty he was going to die. Frank could feel his larynx tightening, and he put a hand on his throat to massage it. The sides of the cab seemed to be closing in, making it hard to breath. He stared outside, saw something fly past, and flinched like he had at the airport.

"You look freaked out, Frank. I didn't mean to—"

"Would you mind if we stopped somewhere for a drink? I mean, I I I don't want to be forward, or for you to think I'm trying anything with you. But I could really really really use one." He winced. "The past... it... *hurts*."

Sara opened her purse and took out a tiny, plastic airline bottle of Southern Comfort. She passed it to Frank, who was shaking so badly he couldn't get the small top off. Sara put her hands over his, helped him to remove the cap, and he downed it in one gulp. Almost immediately, he felt better. But he didn't know whether to attribute that to the booze, or Sara's touch.

"That's... that was... thank you."

She patted his shoulder. "No problem. I get panic attacks too."

Sara turned away, looking out the window. Almost immediately he missed her looking at him. Belgium felt the liquor burn into his belly and wondered how he could draw her attention again. He figured maybe the truth would do it.

"I was locked underground with a..." Belgium chose his next word carefully. "Maniac. I barely got out alive. A lot of people died. Badly."

Without facing him, Sara said, "I was trapped on an island with dozens of cannibals, and several serial killers."

"You were... *seriously*?"

Sara nodded into the window. "A lot of people died. Badly. I guess that's why we're both here."

Belgium had a sudden, overpowering, completely inappropriate surge of affection toward this woman. He wanted to hug her. For her sake, and for his. If she was a kindred spirit, as he suspected, it would do both of them a world of good.

Instead he sat rigidly in his chair, trying to will his heart to slow down.

"I read up on Butler House," Sara said, still not looking at him. "Lots of tragedy there."

Belgium had begun doing some research on the house—the devil you know and all that—but it had scared him too badly to continue.

Sara seemed to be expecting some response, so he grunted noncommittally.

"If any house in the world could be haunted," she continued, "this would be the one." Sara turned, and touched his arm. "Do you believe in ghosts, Frank?"

Belgium didn't believe in ghosts. But there used to be lots of things he didn't believe in.

"I can't rule out that they might exist," Belgium said.

"I think the supernatural is bullshit. I don't believe in any sort of afterlife. But..."

Sara opened her purse. Besides a wallet and a few more SoCo bottles, there was a bible, a rosary, and a vial of clear liquid.

"Holy water," Sara said, snapping her purse closed. "Does that make me a hypocrite?"

Belgium shook his head. "No. It makes you prepared."

"No atheists in foxholes, I guess. Did you bring anything?"

Belgium hadn't. For the same reason he'd never bought a gun.

"Um... no. I guess—this might sound silly—but I sort of feel like I'm living on borrowed time. Ever since... well, let's just say I'm lucky to be alive, and these last few years I've been waiting for my past to to to catch up with me. Whatever happens, happens."

"Kind of fatalistic, don't you think?"

He was surprised by the frankness of her words, and wondered how much she'd had to drink. But perhaps it wasn't the liquor. Maybe Sara was always this straightforward.

He liked that. A lot. And it had been a long time since he could admit to liking anything.

"I don't don't don't think it's fatalistic. More like realistic. When you see dark things—"

"You can't unsee them," Sara said, finishing his thought.

They looked at each other, and Belgium saw understanding in her eyes. This woman was just as wounded as he was. He'd heard about the concept of kindred spirits, but hadn't experienced it before.

"I have a very bad feeling about this trip, Sara," he said in hushed tones.

Then the front windshield burst inward and the car spun out of control.

Pittsburgh International Airport
Mal

Growing more and more uncomfortable as they inched their way through the security line, Mal let his wife go through the metal detector first.

She beeped, as expected, and then got into a conversation with the bored-looking TSA guard. He waved his wand over Deb. That led to her pulling off her jogging pants—which had snaps on the sides instead of seams.

Mal's prosthetic hand always got a few raised eyebrows, but Deb's artificial legs drew attention like a marching band down Main Street. Though Deb was always offered the option of a private search, away from gawkers, she never accepted, preferring to strip down to her shorts and show everyone on the planet her high tech artificial limbs.

Mal knew Deb did it because she didn't want to be treated any differently than anyone else. But they did treat her differently, and Mal watched the crowd finger pointing and murmuring, some assholes actually snapping pictures.

It was made even worse by the fact that Deb was an athlete, and very fit, so standing there in her running shorts like a sexy female Robocop getting ready to pose for Playboy 2054 made him feel jealous as well as overprotective. As expected, after her scan and pat-down, Deb was immediately approached by a smiling Lothario who was better looking, a better dresser, and no doubt younger and richer than Mal was.

So I get to endure her humiliation of stripping down to her stumps, and then nurse my own humiliation because I don't feel I'm man enough for her.

Mal was expertly in tune with his own feelings, thanks to the unrelenting therapy. Besides lacking a hand to touch his wife with, he also felt powerless to protect her. That led to feelings of inadequacy which normally didn't reveal themselves during daylight hours. But as he watched CEO Joe chat up his wife while TSA played stupid with his mechanical hand, Mal felt himself getting angrier and angrier. When they finally let him through, he stormed over to Deb as she was re-snapping her running pants.

"Picked up an admirer, I see," Mal said, sizing up the man. He looked fit, and could probably kick Mal's ass all day long and not break a sweat.

"Just paying the lady a compliment," the guy replied. He looked confident, which Mal hated. Especially because Mal remembered being that confident once.

"I'm the lady's husband," Mal said. "Now go run off to your board meeting."

The guy puffed his chest out. "Or what?"

"Or I'll beat the shit out of you, then make you lick it up."

Doubt flashed across the man's face. He muttered, "Asshole," then turned and walked off.

Deb looked irritated. "Where did all that testosterone come from?"

"The guy was hitting on you, Deb."

"He said it was really brave of me to take my jogging pants off like I did."

Mal rolled his eyes. "He said that because you have a nice ass. Think he would have said that to some fat guy with artificial legs?"

"Can't I be brave and have a nice ass? You know, Mal, I feel like a freak often enough. Some guy innocently flirting makes me feel normal. He wasn't a threat to you."

Mal wanted to turn away. But if he did, it would prove she won and he was wrong. So he forced himself to maintain eye contact. "He saw you as an easy target, Deb."

"I'm not easy. And I'm not a target."

Mal switched tactics. "Deb, there are... guys... who have fetishes about..."

Deb's eyes darkened. "So now he didn't approach me because I had a nice ass. He came over because he's an amputee pervert."

"I'm just saying—"

"You're acting like an asshole."

Mal studied his shoes. He wanted to kneel down, help her put her snap-away pants back on, but he couldn't align the snaps with one hand.

"Look," he said, letting out a long breath. "I didn't like that guy swaggering up to you."

"Him? You swagger more than any guy I ever met."

Maybe, once upon a time. But not lately.

He changed subjects. "Do you have the Xanax?"

"My purse."

He sat next to her on the bench and pawed through her handbag. The medicine bottle had a child-proof cab on it, and after trying to pry it off with his teeth, he simply cradled it in his lap until Deb finished dressing. She reached over, held his hand.

"I'm sorry," he said. "I used to be fine flying. But now..."

"It's okay to be afraid."

He wanted to scream, to smash the pill bottle against the floor and stomp it to bits. Instead he clenched his teeth and whispered, "But I'm afraid of everything."

"I know."

"Including losing you."

"I know." Deb patted his hand. "And that's not going to happen."

"I'm sorry, Deb. You deserve better."

"You're all I need, Mal."

She kissed his cheek. A kiss of pity, not love.

Mal felt his ears get hot. He endured the kiss without flinching away.

"Take a few, Mal. Zonk out on the plane."

Mal nodded. But he wouldn't. Deb couldn't drive the rental car, which meant he had to, and alprazolam abuse and driving didn't mix. So when Deb opened the bottle for him, Mal swallowed one, just to take the edge off, and then they shuffled into the terminal.

With an hour before boarding time, they stopped at the Burgh Sportz Bar in the Airmall. Deb had a chicken salad. Mal had a burger. When the food arrived it looked decent enough, but Mal's stomach was sour and he picked at his French fries while watching Deb inhale her food. She'd talked him into coming to this stupid experiment, and even seemed optimistic about it. Bless her little heart, Deb considered this trip a hybrid of vacation and adventure.

Mal felt differently. He didn't like confronting his fears in therapy, and he knew he'd abhor being purposely frightened. But the thing that bothered him most was being allowed to bring weapons.

What kind of government experiment allows the participants to be armed? What safeguards were in place to prevent someone from getting seriously hurt?

Mal had packed the gun in their check-in luggage, and both he and Deb had taken shooting lessons. But in fright's grasp, Mal wouldn't trust himself to hit a bus from a meter away. What if he fired wildly and hurt someone? What if he shot Deb? What kind of insane tests were going to be conducted on them that required firearms?

"Aren't you hungry?"

He shook his head. Deb took that as an invitation to tear his burger in half and start munching. Mal stared at her, marveling at her resiliency. He wanted to tell her how much he loved her. How proud he was of her. She was two levels away from becoming a black belt. A double amputee, slowly becoming a karate master. Who could have ever guessed all she could accomplish? But instead of gushing his admiration, he thought of that CEO jerk hitting on her, and how she seemed to eat it up.

She's going to figure out I'm a coward, and leave me.

Mal didn't think he'd be able to handle that. But he was sure it was coming.

Someone bumped the back of Mal's chair, and he turned to see a teenager standing next to the table. Chubby, almond-eyed, protruding tongue. Down Syndrome.

"What's wrong with your hand?" the teen said, pointing at Mal's prosthesis.

"I lost it. This one is made of rubber."

"How did you lose it?"

A madman strapped me to a table and cut it off with a scalpel while I begged for him to stop.

"An accident," Mal said. He looked at Deb, who was staring at the boy with wide eyes. While the teen was probably harmless, he was bringing up old memories. Bad memories.

"Where are your parents?" Mal asked, searching around for the child's caretaker.

"You're a freak," the boy said.

Mal blinked. "What?"

"You're a freak and you're going to die." He looked at Deb. "And so are you, lady."

Mal began to stand up. "Look, kid—"

But the teenager stepped back and pointed, then began to yell, "FREAKS GONNA DIE! FREAKS GONNA DIE!"

Mal turned to his wife. Her face had lost all color, and she looked ready to throw up.

"FREAKS GONNA DIE!"

Again Mal looked for the boy's father or mother, but instead he only saw people staring. Not only those in the restaurant, but passersby had also stopped to watch.

"FREAKS GONNA DIE!"

Finally an older woman came rushing over, tugging at the boy's arm, saying "Calm down, Petey, calm down." She offered

Mal and Deb a quick, soulless *I'm sorry*, and then managed to pull her son away from their table as he continued to shout.

"FREAKS GONNA DIE!"

The woman tugged the child further into the terminal, until his voice melded in with the rest of the airport noise. In the restaurant, the clinking of silverware on plates resumed, and conversations picked up to levels prior to the interruption.

Mal, his whole body flushed and twitching, turned to his wife.

"You okay, babe?"

Deb's face pinched, and then she vomited all over the table.

Solidarity, South Carolina

Forenzi

Dr. Emil Forenzi sat on the mattress—the one piece of furniture in his bedroom that wasn't an antique—and squinted at the Bruno Magli loafers he'd just put on. There was a stain on the toe. He pulled it off and licked his thumb, rubbing off a reddish-brown streak.

Blood.

Forenzi couldn't remember wearing the shoes in the lab area, and his mind wandered as to elsewhere he might have trod in bodily fluids. His revere was interrupted by a knock on the bedroom door.

"Enter," he said, dropping the shoe next to the bed.

Sykes came in, holding a sheaf of papers. He silently presented them to Forenzi. It was reports on their guests.

Tom Mankowski, the cop, had just arrived at the airport. Excellent. He would make a sturdy test subject.

The amputees, Mallory and Deborah Dieter, had boarded their plane in Pittsburg. Forenzi had high hopes for them.

Dr. Frank Belgium and Sara Randhurst were due at Butler House any minute. Forenzi's intel provided an interesting tidbit.

"They're sharing a cab?" he said to Sykes. "Do they know each other?"

"I have no idea, sir."

Forenzi glanced at him, caught a glimpse of the man's sharp dentata.

"Do you mind if I ask you a personal question, Sykes?"

"Nothing is personal to me, sir."

"Do you ever bite your tongue while eating?"

"As much as anyone else."

Sykes didn't elaborate. Forenzi flipped through more pages, seeing who else was attending, and frowned at the lack of a dossier on the VanCamps.

"Josh and Fran VanCamp didn't confirm?"

"No, sir."

Forenzi clucked his tongue. That was a shame. They would have been ideal.

No matter. This weekend would proceed without them, and it would be a success nonetheless.

"Have you spoken to your team?" he asked Sykes.

"Yes, sir. We're ready."

"My team?"

"I checked on them half an hour ago. Proceeding as scheduled."

"Dinner?"

"Planned for seven, as requested."

"Will we have those little Swedish meatballs? Those are wonderful."

"Those are listed on the menu, sir."

Forenzi nodded. In the hallway, floorboards creaked.

Both Forenzi and Sykes turned to look. No one was there.

"The ghosts are getting anxious," Forenzi mused.

The paranormal history of Butler House was well-documented, and Forenzi had lost count of the strange phenomenon he'd encountered since coming here. Doors closing by themselves. Sharp drops in temperature. Strange odors. Creepy sounds. Last week, he was awoken from deep sleep, absolutely positive someone had been at the foot of his bed, watching him

"Do you believe in ghosts, Sykes?"

The man shrugged.

"So you aren't afraid of the supernatural?"

"I'm not afraid of anything, sir."

"Of course you're not. Dismissed."

The man left, closing the door behind him. Not much of a conversationalist, Sykes. But he had other areas of expertise.

Forenzi stood up and looked into the ornate, full-body mirror hanging above the bureau. He laced a tie through his collar and fussed with a half Windsor knot, trying to get it even. As he fought the fabric, he noticed something moving in the lower corner of the mirror.

The dust ruffle of the bed.

Forenzi looked down, behind him, and the rustling stopped.

Mice? Rats?

Something else?

And what happened to my shoe?

Forenzi searched the floor, turning in a full circle, looking for the loafer with the blood stain. He could have sworn he'd dropped it on the floor before Sykes came in.

Under the bed?

The doctor got on his hands and knees, ready to lift up the dust ruffle. But something gave him pause.

Behind the dust ruffle, something was making a sound. A distinct, recognizable sound.

Chewing.

I hear chewing.

A streak of panic flashed through Forenzi, and he crabbed backward, away from the bed. Then he quickly scanned the room for some sort of weapon. His eyes settled on an old, cast iron stove. Atop the bundle of kindling next to it was a fireplace poker.

Forenzi got to his feet and snatched the poker, turning back to the bed. Then he held his breath, listening.

The chewing was now accompanied by a slurping noise.

What the hell is that?

He knelt next to the bed, firmly gripping the poker with his right hand, reaching toward the dust ruffle with his left—

—and hesitated.

Do I really want to know what's under there?

The chewing and slurping sounds stopped.

Forenzi continued to hold his breath, focusing on the silence.

After ten seconds, he let out a sigh, already starting to convince himself he'd imagined the whole thing.

Then he heard something else.

Scratching.

From under the bed. As if something was raking its nails on the floorboards.

Acting fast, before he lost his nerve, Forenzi lifted up the dust ruffle and jammed the poker underneath, flailing it around.

He didn't hit anything. And the scratching sound stopped.

Forenzi leaned down, squinting under the bed. But it was too dark to see anything.

Moving the poker slowly, he swept it across the floor, kicking up vast colonies of dust clods. When his poker touched something solid, he retracted quickly—

—pulling out his missing loafer.

He stared at it, trying to make sense of what he saw. The shoe was damp with a viscous goo, and the toe had a large hole in it, surrounded by what appeared to be...

Bite marks.

Charleston, South Carolina

Tom

Fetzer Correctional Institution was known as a Level 3 prison. It housed the worst of the worst. Violent offenders and lifers did their time here, as did the death row inmates, up until their appeals ran out. In order to arrange a last-minute visit with one of its prisoners, Tom had to call in a big favor with his old boss, a retired Chicago Homicide Lieutenant named Daniels. She'd pulled a few strings and gotten him an audience with possibly the most depraved and sadistic murderer in this nation's history, Augustus Torble. The millionaire heir who bought Butler House then tortured several women to death.

Tom drove the rental SUV to the perimeter fence, and an armed guard looked at Tom's badge and checked his name on the visitor roster. Tom was allowed through the double fence, electrified and topped with razor wire, and he drove past one of the prison's five gun towers. The main building was a red brick monstrosity that was among the drabbest, ugliest buildings Tom had ever seen. It had a flat façade devoid of any embellishments, save for barred windows and an arched entryway with ugly steel doors.

He parked in the visitor lot, and walked down a cracked, sun-baked sidewalk to the entrance. It was overcast and hot, the gray sky looking like it was ready to rain, but the humidity seemed strangely absent. Tom was buzzed in after being directed via intercom to look up into the security camera, providing them with video footage of his face.

Inside, he was met by two more armed guards, who led him without fanfare down a harshly lit hallway to a waiting room, where he was told to have a seat. Tom parked his butt on a steel bench bolted to the floor, and watched the clock on the wall—a clock housed in wire mesh. It was much more humid in the prison than outside. In fact, Tom almost immediately began to perspire, and wished he'd had a handkerchief to blot his forehead.

When two minutes passed, a dour woman in a frumpy pantsuit entered and frowned at him. She was accompanied by a guard.

"I'm the assistant warden, Miss Potter. You couldn't have come at a worse time." Her southern lilt making the last word sound like *tahm*. "The prisoner is being readied for transport."

"Where is he going?" Tom asked.

"Out of my hair. Prisoner transfers are common, and I'm not always told the particulars."

"Do you know the reason?"

"I wasn't informed." The way her mouth pursed told Tom that this annoyed her. "What is it you want with the prisoner?"

"I have some questions to ask him. About Butler House."

Potter snorted. She removed a handkerchief from her jacket pocket and blotted the sweat on her neck. "That house is a blight on the beautiful state of South Carolina. Needs to be razed flat, if you ask me."

"What have you heard about the house, Ma'am?"

"You mean, is it haunted? I deal in the real world, Detective. I see enough hatred and evil in men's souls without having to blame the supernatural for it. But I'll tell you something. I've had several interactions with Mr. Augustus Torble. And if there was ever a man possessed by demons, it's him. Just last week he had an altercation with another prisoner over the last bag of potato chips. Mr. Torble bit the other prisoner's finger off. When questioned about the incident he had to be restrained, because..."

Her voice drifted off, and Tom could detect a bit of flush in her cheeks.

"Ma'am?" he asked.

She blew out a stiff breath. "Because Mr. Torble was noticeably aroused by the incident, and kept playing with himself while being questioned."

Tom kept his face neutral, professional.

"Has Torble had a lot of incidents like that?"

"More than his share. The other prisoners are afraid of him. Are you armed?"

Tom had left his gun in his luggage. "No, Ma'am."

"Regulations insist on a pat down, to prevent weapons or other contraband from being passed to the prisoner. Would you mind standing up and raising your arms, Detective?"

Tom did as instructed, and the guard did a thorough frisking, going so far as to check each of Tom's pockets.

"I'm to understand you've dealt with murderers before," Potter said. "Your boss, Lieutenant Daniels, spoke highly of you. She apparently knows some very important people. Normally a spur of the moment visitation request from an out of town police officer would be denied. Especially during the time-sensitive and delicate procedure of transfer."

"I'll be sure to let Lt. Daniels know how hospitable and accommodating you and you staff have been."

He didn't bother to tell her Jack was retired, and the assistant warden's efforts to get a pat on the head were likely for nothing.

"You have ten minutes," Potter said.

"Has anyone told him I'm coming?"

"No. Only that someone wants to speak to him. But Torble is used to that. People are always coming by to pick his brain about something. Cops, psychiatrists, reporters. He gets so many visitors he could use a secretary. Or a press agent." She turned to leave. "Don't touch the prisoner, don't pass anything to the prisoner. Your entire visit will be monitored and recorded. And Detective..."

"Ma'am?"

"Watch yourself. This one is as bad as they come."

Potter nodded a goodbye, and the guard led Tom down another corridor and into a room with a reinforced door. Inside, an older man was sitting at a steel table attached to the floor like the one Tom had recently used. He wore an orange prison jumpsuit, and leg shackles, locked to a steel U bolt in the floor. His hands were also shackled to a thin chain encircling his waist, preventing him from raising his arms.

His gray hair was wild, uncombed, his face sporting three days of stubble. He was thin to the point of gaunt, and though his records stated he was sixty-two years old, he didn't look much older than fifty. The killer's eyes were deep set, dark, and had a glint to them. Intelligence, insanity, mirth, or maybe a combination of all three.

"Mr. Torble, my name is Detective Mankowski. Thank you for your time."

"Call me Gus," he said. His voice was unusually deep, and decidedly less southern than Miss Potter's. "What's your name?"

"I prefer to go by Detective. Or Mr. Mankowksi."

"Have a seat, Detective. We have lots to talk about."

Tom sat across the steel table from him. The killer crouched down a little, like a coil ready to spring. It was just as humid as the waiting room, and Tom continued to sweat. Torble, on the other hand, appeared cool and comfortable.

"I'd like to talk about Butler House."

Torble smiled. "Good times. It has a torture chamber, you know. I called it the Happy Room. I had a hooker down there once, tied to a rack. Used boiling lard on her. Poured it all over her body, inch by inch. Did it every day for weeks. Put an IV in her to keep her hydrated. You know the smell of breakfast sausage, frying up in the pan? That's what she smelled like. I swear, as often as not I'd be drooling after a session with her."

Tom had prepared himself for this. Sadists like Torble got off on their ability to manipulate, to shock. So Tom forced his facial muscles to remain lax, and made sure his breathing was slow and steady. Reacting to psychopaths only egged them on.

"Did you ever do anything like that before buying Butler House?" he asked.

"You mean, did I skin kitty cats when I was a toddler? Or rough up whores?"

"Anything of that nature," Tom said blandly.

Torble's lips pressed crookedly together, and he looked off to the right, a poker tell that someone is searching for a truthful memory. "Nope. Can't say that I had."

"Did you ever notice anything odd about the house while you lived there?"

Torble studied him. "This is about the house? Not about trying to pin some old, unsolved crime on me?"

"I'm curious about the house."

"You mean you're curious if it's haunted."

Tom stayed silent.

Torble leaned back as far as his shackles allowed him. Tom couldn't understand how the man wasn't sweating. Tom himself felt like he'd dressed quickly after a particularly hot shower.

"My lawyer pressed for the insanity defense. Said we might persuade the jury that Butler House drove me crazy, based on its notorious reputation. That the devil was perched on my shoulder, whispering things in my ear. Tell me, is it insane to give your wife boiling water enemas? That was one way I punished her if she didn't help with the whores. Also, I have to tell you, as far as gaining spousal compliance goes, nothing beats a sturdy pair of pliers."

Breathe in, breathe out. Remain calm.

"Did Butler House drive you crazy, Gus?"

"Do you know how certain places have an energy to them, Detective? A vibe? Take this shithole, for instance. I bet, when you were driving up to the prison, you could feel the despair. The hopelessness. The desperation. I bet, if you closed your eyes and tried to tune into your senses, you could tell you were in a prison, even if you didn't know. Care to try it?"

Tom wasn't going to close his eyes in front of this loon. "I'll take your word for it."

"You want my opinions, but you don't offer yours. That's not very sociable."

Tom breathed out. "Yeah, this feels like a prison."

"Well, Butler House also has an energy. And I'm betting you haven't been there, because you'd immediately know what energy I'm talking about."

"What kind of energy, Gus?"

"That house feels *evil*. It exudes it, like a bog steams on cool nights. Terrible things have happened there, going back almost two hundred years. And terrible things will continue to happen there, as long as it stands."

"Did you ever see anything supernatural while you were living there?"

"Do you mean ghosts, Detective?"

"I mean anything at all."

"Have *you* ever seen anything supernatural?"

Tom has seen plenty of strange things, some practically impossible to comprehend. But the closest he'd gotten to anything supernatural was the writing on his bathroom mirror.

"Maybe," Tom said.

"I had this one hooker, name was Amy. Sixteen years old, sweetest little smile on her. I started on her legs, using a branding iron, working my way up. I came back down to the chamber the next day, her chest is all branded. Someone wrote the word BITCH on it. But here's the stinger. It wasn't me. I didn't brand that word on her. It wasn't my wife, either, because she was in the punishment box. And I don't think sweet little Amy did that to herself. That's just one of many unexplainable things that happened at Butler House."

"Is Butler House haunted, Gus?"

Augustus Torble smiled, and it was an ugly, twisted thing. "If ghosts and demons really do exist, Butler House is where you'll find them."

Despite the heat, Tom shivered.

"Do you know anything about experiments being done at Butler House?" he asked. "Tests?"

"What sort of tests?"

Tom didn't answer, instead waiting for Gus to fill in the silence. The seconds ticked past.

"In prison, you hear things," Gus finally said. "Things about the government, trying to cure soldiers of their fear. Let me tell you something, Detective. I know fear. I've seen it, up close. When you come at someone with a scalpel, and look them right in the eyes as you slip it into their thigh, you can witness fear in its purest, freshest form. And if they could come up with a cure for that, it would be quite a trick indeed." Gus winked. "But it would also ruin a lot of fun."

"So you've heard about a program like that?"

Torble shrugged. "I've heard lots of things."

"Have you heard about any connection between government experiments and the Butler House."

"I'll answer that, but first I want you to answer something for me, Detective. What do you know about fear?"

Without being able to prevent it, Tom thought back to when he had first met Joan. What they'd gone through together in Springfield. The maniacs that tried to kill him. The horrors in the basement.

"Yes," Torble said, studying him. "You know fear. But unfortunately for you, I cannot confirm nor deny any connection between government experiments and Butler House. But I can show you something that might surprise you. Interested?"

Tom offered a slight nod.

Torble grunted, then began to shake all over. His face turned deep red, the veins in his neck bulging out. Tom was wondering if the guy was having a stroke, or a heart attack. He was about to call for the guard when, quite suddenly, Torble's hand slapped onto the metal table between them with a *BAM!* His bleeding wrist still had the cuff on it, but the chain that had wound around his waist was broken.

"I SEE YOUR FEAR!" Torble thundered as the guards rushed in and pounced on him. "YOUR FEAR WILL BE THE DEATH OF YOU, TOM!"

Torble was tackled, pinned to the table while screaming incoherently, and Tom stood up and moved back, too surprised to speak. Another guard escorted him out into the hall, leading him to the exit.

Tom wasn't sure what he'd actually come here to learn, and wasn't sure he'd learned anything. Maybe Torble knew something. Maybe he was just a nut who got his jollies trying to scare cops.

If that was the case, it worked. Tom was thoroughly mortified. Not because of his crazy admissions to atrocious deeds. Tom had met plenty of terrible specimens of humanity. Not because he broke his shackles. That was surprising, but not unprecedented. It was well known that people on drugs, or just insane in general, could snap handcuffs.

No, what bothered him most was what Torble had said. Potter had stated Torble hadn't known Tom was coming.

Yet, somehow, without being told, Torble had called Tom by his first name.

Outside of Charleston, South Carolina

Sara

"Do something, Frank," Sara said. "It's suffering."

They were staring at the side of the road. On the asphalt, in the middle of a small spattering of blood, a cardinal was twitching its broken wing.

"It's dead, Sara. That's just a reflex. It hit our windshield going over seventy miles an hour."

"Are you sure."

"Yes yes yes. But if this makes you feel better…"

Sara looked away as Frank stomped hard on the cardinal with a sickening *crack*.

She immediately dug her hand into her purse, locking her fingers around one of the miniature bottles of Southern Comfort. Her buzz was wearing off, and the situation wasn't improving. They'd tried calling for another cab, but none would take them to the Butler House. Frank was in favor of going back to the airport and renting a car, but their bags were in the cab's trunk, which wouldn't open. After hitting the bird, the car swerved off the road and the tail end smacked into a tree. They had to wait for the tow truck driver to arrive with tools to open the back.

Just one sip. To make the fear go away.

She released the bottle. Sara knew she used alcohol to cope. But she refused to believe she was dependent on it. Also, she was starting to like the odd, soft-spoken Dr. Belgium, and wanted to stay relatively clear-headed because she enjoyed his company.

It had been a long time since she enjoyed anyone's company. After what happened on Plincer's Island, Sara was certain she'd never trust a man again. But there was something about Frank that was, well... *frank*. He seemed kind, sincere, and even kind of cute. She didn't even mind the odd way he spoke, repeating words.

But most important of all, he made Sara feel safe. If she'd been alone in the cab when they hit the cardinal, she would have been hysterical and drinking SoCo like water. But Frank's presence soothed her. Maybe because he lived through a hellish experience, like she had. Or maybe it was just chemistry.

Sara took her hand out of her purse, and tried to seem nonchalant about it when she placed it in Frank's. He glanced at her, his eyes widening. But his fingers clasped softly around hers, and all thoughts of drinking slipped from Sara's mind.

"Thanks for doing that," she said.

"I could, um, step on it a few more times, if you want."

"That's okay. This is really forward of me, Frank, but are you seeing anyone?"

"No. I haven't... I... it's been a very long time, Sara."

"For me, too."

As Sara stared at him, it occurred to her she'd forgotten how to flirt. She wondered how she looked, no make-up, hair probably a fright. She also wondered how Frank would react to the fact she had a child. Sara hadn't tried to date anyone recently, but she guessed most men wouldn't be interested in a pre-made family.

"I have a son," she blurted out. "Jack. Would you like to see a picture?"

She watched his eyes, searching for any hint of rejection.

"Of course," he said.

Sara reached into her purse with her free hand, took out her wallet. The only picture in it was of Jack, in his high chair, smiling and eating strained peaches.

"He's adorable. And his father?"

Sara shook her head.

"I don't mean to pry, but that painting on the wall behind him," Frank said. "Is that Van Gogh's *Portrait of a Woman in Blue*?"

"It's a fake. Long story. I thought it was real. But the real one is in a museum in Amsterdam."

"I'd like to hear that story someday."

"I'd like to tell it someday. Maybe when we're done with the weekend. Where do you live, Frank?"

"Pittsburgh. You?"

"Michigan. Near the coast."

"Which coast?" Frank asked, holding up his left hand with his fingers together and his thumb slightly out.

Sara smiled. Because Michigan looked like a mitten, that was how residents showed where they lived. She touched the base of his index finger.

"So who is taking care of Jack while Mom is off visiting haunted houses?"

"After… what happened to me, I was having some trouble coping. Jack was taken by social services. I haven't seen him in six months."

"I'm sorry." Frank gave her hand a squeeze. "I can't even imagine what that must be like."

"That's why I'm here. If I get the money, I can hire a lawyer, get my son back."

"Are you well enough to care for him?"

The question pinned Sara there as surely as if she'd been staked to the ground. Was she well enough? Her recent behavior didn't indicate she was. If anything, she'd gotten worse since they took Jack away.

So how do I respond? Bravado? Lie so I don't look like a bad person?

Or the truth?

Frank seemed patient. Understanding. Sara didn't know if anything would become of this chance meeting, but she didn't want to start their relationship with lies. Even if it made her look weak.

"I don't think I am well enough, Frank. But right now, my hope is gone, because it isn't possible to get him back. If I had some hope again, I think I could pull myself together."

Frank nodded, slowly. "I don't know you at all. But—and this is odd—I I I feel I do. You remind me of a woman I know named Sunshine Jones."

Sara raised an eyebrow. "Former girlfriend?"

"No. I worked with her, every day, and never had a chance to tell her how much I thought of her. Bright. Tough. Pretty. She had this indefatigable spirit. I think you do, too."

"That's kind of you to say."

"I wouldn't say it if I didn't believe it."

"What happened to Ms. Jones?"

"She married someone else. It was best. He's a good man. But I always wonder what might have happened if I just just just… tried."

"Sometimes trying is the hardest thing in the world."

"I know a little something about hope, Sara. But I don't think you've given up yet. I think you've just been kicked really hard."

Sara really wished that was true. "Why do you think that, Frank?"

"Because I've been kicked pretty hard, too."

She moved a little closer to him, trying to read his eyes. Frank Belgium had the kindest eyes Sara had ever seen.

Then a car pulled up next to them, and a guy yelled through the window.

"Everyone okay?"

"Yeah," the cabbie said. He was leaning up against the crumpled trunk of the car, smoking a cheap stogie.

"Does anyone need any help?"

"No no no," Frank said, smiling at Sara. "We're doing fine."

The man began to pull away when Sara yelled, "Wait!"

The car stopped, then backed up.

"Do you have a crowbar?" Sara asked.

"It's a rental. There's probably one."

"Our luggage is stuck in the trunk. Can you give us a hand?"

He continued backing up until he was behind them, then pulled over to the side of the road. When he exited the vehicle, Sara saw he was tall, over six feet, moderate build with longish light brown hair streaked with gray. He opened his trunk, poked around for a bit, and found a crowbar.

The taxi driver spat on the street. "Hey buddy, you touch my cab with that, I'll call the police."

"I am the police," the man said, producing a badge.

The cabbie shrugged.

"Thanks so much," Frank said. "Several cars have passed, but you're the first one to stop."

"What happened?"

"Bird flew into the windshield."

The cop eyed the dented trunk. "Must have been one helluva bird."

"I'm Frank," he offered his hand, which the cop shook. "This is Sara."

"Tom. Nice to meet you both."

Tom pressed the flat end of the crowbar between the trunk lid and the fender, and gave it a fierce twist. It instantly popped open.

"Thanks, Tom." Sara reached into the grab her bag, grateful it was dry. She had two more bottles of Southern Comfort in it, and a leak would have been both embarrassing, and worrying. If she was going to be involved with a fear experiment, she wanted to have liquor nearby.

"I know it's a lot to ask," Frank said. "But would you mind taking us back to the airport to rent a car? I'll pay you for your time."

"I'm kind of running late," Tom said. "Can't you call a cab?"

"We're going to a place cabs are afraid to go," Sara chimed in. "It's called Butler House."

"In Solidarity?"

"You know it?" Frank asked.

"No. But that's where I'm headed. Some kind of fear study."

"So are we," Frank said. "Would you mind if we tagged along?"

"Not at all."

"Sara?" Frank turned to her.

She really liked that he asked her opinion. "Can I see your badge again?"

Tom offered his star.

"Chicago," she said.

"The Windy City. I'm a detective."

Frank appraised him. "Did anyone ever tell you that you look like Thomas Jefferson?"

"I may have heard that once or twice. You guys coming along?"

Sara handed his badge back. "Thanks, Tom. I think we will."

Tom held out his hand to take Sara's bag, and he placed it and Frank's in his trunk along with the crowbar.

"Would you like the front front front seat, Sara?" Frank asked.

He was doing the nice thing by offering, but still looked slightly disappointed. Sara thought it was adorable.

"Thank you, Frank. But would it be okay if I sat in the back with you?"

Frank nodded several times in rapid succession. "Of course."

Sara looked at Tom's rental car. It was a compact. Which meant it would be cramped in the back.

She was looking forward to it.

Deb

"You gotta be fucking me with a wet noodle."

The woman in the rental car line ahead of Deb and Mal had pink and green hair, a mouth that would make a trucker blush, and an apparent problem with her credit card.

"I ran the card twice, Ms. Draper. I'm sorry, but I'm going to have to ask you to get out of line."

"I've got a five hundred dollar limit on that goddamn card, pencil dick. And a zero fucking balance. The car is only fifty bucks a day, and I'm returning it tomorrow."

"The deposit is five hundred dollars, Ms. Draper. Unfortunately, that maxes out your credit card and leaves you nothing to pay for the rental."

Deb felt bad for the woman. She'd been in a situation like that before.

"I've only got thirty bucks on me. I'm running cash poor today. Can't you help a fucking lady out?"

"I'm sorry, Ms. Draper."

"I'll blow you."

The clerk did a double-take. "Excuse me?"

"I'll take you in the guy's shitter and suck your Slim Jim if you get me this car."

"Uh… as romantic as that sounds, I'm married."

"Which probably means you need head more than most."

Mal, who had been sullen and inconsolable on the airplane, actually snickered at that and gave Deb a nudge.

She whispered to Mal, smiling. "What? I give you head all the time."

"Once a week is not *all the time*, Deb," he whispered back.

"If it were up to you, it would be every two hours."

The rental car clerk raised his voice. "If you don't leave the line right now, Ms. Draper, I'm calling airport security."

Ms. Draper was seemingly unperturbed. "If you're shy because you have a micropenis, don't be. I've seen all types. It actually makes it easier for me to deep throat. And if you got a problem getting it up, I can stick my finger up your ass, work that prostate."

The rental car guy reached for the phone on the counter.

"You know what, assbag?" Ms. Draper said. "Tomorrow I'm going to be a million dollars richer. And I'm going to buy your goddamn little car rental business here, and make you clean toilets with your tongue for six bucks an hour."

She threw up her hands in a dismissive matter and spun around, facing Mal and Deb.

Several things flashed through Deb's mind at once. The first was Draper's million dollar comment. Obviously she had been invited to Butler House as well. The second was that this green and pink haired woman had pocked scars covering her face, as if she'd had a severe case of acne as a teen. But these also covered her neck, and as Deb's eyes travelled down her low-cut blouse, her cleavage as well.

Those weren't acne scars. They were man-made.

"Enjoy the show?" she asked Deb, a sneer on her face.

"Very much so," Deb replied. "You want to ride with us? We're heading to Butler House."

The woman raised an eyebrow. "No shit. Really?"

"Sure," Mal said. "And you don't have to suck my Slim Jim."

"But if you want to stick your finger up his ass," Deb said, "be my guest."

"Please don't stick your finger up my ass," her husband said. "I'm cool."

Ms. Draper eyed each of them up and down, apparently taking notice of Deb's prosthetic legs and Mal's rubber hand. Then she smiled.

"I'm Moni Draper. Pleased ta meetcha both."

There was a round of hand shaking, and Mal approached the clerk at the desk.

"Would you really have blown the rental car guy?" Deb asked.

"Girlfriend, I've done a lot more for a lot less, back when I was strung out." She dug into her shoulder bag and took out a pack of cigarettes, even though there were No Smoking signs posted everywhere throughout the airport. She lit up with one of those jet lighters, where the flame was blue-green and hissed. Deb noticed her hands were also covered with pock marks.

"So what do you do?" Moni asked.

"I'm an athlete."

"With no legs? No shit. Good for you, babe. What sport?"

"Marathons. Triathlons."

"You can make money like that?"

"I've got sponsors," Deb answered.

"Wait a sec. Were you that bitch in that energy drink commercial?"

Moni used the word *bitch* like she used the word *babe*, with obvious affection.

"That was a while ago."

"I used to drink that stuff all the time. I remember you, on that bicycle and shit. In those cute little biking pants."

Deb still had those biking pants, and they were, indeed, cute.

"What do you do?" Deb asked.

"Model."

Deb wasn't sure what to say to that, then Moni winked.

"Kidding, of course. I'm actually an escort. Topping. Domme stuff."

"Like a prostitute?"

"Back in the day I was. Streetwalker. But I had a close encounter with a maniac who cut me up pretty good, as you can plainly see. So now I only do in house calls to select clients. The scars are actually a plus, because they make me look scarier."

"So a domme is a dominatrix?"

"You betcha. Money is better, and I don't have to fuck them."

Deb was curious. "So what do you actually do to guys if you aren't sleeping with them?

"All kinds of crazy shit. Tie 'em up. Slap them around. Spank them. Make them lick my boots. Pee on them. Figging."

"Figging?"

"You don't want to know. Point is, I'm in control, the bottoms love it, and the money is good. At least, it used to be good. I've been semi-retired for a while." Moni took a big draw on her cigarette, then blew the smoke out of her nostrils. "Went back to school. But I'm almost out of money, and I figured I'd have to start scheduling clients again. Then I got the invite to this fear thing, and I was like, holy shit, I finally got a lucky break. Hopefully I'll never have to fig a guy again."

"You have to tell me what figging is."

Moni grinned and winked. "Trust me. You're better off not knowing."

Mal motioned for them to follow him, and they were led to the parking garage and a mid-size sedan. The clerk made a concentrated effort to ignore Moni. Deb, however, was really starting to like the woman. The incident at the restaurant back in Pittsburgh had really rattled her. But Moni was getting Deb's mind off of that, and also helping break the tension between her and Mal. Deb knew her husband was going on this trip for her, and didn't think any good could come from it. What Mal didn't understand was that Deb needed to do something, anything, because it beat doing nothing. Even if it didn't work, it was worth a try.

"So you can run with those fake legs on?" Moni asked.

"Not well. These are my walking legs. I've got a different pair for running."

"Cool. And your husband, does he have different hands too?"

"Mal just has the cosmetic hand. It isn't functional. It's just for show."

"But they have functional ones. I've got a client, a real live private eye, he's missing a hand. He can break a beer bottle with his fake one. Also, it vibrates."

Deb shot Moni a *that's bullshit* look. "Seriously?"

"Variable speeds and everything. The guy is a bit of a nut, but that fake hand is something every man should have. Make your hubby buy one."

Mal never bought a mechanical prosthesis. He felt it would be a constant reminder of what he no longer had. Instead, he tried to pretend that his entire left arm no longer existed.

"Thank you very much, Mr. Deiter," the clerk said after having Mal walk around the car and signing the agreement stating it had no damage. "Enjoy your stay in Charleston."

"Oh, we're not staying in Charleston. We're going to Solidarity."

"Not… *Butler House*?" The clerk's voice had gone up an octave.

Mal didn't answer, and Deb knew why. When they'd called to confirm their attendance, the recording said informing others about the experiment would disqualify them.

"What's Butler House?" Mal asked, obviously playing dumb.

"It's… it's the most evil place on earth. Whatever you do, stay away from that house, Mr. Deiter. And may God go with you."

The clerk did a quick about-face and rushed past Deb and Moni, in a sudden and unwarranted hurry. Deb watched the man as he passed, and the expression on his face was pure fear.

He looked like he'd just seen a ghost.

Tom

The private driveway leading up to Butler House wasn't paved, and Tom almost missed the turn because the entrance was overgrown with brush. Only a sign reading 683 AUBURN ROAD, hanging on a wooden post mostly obscured by vines, gave any indication there was a road there.

"We're about to get bumpy," he told Frank and Sara as he pulled the car off the paved street and onto a dirt trail.

Bumpy was an understatement. Ten yards into the woods, Tom realized he should have rented something with all-wheel drive. First they hit a ditch that made their undercarriage scrape against the ground, then the car almost got stuck on a mound of dirt, Tom having to gun the engine before the tires gained traction.

The pair in the back seemed to be enjoying themselves, the rough terrain giving them an excuse to bump into each other. During the car ride, Tom had ascertained they'd just met, but they seemed to be hitting it off very well. The Dutch courage he smelled on their breath might have been one of the reasons for that, but Tom also felt strangely comfortable with the duo. Tom remembered meeting Joan, and at the same time he'd also met two guys named Abe and Bert. Tom still spoke with Bert regularly, and he and Bert visited Abe in the hospital six months ago. Abe, a used car salesmen, had sold a clunker to a man who was unhappy with his purchase, and even unhappier with Abe's refund policy. The guy had expressed his displeasure by chasing Abe around the car lot with a baseball bat and ultimately breaking his leg.

When he'd met Bert, Abe, and to some extent, Joan, there had been a familiarity there that was unusual. Akin to going to a high school reunion and seeing people you hadn't seen in twenty years. But he hadn't met Abe, Bert, or Joan before, just like he hadn't met Frank and Sara. Yet Tom felt immediately comfortable around them. Like they were destined to be friends.

It might have had to do with shared experiences. Like Tom, both Frank and Sara had apparently lived through something awful. So even though they each came from different walks of life—a homicide cop, a counselor for wayward teens, and a molecular biologist—they were still birds of a feather.

Tom drove through the thicket, which then opened up into marshland, acres of cattails in all directions. The mild wind blowing made them sway, like waves rolling across a brown and green sea. The effect was weirdly hypnotic, made even more so because some of the cattail spikes—thick tubes on the top of each stalk that resembled cigars—had begun to seed, turning them into white tufts. Like dandelions, the white seeds floated on the breeze, giving the appearance of a snow flurry. It made Tom feel eerie, and somehow alone. Even the duo in back, who'd spent a majority of the car ride gabbing, went silent at the spectacle.

"This is… creepy," Sara finally said.

"I don't believe in a netherworld," Belgium said. "But if one exists, this is how I picture it."

They drove more than a kilometer through the undulating plants, and then things got creepier when Butler House came into view.

It seemed to rise up out of the cattails, looking both incongruous to its surroundings, and also as if it had been there since time began. Gray, sprawling, and decrepit, it might have once been regal, but now appeared way past its prime. Even from the distance, Tom could sense its decay. The roof seemed to slump in the center. The walls looked slightly crooked. The entire house appeared to lean to the left, ready to collapse during the next big storm. Which, judging by the ominous gray clouds overhead, could be any minute.

When they got within a hundred meters of the house, Tom saw a small guard station, no bigger than a porta-potty, and a steel gate barring the path. As Tom approached, a man in a suit and tie came out of the tiny building and held up his hand to stop them. He wore sunglasses, even though it was overcast, and Tom saw a glimpse of a shoulder holster beneath his jacket.

Tom stopped next to him and rolled down the window. He immediately wrinkled his nose. The air stank of sour, like carnations going bad.

"IDs," the guard said.

Everyone fished out their driver's licenses, and when Tom collected all three he passed them over. The guard gave each a cursory glance, and handed them back. Then he returned to his little booth and the gate swung open.

"Talkative fellow," Belgium said.

"Even money he's former military," Tom told him.

"How do you know?" Sara asked.

"He had a bearing about him. A stillness, but alert at the same time. A lot of cops have that, too."

"How do you know he wasn't a cop?"

"Cops ask questions. Soldiers follow orders."

Tom continued on to the house, which seemed to grow in size faster than they approached. By the time they parked on the grass near the front door, Butler House blocked more than half the sky. It wasn't particularly bright out to begin with, but in the house's shadow it felt dark as night.

"Well well well," Belgium said. "It's even uglier up close."

Tom agreed. They could now see the broken shutters, the peeling paint, the cracked masonry. Thorny weeds jutted out of the ground next to the crumbling foundation. One of the chimneys had several bricks missing.

"Looks like someone picked up the house and dropped it," Sara said after they exited the vehicle.

Tom couldn't help but remember the Butler House website, and all of the atrocities committed here. Augustus Torble's words popped into his mind.

That house feels evil. It exudes it, like a bog steams on cool nights.

Tom had dismissed the words as lunacy. But standing in front of the house, it didn't feel a part of his world. Almost as if, at any moment, it would sprout hundreds of black, oily tentacles and devour them all.

He did *not* want to go inside.

"You look like I feel, Tom," Belgium said. "I don't see how any good can come from us going in in in there."

The front double doors, arched and barred with wrought iron *fleur de lis*, opened outward. The trio immediately took a step backward, and Tom's hand went to his chest, seeking the shoulder holster and gun that weren't there, still packed in his bag.

Standing in the doorway, flanked by two military men in gray suits, was Dr. Emil Forenzi. Tom recognized him from online pictures. He was a wisp of a man, tufts of white hair over his ears that looked a lot like cattail seeds, back beginning to bend with age. His suit was blue poplin, tailored, his necktie tan. His smile was broad and looked genuine.

"Welcome to Butler House. I'm so pleased to see you all. Three of our guests have already arrived, and we're expecting three more. Detective Mankowski, if you'd be so kind as to give my men your keys, they'll park the car and take your bags to your rooms.

Tom handed over the rental car automatic starter, then took Forenzi's outstretched hand. It was delicate and boney, like a fledgling bird.

"I am Dr. Forenzi. It's a pleasure, Detective. I've followed your exploits closely. You're a remarkable man, on so many levels."

Then the doctor turned to Sara. "Greetings, Ms. Randhurst." He clasped her hand in both of his. "I've read about your extraordinary bravery. It is an honor to meet you in person. And Dr. Belgium…" Another handshake with Frank. "I'm so eager to talk to you. Apologies for the… *crude*… way you were beckoned here. Come in, come in, meet the others."

Forenzi led them through the doors, and when Tom crossed the threshold he heard a strange humming sound. It disappeared immediately, and before he could think about it Tom was facing Butler House's great room.

The website pictures didn't do it justice. The space was massive, a two story cavernous area that was big enough to comfortably seat King Kong. The light came from three gigantic deer antler chandeliers, hanging from the rafters on thick chains. Each contained at least a hundred antlers, and they were asymmetrical and seemed thrown together. Like big heaps of bones.

The centerpiece of the great room, a ceiling high stone fireplace, easily utilized several tons of granite. Impressive as it was, it wasn't lit, and Tom felt a chill when he stared at it.

Various chairs and tables were scattered around the room, some obviously new, others outdated and in need of repair. Though the chandeliers were big, they weren't enough to adequately light the space. Plus they threw strange shadows across the walls and floor.

Seated near each other were two men and a woman. Forenzi led them across a frayed, drab Persian rug and stood in the middle of everyone.

"Might I introduce our new arrivals. Chicago cop Tom Mankowski, who has worked several serial killer cases, but his claim to fame has to be the part he played in the tragedy at the late Senator Philip Stang's mansion."

Tom remained calm, even though those words hit like a blow. He had no idea how Forenzi found out about that. But he intended to ask him as soon as they were alone. That, and questions about Roy. But for the time being, he needed to just watch and listen.

"Sara Randhurst survived a terrifying ordeal on Rock Island in Michigan, including several encounters with feral cannibals, and a well-known serial killer named Lester Paks. A sadist who filed his teeth down to points and chewed his victims to death."

Tom glanced at Sara, and even in the dim light he could see her face had gone white.

"And Dr. Frank Belgium, a molecular biologist who actually encountered Satan himself."

Sara's head jerked in his direction. "Frank? Really?"

"I really can't talk about that that that, Dr. Forenzi. It's highly classified. And how did you happen to hear about…"

"Dr. Belgium, meet Aabir Gartzke, psychic medium, sensitive, and clairvoyant extraordinaire."

Aabir stood and gave a theatrical bow. She was a tall woman with dark, Slavic features, her long black hair pulled back in a severe ponytail. Her dozens of silver and gold bracelets jangled as she moved, and the loose blouse she wore wouldn't have been out of place on an eighteenth century gypsy.

"I have met you all already, in my dreams and visions. Detective Mankowski, how is Joan's latest movie coming along?"

Tom played coy. "If you're clairvoyant, shouldn't you already know that?"

Aabir smiled. "Indeed. The writer acquiesced, changed the scene as instructed. Right now, your girlfriend is in the star's trailer, discussing wardrobe. And Sara, no need to worry, my dear. Jack will be returned to you soon."

"It doesn't take a psychic to know that," Sara said.

"Of course not. I could have easily gotten that through the court records. But you will be pleased to know that Jack is walking now. He's doing well with his foster family, but he still has memories of you and misses how you used to sing to him."

"I… I need to use the bathroom," Sara's voice cracked, and she began to walk off.

"Down that hallway," Forenzi pointed, "third door on the right."

"Sara?" Belgium began to go after her. But she stopped him by saying, "I'm fine, Frank, I just need a minute."

"Dr. Belgium," Aabir continued, "have your friends Sun and Andy told you yet they're pregnant?"

He looked at his shoes. "No, they haven't."

"If it's a boy, his middle name will be Frank. And it will be a boy."

"Impressive, Ms. Gartzke," Forenzi said. "Aabir's skills have helped police find four missing children, and two murderers. But, like each of you, she is here at Butler House to face one of her greatest fears."

"There are many kinds of spirits," Aabir said. "Ghosts are the residual energy of human beings after they have died. Poltergeists are attached to particular locations. They reenact the same scene, again and again. Usually scenes of violence or death. But the last type of spirit is the dangerous one. The kind that has no earthly counterpart."

"Demons," Dr. Forenzi said, nodding.

"Demons are malevolent entities that feed on the energy of the living. I have encountered demons in the past. They are extremely dangerous. In some cases, they can even kill. Demons frighten me deeply."

"You don't seem frightened right now," Tom stated.

Aabir put her hands on her hips and stuck out her chin. "I performed a cleansing ritual on this room, so they can't enter. But there are many demons in this house. I can feel them, like eyes on the back of my neck."

Tom recalled how he was sure someone had been watching him while he was sitting at Roy's desk, but no one had been there.

"Have you ever encountered a demon, Mr. Pang?"

"No, I haven't," said the Asian man sitting next to Aabir. He had broad shoulders and a compact frame, and a pencil mustache on his upper lip. "That's because demons, like ghosts and poltergeists, don't exist."

"Woo-jin Pang runs a company that specializes in debunking paranormal activity."

"Science has been unable to prove the existence of a spirit world."

"Science also hasn't been able to prove it doesn't exist," Aabir countered.

"It isn't up to science to disprove a wild claim, bro. It is up to the person making the wild claim to show scientific evidence of it. If I say I have a leprechaun in my backpack, the burden of proof is on me."

"And you've never encountered anything you can't explain?"

"Of course I have. But not being able to explain a phenomenon doesn't mean it should be automatically attributed to the spirit world. I was using my EMF meter at a client's home two weeks ago—"

"Excuse me," Tom said. "That's the second time I've heard those initials. What's an EMF meter?"

The ghost hunter rolled his eyes. "It tests for electromagnetic fields. Supposedly EMFs are disrupted by supernatural activity. It's one of many tools used to measure conditions we can't see, bro. So I was using the meter, and it kept spiking. We ruled out appliances, cell phones, fuse boxes, the air conditioning. We even killed the main power at the breaker. It still kept spiking."

"And you're saying that wasn't a spirit?" Aabir asked.

"It wasn't a spirit. There was a storm ten miles away. My equipment is so sensitive it was picking up lightning strikes."

"Mr. Pang claims he's never been frightened while doing paranormal research," Forenzi said, smiling politely. "We'll see if Butler House changes his mind."

Pang crossed his arms over his chest. "If ghosts do exist and they're here, I'll find them."

"And last," Forenzi said, "but certainly not least, is perhaps the only person in the world more skeptical than Mr. Pang, bestselling author Cornelius Wellington."

Cornelius Wellington was in his fifties, wearing a sweater vest, glasses, and a graying Van Dyke beard.

"Pleased to meet you all," Wellington boomed. He pronounced all as *awl*, and sounded a lot like John Lennon. "I'm very much looking forward to the proceedings, Dr. Forenzi. I'm sure you have quite the little show concocted for us."

Forenzi chuckled. "Mr. Wellington is known for his books that debunk the supernatural. Due to his certainty that spirits do not exist, he's convinced I have turned Butler House into something akin to the Haunted Mansion at Disneyland. Animatronic specters and people in masks jumping out to yell 'Boo!'"

"I certainly hope so, Doctor. That will be exceedingly more exciting than sitting around waiting for ghosts to make contact."

There was a booming knock on the front doors, and everyone turned to watch as one of the guards opened them up, revealing three people, two women and a man.

"Ah, the rest of our party has arrived." Dr. Forenzi smiled so broadly Tom could see his molars. "And so it begins."

Mal

Mal winced at the steak on the plate in front of him. It looked, and smelled, divine.

But try cutting filet mignon with only one hand.

The enormous banquet table everyone sat at was one of the original furnishings, according to Dr. Forenzi, who held court at the head of it. He'd been telling stories about the various ghosts said to haunt Butler House. They included:

Blackjack Reedy, a one-eyed slave master who roamed the hallways with a whip.

Sturgis Butler, who was charred to the bone and smelled like burnt pork.

Jebediah Butler, who floated from room to room on a puddle of his own blood, which constantly leaked from his flayed skin.

Ol' Jasper, a slave with four arms who dragged a machete around. You knew he was close when you could hear the sound of him dragging his long blade across the floor.

The Giggler, a masked demon who would mutilate himself in order to instill fear.

Colton Butler, carrying his bag of ghastly surgical instruments, still trying to conduct his insane experiments upon the living.

Mal was only half-paying attention. His mood had brightened a little since the awful airport experience, mostly due to Moni Draper's irrepressible personality. She talked nonstop about unrelated topics—what Mal referred to as diarrhea of the mouth—but was so upbeat and foul-mouthed that it was like watching a stand-up comic.

But Moni's energy evaporated once they entered Butler House. As pleasant a host as Dr. Forenzi attempted to be, there was a very real and very bad feeling that hung in the air, like a blanket pressing down upon them all. Mal was nervous, boarding on paranoid. He was also hungry, and staring at the slab of meat before him made him depressed as well.

A moment later, his plate was switched with a steak already cut into pieces. He glanced at Deb, sitting next to him, and she was now busily cutting her new steak, not even acknowledging what she'd done.

"A wonderful set-up, Doctor," Wellington said after patting his lips with a linen napkin. "So now, when we see one of your actors limping through the hallways with a satchel of scalpels, we're supposed to be terrified. The power of suggestion leaves us more receptive to strange phenomenon, and more susceptible to accepting them."

"Indeed, that would be the proper way to conduct a fear study," Forenzi admitted. "But all I can offer you is my word that I haven't hired any actors to try to scare you people."

"What exactly are we supposed to do to get our million bucks?" Moni asked, her mouth full of baked potato.

"It is simple. After dinner, my associate Dr. Madison will take a small sample of your blood and conduct a brief physical to ascertain your general health. Then, tomorrow, another sample of your blood shall be taken." Forenzi winked. "Should you survive, of course. Which is why I've had all of you sign waivers."

"You've conducted this experiment before?" Tom, the cop, asked.

"Not quite in this way. But we have had guests before."

"And what happened to them?" Tom continued.

The doctor laughed. "Naturally, they all died of fright."

There were a few nervous titters around the table, but the cop didn't join them.

"Allow me a self-indulgent moment to explain my research, and why each of you are so important." Forenzi pushed back his chair and stood up, spreading his hands.

"Ladies and gentlemen, we're all here today as self-aware, sentient beings. Perhaps some of you believe in the afterlife, spirits, souls, God and the devil. Perhaps some of you find all of it, to use one of Mr. Wellington's words, poppycock."

Mal hadn't heard the writer use that word yet, but he could imagine it easily enough.

"But what makes us believe what we believe? Our differences really are tiny compared to our similarities. We're all made of the same stuff. We're all 99.9% identical, genetically. Am I correct, Dr. Belgium?"

"Yes yes yes, you are so far."

"Doctor, if you wouldn't mind, can you provide the group with your learned definition of life?"

"Life? Well, all living things, in order to to to be considered alive, have to meet certain criteria. These criteria vary, depending on the scientist. But I'd define life as a structure that can reproduce, respire, create energy for itself, and respond to environmental changes. Also, life can cease."

"By that definition, fire is alive," Forenzi said.

"Fire is a chemical process known as combustion."

"But isn't life also a chemical process?"

"Well, yes." Belgium nodded several times. "It certainly certainly certainly is."

"We are all made of chemicals." Forenzi swept his hands across the table, grandiosely indicating all seated there. "Chemical reactions allow us to metabolize food and oxygen, and excrete waste. They are responsible for cell division. Aging. The very thoughts we have in our heads. *Emotions*. Dr. Belgium, can you elucidate the chemistry of emotion?"

"Well, in response to a stimulus, or in some cases due to a problem with the limbic system, our body releases neurotransmitters and hormones, which dictate how we feel feel feel about certain things. Watch a sad movie, we cry. When we meet someone we like, we bond. These are chemicals we manufacture ourselves, which we've evolved to help us adapt to various situations."

"A mother's instant affection for her child when it is born isn't due to love," Forenzi said, focusing on Sara. "At least, not love alone. It is because, during childbirth, the mother's body floods with oxytocin. Not only does that jump start lactation, but it also forces the incredibly strong emotion of maternal love. Which brings us to fear."

Forenzi spread out his palms, like a preacher orating to his congregation.

"My friends, I have isolated the neurotransmitter that activates the fear response. Which means, very soon, I'll discover a way to control fear."

Mal, who'd been greedily devouring the steak his wife had cut for him, suddenly gave Dr. Forenzi 100% of his attention.

"You can cure fear?" he said.

"I'm very close, Mr. Deiter. Fear begins in the amygdala, which is located in the medial temporal lobes of the brain. When you are frightened, it releases hormones and neurotransmitters that stimulate the fear response. You are aware of the symptoms. Paranoia. Increased heartbeat. Dry mouth. Sweating. Shortness of breath. Lightheadedness. The feeling of hopelessness. Because many of you survived some horrific events, your brain chemistry has physically become altered.

Which is why you continue to be afraid all of the time. Your mind still believes it is in danger, and it keeps pumping chemicals into your body. "

"So you're going to test our blood for these these these chemicals," Dr. Belgium said, "then scare us, and test our blood again. And then am I to assume you'll then try to block the fear somehow?"

"All in good time, Doctor. All in good time."

"So why are Mr. Wellington and I here?" Pang asked.

"Every good experiment needs controls," Forenzi said. "Your skepticism will provide a baseline metusamine level."

"Metusamine?" Belgium said. "*Metus* is latin for *fear*. So metusamine—"

"Metusamine is the neurotransmitter I isolated that is responsible for the fear response. Correct, Dr. Belgium. And I'm synthesizing the transporter protein—"

"Which will terminate effects of of of metusamine!" Belgium yelled, obviously excited. "How close are you to synthesis?"

"I've been able to induce fearlessness in a primate, a Panamanian night monkey."

"I'd be honored and excited to go over your data."

"In time, Doctor."

"And will we be able to try this for ourselves?" Mal asked. A fear-free life was a gift almost too valuable to fathom. To be able to sleep well again, to live without the constant paranoia. A drug like that would be a miracle.

"Very soon. And your presence here, Mr. Dieter, will help speed the process."

Deb reached over, touched Mal on the arm. He looked at his wife and saw she was teary eyed. He realized he was as well.

"So let us finish our meals," Dr. Forenzi said, raising his wine glass, "and then begin the process of scaring the hell out of you fine people."

Everyone toasted. Everyone seemed excited, except for the cop, whose face remained neutral. Mal said to his wife, "Maybe you were right, honey. Maybe this trip was the answer to our prayers."

"I love you, Mal."

"I love you, too."

They shared a quick kiss, and Mal went back to his steak. The cop, Tom, looked over at him, and his calm expression was replaced by something else.

Concern.

Did Tom know something the rest of them didn't?

Mal's relief evaporated, and the uneasiness returned.

After dinner, he'd confront the Detective, pick his brain.

Maybe this really was as it seemed, a million bucks and a cure.

But maybe, just maybe, Forenzi was playing them all.

Like fattening up the turkeys before Thanksgiving dinner.

Frank

Dr. Frank Belgium walked up to the second floor with Sara and marveled at the curve balls life threw.

A few days ago he'd been hating his job, and his life. He'd been lonely, depressed, and living in constant fear.

Now he was next to a wonderful woman and actually daring to think about the future for the first time.

Belgium wasn't prone to daydreaming. Others would consider him a fatalist, but to Belgium that meant *a realist who truly knew how bad things were*. But there, in Butler House, Belgium indulged in a mini-fantasy where he and Sara and Jack had a house somewhere. They were playing a game of Monopoly, which he used to love as a kid. He saw himself land on Boardwalk with a hotel and start laughing, and his new family laughed along with him, and there was the scent of baked apples coming from the pie cooling on the windowsill. He and Sara took Forenzi's metusamine pills, and neither were afraid anymore. Life wasn't something you endured. It was something you appreciated.

A ridiculous notion, of course. But the idea of it pleased him, and he clutched it to his being like a life line.

"Here's your room."

Belgium snapped out of his reverie and saw one of the men in suits had opened a door for him.

"You're the next door over," the man told Sara. She smiled shyly at Frank, and followed him a few meters down the hall.

"See you in a bit, Frank," Sara said.

Frank nodded, and watched her disappear through the door. Frank went inside his, closed the door behind him, and took a look around.

A bed, some old furniture, and some drapes replete with cobwebs, none of which would have been out of place in Dracula's castle. No bathroom.

Belgium found his suitcase next to the dresser. He considered changing into a fresh shirt, but figured it would be wrinkled, and he hadn't packed a travel iron.

Maybe he could ask Sara if she had one. Maybe that would be a good excuse to go to her room, because even though they'd only been apart for less than a minute, he missed her already.

Frank went back to the door and opened it—

—Sara was already standing there.

"I wanted to do this in case we don't have a chance later," she said.

And then Sara's arms were around Frank's neck and her lips were against his.

Belgium was so surprised he couldn't move. He just stood there, not knowing where to put his hands, or how to move his mouth. He hadn't kissed a woman in so long he'd forgotten how.

Would she figure out how bad he was at this?

Did his breath stink?

What if he used too much saliva? Or if they bumped their teeth together?

What was he supposed to say when the kiss ended?

But Frank's doubts quickly began to vanish as he lost himself in the sensation. Sara was tender, persistent, and she pressed her body closer to his, and when he touched her waist she sighed, and when his tongue touched hers it felt like an electric shock, making Frank moan in his throat.

She finally broke the kiss and looked at him, her pupils so big, a slight blush in her cheeks, and Belgium had to reach out and run a finger along her neck, just to prove she was real.

"I like you, Frank."

"I like you, too."

She gave him another kiss—just a peck on the cheek—and walked off, back to her room, leaving Frank to wonder that maybe his ridiculous little daydream wasn't that ridiculous after all.

Sara

Sara chewed her lower lip as she pulled a sweater on over her head.

She could still taste Frank.

In the past, Sara never would have been so brazen. Kissing was an intimate act, and all she had been intimate with lately was a bottle of booze. But she'd never felt such an immediate chemistry before. Part of it was the obvious fact that he was such a nice guy. But it went deeper. Something about being with Frank gave her hope.

And she needed some hope in her life.

Living without Jack was a constant reminder what a failure she was. As a mother. As a human being. The alcohol amplified this feeling, but without the liquor the horrors of Rock Island kept haunting her.

While it would be amazing to take a pill and not have nightmares, or panic attacks, Sara was a lot more skeptical about it than the others seemed to be. She didn't like Dr. Forenzi. His constant mentions of babies and children seemed less like reassurances, and more like attacks. Sara didn't like this house, either. Even though the location was vastly different, it gave off the same vibe as Rock Island. There was something bad happening here, and she couldn't wait to leave.

That was another reason she went to Frank's room. Yes, she found him attractive, and yes, he gave her hope. But the most important thing of all was how she felt when she was with him. When Sara was around Frank, she no longer felt afraid.

So she threw herself at him, the desire for him to kiss her back stronger than her fear of rejection.

And he had kissed her back.

And he was pretty good at it.

She shivered, thinking about his hands on the small of her back, and then turned to the dresser mirror to fuss with her hair again.

That's when she noticed something in the mirror. Something behind her.

The rocking chair in the corner of the room.

A brittle-looking thing, made of old wood, so dark it was almost black.

Had it just moved?

Sara stared at its reflection.

The chair remained still.

I'm seeing things.

Sara went back to finger-combing her bangs, wishing she'd packed some gel. Hindsight being 20/20, she should have also packed some make-up. A little lip gloss, and a little eyeliner would—

The rocking chair moved.

Sara watched, her breath caught in her throat, as it rocked all the way forward, held it there for a moment, and then rocked back.

Just as if someone was sitting in it.

Sara knew she needed to turn around, to look directly at it. But every muscle in her body had locked.

What was the monster that didn't cast a reflection? A vampire? Were there others that didn't show up in mirrors?

If I turn around and check, will I see some hideous creature in the chair, grinning at me?

A ghost?

A poltergeist?

A demon?

The chair rocked again, creaking as it did.

Turn around and look.

Just do it.

Sara closed her eyes, and through brute force of will turned on her heels to face the chair.

Now open your eyes.

But she was too afraid.

Do it!

Open your eyes!

Sara peeked.

The chair was empty.

Tom

One of the suited guards showed Tom to his room after dinner, and it was both as opulent and as creepy as Tom expected.

The bed was a large four-poster, with a crushed velvet bedcover. The dresser was heavy, Renaissance Revival, with a matching bureau. There was an iron, woodburning stove, an Oriental carpet on the wood floors, a rolltop desk, and portraits on the walls Tom recognized as Colton and Jebediah Butler. The light was dim, due to an antique lamp with a low wattage bulb and a very large tasseled shade. There were candles throughout the room, all unlit.

The room's sole window faced west, and Tom looked out into the waving fields of cattails. The sky had gotten darker, and had taken on a reddish tinge. He checked the window clasp, but it, like the sash, had been thickly painted over.

Tom put his suitcase onto the bed and opened it up. First he checked his gun, a Sig Saur 9mm, and put in a fresh magazine. He holstered it, put on his holster, and then checked his fanny pack. Inside were three more mags, fifteen rounds each, twenty glow sticks, a tactical flashlight, a Zippo lighter, a Swiss Army Champion Plus knife, some handcuffs, and a Benchmade Mangus butterfly knife with sheath.

He strapped the Mangus sheath to his ankle, and was inventorying the first aid kit he'd packed when someone knocked at the door.

"Come in," Tom said, facing the doorway.

It was Moni Draper. "Got a minute?"

"Sure."

She strutted in, and Tom admired her moxie. Especially after what she'd gone through. Tom knew Moni from her association with a serial killer named Luther Kite. He'd tied her up and tortured her using an antique medical device called an artificial leech. It was used by doctors in the 1800s for bloodletting, back when it was thought that bad blood caused ailments and bleeding cured people.

Tom had encountered Kite in the past, and had done a lot of research on him. Moni has over two hundred scars on her body, where Kite had used the device on her. She'd been found nearly dead, but somehow had rebounded. And, judging by her general attitude, she'd moved on with her life.

Tom had his share of nightmares, mostly due to what had happened at Senator Stang's mansion in Springfield. But he'd never been at the total mercy of a maniac who was excited by causing pain. He didn't know if he'd be able to adjust like Moni seemed to. And he hoped he'd never have to find out.

"You smell bullshit," Moni said.

"If something seems too good to be true, it usually is."

"Stay with me."

"Excuse me?"

"They're going to try to scare us. Maybe the threat won't be real. Maybe it will. Either way, I want to be with the strongest guy in the room, and that's you."

Tom nodded.

"We can..." Moni smiled slyly, "seal the deal if you like. I've done lots of cops."

Back when Kite had done that to her, Moni was a prostitute. Apparently the attack hadn't scared her out of the profession.

"Kind of you to offer, but I'm okay."

"Is it because of the scars?"

"It's because I'm in a committed relationship."

Moni pulled her shirt down, revealing her pock-marked cleavage. "So this doesn't disgust you?"

She jiggled a bit. Tom didn't reply. Moni continued to pose for another five seconds before saying, "So are you disgusted or not?"

"I'm still deciding," Tom said. "Give me a minute."

Moni giggled, walked over, and gave Tom a friendly punch on the shoulder. "You're okay for a pig, you know that?"

Tom wasn't offended by her use of the word *pig*. If anything, it amused him. "Thanks. And I promise I'll do my best to protect you if things get crazy."

"I believe you. Who's the special lady?"

"Her name is Joan. She's a Hollywood producer."

"She have any interest in the story of a plucky whore who survived multiple attacks by maniacs and then went on to become a millionaire?"

"I'll ask her."

"What's that?" Moni pointed at a wrapped plastic disk in Tom's kit.

"A Bolin chest seal. For sucking chest wounds."

"Like getting stabbed in the lungs?"

"Or shot."

She continued to point. "I know that's a tourniquet, and that's one of those airway breathers. What's in that package? Celox?"

"Clotting powder. Stops bleeding quickly."

"You came prepared. But I bet you don't have one of these."

Moni reached for her purse, then stopped. "Where are you from?"

"Chicago."

"A Chicago pig has no jurisdiction in South Carolina."

"True."

Moni pulled out a large syringe and held it up, triumphantly.

"What is that?" Tom asked, feeling like he already knew.

"Heroin. Enough to make a charging bull OD. I didn't think I could get a gun through TSA because I'd get into trouble, so I brought this to protect myself."

"Instead of a gun you brought a lethal dose of heroin," Tom said. "You don't think if you got caught with that, you'd be in more trouble?"

Moni's eyebrows crinkled and her lips pursed. "When you say it like that, it sounds like a bad idea."

"Am I interrupting?"

They looked at the open door and saw Mal, the sports reporter missing a hand.

"The more the merrier," Moni said, waving him in.

"Forenzi wants us to line up for our physicals, but I just wanted a moment of your time, Detective. Are you both… busy?"

"I'm just showing the pig my heroin," Moni said.

Mal frowned. "I could come back…"

"How can I help you, Mr. Deiter?" Tom asked.

"At dinner. You didn't seem excited about Forenzi's experiment. You seemed like you knew something no one else did."

Both Mal and Moni stared at Tom. He wondered what to do, but strangely he felt comfortable around them, in the same way he felt comfortable around Frank and Sara.

In that moment, he decided the benefits of telling them outweighed keeping it a secret.

"My partner, Roy Lewis, came to this house last week, supposedly doing the same thing we're doing tonight. He never came back."

Tom watched Mal's frown deepen. "Shit."

"You look so sad," Moni told him. She offered the syringe. "Need a little pick me up?"

"Moni," Tom kept his voice even, "can you please put away the heroin? And Mal, I don't know what happened to Roy, so I can't cry *foul play* yet. Maybe Forenzi is legit, and this will all be smooth sailing."

"But you don't believe that."

"No. I don't." Tom felt like he was telling a child there was no Santa Claus.

Moni put her hand on Mal's neck. "Buck up, little soldier. Would a little three-way action with me and your wife make you feel better?"

Mal choked out a laugh. "You know, it probably would."

"Is she into chicks?"

He lost his mirth again. "No."

"Too bad. Well, maybe some figging will take your mind off things."

"What's figging?" Mal asked.

"It's when you take a—"

"Mal?" His wife, Deb, stuck her head into the room. "Everything okay?"

"He's moody," Moni explained, "so I offered him smack and a three way."

Tom decided it was time to take some control of the situation. "I don't know how this is all going to play out tonight, but I think we all need to stick together, and watch out for each other. Did anyone bring weapons?" He looked pointedly at Moni, who was waving her hand. "Weapons other than narcotics?"

"I packed a .38 in our suitcase," Mal said.

"Extra rounds?"

Mal shook his head. "Just the five in the cylinder."

"Are you a good shot?"

"I'm so-so. Deb is better."

Tom took out his Sig, removed the magazine, and pulled back the slide to make sure the barrel was clear. Then he did a quick explanation of how to load, how to use the decocker, and what double action meant. As he was passing his gun around, one of the suited guards knocked on the door frame.

"We're ready for you."

Tom took his Sig back, tucked it into the holster, and followed the others into the hallway. They'd been given rooms on the second floor, all in a row, and there was an ornate wooden railing that overlooked the great room. As they headed for the stairs, they passed a marble statue of a cupid on a pedestal. Tom did a double-take, then went back for a closer look.

In the baby's mouth were sharp fangs.

Moni, who was behind him, said, "Wouldn't want to breastfeed that little bastard. And look at the wings."

At first glance, they seemed like typical, feathered cherub wings. But the individual feathers weren't feathers—they were tiny daggers.

"Dr. Madison is waiting."

Tom turned, startled, and was surprised to see yet another guard in a gray suit standing next to him. That made five he'd seen so far. Why did Forenzi need so many guards? To protect him from ghosts? And how had he managed to sneak up on Tom? Like the others, this guard was tall, muscular, and wearing military boots. But he hadn't made a sound during his approach.

"What branch of the military were you in?" Tom asked.

The man's face remained blank, and he didn't answer.

"Do you work for the government, or for Forenzi directly?"

"Please move along," the guard said.

Tom shrugged, and he followed Moni and the others down the stairs, across the great room, and to a hallway lined with drab paintings depicting plantation life. They looked old, paint peeling and a decade's worth of grime on them. Slaves in the field, picking tobacco. Blackjack Reedy astride a horse, whip in hand. An endless field of cattails, stretching off into the horizon. Everyone had stopped next to a closed door, and Tom assumed it was the queue for the examination room. But he quickly figured out the group had huddled around another painting, this one of Butler House.

It was massive, perhaps a meter tall and twice as wide, in an ornate frame and protected behind some non-reflective glass. The picture depicted the house in the 1800s, when it was still new, and the fields were filled with cotton. Tom didn't understand the interest until Frank pointed to a figure in one of the windows.

It was a woman, her hair tied back, a pensive look on her face. Tom squinted at it, then turned to Sara, who had gone ashen.

The woman in the painting was a dead-ringer for her.

Tom moved in closer, checking the figures in the other windows.

He saw Frank's face peering out between half-closed shutters on the second floor.

Deb, opening the front door to the house. Mal in the shadows behind her.

Moni's face, complete with her pock marks.

Wellington, in the cotton field with a scythe.

Two people in a horse-drawn buggy, approaching the house. Pang and Aabir.

Tom looked for himself, dreading the search, holding his breath.

"You're here," Belgium said, pointing to the side of the house.

Tom didn't understand what he was seeing. It was definitely his face, lying sideways on the ground, but his body was obscured by scrub brush.

"And over here," Belgium continued, moving his finger.

Then Tom understood.

His body wasn't in the bushes. His body was sitting against the house, holding a knife, his shirt drenched with blood.

Tom had apparently cut off his own head, and it had rolled away.

Deb

Mal was in much better spirits since Dr. Forenzi's talk at supper, which was just in time for Deb's mood to take a nose dive.

They passed co-dependency back and forth like two hobos sharing a cigar. So it was Deb's turn to feel awful, and Mal's to buoy her up.

But he'd gone out to ask the cop some questions, leaving Deb alone in her room.

Which was when a painting in the bedroom fell off the wall.

It scared the shit out of her, and when she went to look for him she found a convention of sorts in Tom's room.

Now, first in line to be examined, she still hadn't had the chance to tell Mal what had happened. The painting—a ghastly picture of a brooding southern gentlemen standing calmly in the middle of a storm—had dropped off the wall just as she was wiping the sweat off her stumps.

It could have been a coincidence. Or it could have been supernatural.

What was behind it didn't matter. What mattered was Mal hadn't been there for her, when she'd been there for him since the airport in Pittsburgh.

It wasn't fair. So now she was coping with resentment as well as fear, and having to go in first made Deb even more on edge. Add in seeing herself on the hallway painting, and Deb wanted to either cry, rip all her hair out, or both.

"Tom's partner disappeared here last week," Mal said, whispering over Deb's shoulder.

Deb sensed the worry in her husband's voice. But she was worried, too. She needed him to be strong for a while. The fact that he wasn't made her angry as well as scared.

"Deb, did you hear me?"

She turned around so fast that she lost her balance, which for Deb was about the most humiliating thing she could do. That Mal had to quickly reach out and steady her made it even worse.

"Leave me alone," she said, teeth clenched and trying to pull away.

He recoiled like he'd just seen a snake. "Deb? What's wrong?"

"It isn't all about you, Mal. I'm hurting, too. I need support just like you do."

"Deb, I—"

"I don't need this right now."

The door to the examination room opened, and a male voice from inside said, "Come in."

Deb began to enter, but Mal held her back.

"Let go, Mal."

"Let's talk about this. We can let someone else cut ahead."

"Let. Go."

"At least let me go first so I can tell you what to expect. I know you hate doctors. Let me—"

Deb pulled away, wobbled into the room, and slammed the door behind her.

She immediately regretted her decision.

The exam room looked like it jumped off a postcard from the 1800s. The examination table was made of wood, with a cracked leather cushion, and metal arm rests with buckled straps. A dusty apothecary shelf, filled with old glass bottles, took up most of the left wall. Along the right wall were a desk, a water basin, and a shelf of moldering, leather-bound books. On the desk was some sort kind of organ—a human lung maybe—floating in a specimen jar of gray liquid.

"Take a seat."

The doctor still hadn't turned around. Her husband had been right; she was afraid of going to the doctor. She'd seen too many in her lifetime, and they always hurt her in some way.

Deb considered walking back out, letting Mal go first. But stubbornness won out over nerves and she went to the antique examination table and sat down.

"Name?" the doctor asked. He was filling out something on a clip board.

"Deborah Dieter."

Deb looked at the old medical cart next to the table. On it were filthy old medical tools. A bone saw with crusted brown flecks. Pointy forceps. A large, curved scalpel. A jagged pair of oversized snippers. A hand drill that seemed more suited to a woodworker than a doctor. Rusty trocars. A rough-edged metal speculum that was open wider that a human being could accommodate.

Deb could feel her mouth go dry and her heart rate kick up. Getting an exam was bad enough. Getting an exam from some quack stuck in the nineteenth century was much worse.

Of course it's much worse.

That's the point.

Deb closed her eyes and slowed down her breathing, controlling her fear. This had to be part of Forenzi's experiment. To try and scare her. What could be scarier than a collection of barbaric surgical implements from the past?

After ten seconds or so, Deb was able to reign in her panic. Then she opened her eyes and found herself face-to-face with—

Oh my god.

She recognized this so-called doctor. He was the hotel clerk who sent her to the Rushmore Inn. The same pale, pasty face. The same crooked toupee.

But he's still in prison!

Isn't he?

"I'm going to take some of your blood, Mrs. Dieter." His breath smelled like sour milk.

"I need to…" Deb said weakly. "Are… are you…?"

"I'm Dr. Madison. I assist Dr. Forenzi."

He was tugging on some rubber gloves, and gave Deb a crooked smile.

Is this the guy? Or does he just look like the guy, and my imagination is doing the rest?

Deb sometimes thought she saw people she knew in crowds, only to look closer and realize they just resembled the people she knew. Her mind filled in the blanks, jumped to conclusions. It happened to everyone.

Is it happening to me now?

"Why, Mrs. Dieter. You look like you've seen a ghost." He opened up a plastic package, taking out a long needle attached to a clear tube.

Maybe this isn't the guy. Maybe Forenzi hired him because he looked like the man Deb knew.

To scare her.

After all, this is a fear study.

"You… remind me of someone."

"I get that a lot. George Clooney, right?"

More like Boris Karloff.

"Please put your arm on the armrest, Mrs. Dieter. I'm going to strap it down so you keep still."

He buckled a strap around her wrist.

"So, are you from around here, Doctor?"

"Oh, no. I'm from West Virginia."

Where the Rushmore was.

"Been here a while?"

"Only recently. For the past few years I've been… busy."

"Busy doing what?"

He smiled again. "Just hold still, Mrs. Dieter. This will only pinch for a moment."

The needle was jammed into her forearm. The agony was immediate.

Then he began to move it from side to side.

"Where is that vein? I can never find it."

Deb ground her teeth, locking her jaw. The doctor wiggled it, going deeper, so deep Deb was sure he'd hit bone.

The pain was bad. But the anxiety was nuclear.

Deb shut her eyes again, begging the universe for it to stop.

"You have such tiny veins. I may have to get a smaller needle."

Yes! Please please please do that!

Her whole world had been reduced to that needle in her flesh, probing, twisting, poking left and right like she was being tenderized instead of giving blood.

"Maybe I should try the other arm."

No!

"Yes, I think that'll I have to… ahh, there it is."

Deb chanced a look and saw him attach a vacuum vial to the end of the tube, and it began to fill with blood.

"Was that so awful, Mrs. Dieter?"

Deb's hair was stuck to her head from sweating. She blew out a deep breath, and pumped her fist to make the blood go faster.

"Looking good, Mrs. Dieter. Looking... oh, wait. We're slowing down."

He flicked the vial with a fingernail, which tugged on the needle and caused Deb a spike of pain.

"I believe your vein has collapsed." He roughly grabbed the needle, then pulled it out.

"Do we have enough blood?" Deb whispered.

He shook his head. "I'm afraid not."

"So...?"

"So I guess we'll have to try that other arm after all."

Before Deb could object, the doctor was pinning down her other wrist and buckling it to the armrest.

She was trapped.

"What are you doing?"

"You recognized me. From the hotel. I can see it in your eyes. Don't you lie to me, girl."

Deb immediately began to thrash and yell, but the moment she opened her mouth, the man waved his hand over her face and Deb could no longer make a sound. It felt like something foul had crawled inside her throat and was choking her from the inside out, even though she was still able to breathe. Deb screamed, loud as she could, but it only came out as a hiss of air. She tried to kick him, but he caught her left prosthetic and pressed the vacuum release, letting it drop to the floor. He did the same with the left one.

"Ya know my name is Franklin." His voice was getting deeper, the southern accent more pronounced. "Ya know I'm very angry about what y'all did at the Rushmore."

Deb pulled on her arms as hard as she could, until her elbows felt like they were going to pop. But old as the examination table was, it was built solid.

She was trapped.

Franklin strolled over to the equipment cart. He ran his hand over the antique medical tools, his fingers caressing the rusty speculum.

"Ya know I'm angry about going to prison. I'm really, *really* angry about that, girl. Do ya know why?"

He picked up the hand drill.

"I'll tell ya why."

Deb was growing light headed from her attempts at screaming. She tried to push Franklin away with her stumps, but he simply moved to the side of the table.

Then he placed the drill bit on Deb's thigh, pressing down hard.

"Because," he whispered to her, "one year ago today, I died in prison."

He reached his hand down the front of his pants—

—and pulled out a handful of something, throwing it in Deb's face.

At first, she thought it was rice.

Then the rice began to wiggle.

Maggots.

Franklin put both hands on the drill.

"I don't like being dead, girl. The spirit world is all fucked up. So I'm going to hurt ya. I'm going to hurt ya so bad. And then I'm going to hurt that husband of yours even worse."

Just as he began to turn, the back door to the examination room began to slowly open.

Then the lights flickered and went out.

Deb screamed in the blackness, making no more noise than a leaky tire.

A moment later, the lights came back on, just as the drill clattered to the floor.

Deb saw a man in a lab coat standing in front of her.

"I'm Dr. Madison," he said. "What in God's name has happened to you?"

Deb tried to talk, but she had no voice. she tried to point with her chin where Franklin was standing.

But Franklin wasn't there.

Franklin had disappeared.

Mal

When the door opened, and he saw Deb crying and hysterical, something in Mal snapped. He stormed into the exam room, demanding answers from the doctor, listening to his wife try to talk but unable to.

Someone—Tom—finally figured out that she couldn't speak, and Dr. Madison gave Deb a pen and some paper to relate her story.

Deb's handwriting was erratic, and didn't make much sense, but the part that stuck out the most was the word she wrote and circled several times.

GHOST

"So he bound your arms, tried to take blood, then threatened you with the drill?" Tom asked.

Deb nodded. Mal felt sick.

"And you say it was a man named Franklin? Someone you'd met before?"

Another nod.

"He's in prison," Mal said. "But he could have gotten out."

Deb beckoned for the paper and wrote "Franklin said he died in prison."

"That's easy enough to check," Tom said. Then he pointed to the floor. "So is this drill. My guess is that ghosts don't leave fingerprints."

Deb shook her head and wrote "gloves".

"Careful ghost." Tom looked at Madison. "And you're sure no one went past you, Doctor?"

"Positive. I was standing in the doorway the whole time. And..."

The doctor's face pinched.

"And?"

"When I came in here, before the lights went out, I saw Mrs. Dieter. But... I didn't see anyone else." He turned to Deb, looking pained. "I'm sorry, but you were alone in here, dear."

Mal wanted to hit somebody. "This qualifies as assault, right Detective?"

"Absolutely."

Mal pulled a cell phone from his pocket. "I'm calling the police."

By now, everyone was in the exam room, huddling around Deb. Moni was helping her put her legs back on, and Dr. Madison was peering down his wife's throat with a lighted opthalmoscope.

"Your vocal chords are swollen, but I don't see any damage. How did you lose your voice?"

Deb shook her head and mouthed "I don't know."

Mal was walking around the office, waving his cell phone around like it was a talisman to ward off evil spirits. "Goddammit, no signal. Anyone else have a cell phone?"

Tom checked his. "No bars."

"Doctor, where's the phone in this place?"

Dr. Madison shrugged. "There aren't any phones at Butler House. No electricity either, except what's powered by the gas generators. No Internet. We're completely cut off from the grid here."

"This is insane," Mal said. He turned to his wife, who was still shaking from her ordeal. "We're leaving, Deb. Right now."

But rather than get the expected nod, Mal watched in amazement as Deb shook her head.

"Honey, you were attacked!"

"If it was a ghost," Deb said, her hoarse voice barely a whisper, "he went away. If it was a trick to scare me, that's the point of this experiment."

She reached out, held Mal's hand. He gripped it tight.

"Let's stay," she said.

Moni grinned. "I'm with you, girlfriend. And if the ghost comes back, we kick his Casper ass."

Mr. Wellington was feeling the walls. "I can't find any secret passages or trap doors or mirrors. But any magician worth his salt can do a disappearing act. This didn't have to be a ghost. There could be a rational explanation for all of this."

Pang was setting up his spirit hunting equipment. Frank and Sara were holding hands in the corner of the room. Aabir had her eyes closed and was swaying where she stood.

"So much sorrow in the room," the medium said. "So much misery. And something else. A strong presence. An evil presence. Hatred. Toward you, Deb. Toward your husband. Something to do with West Virginia. Many people died there." She opened her eyes. "Deborah, can I touch your hand?"

Deb let go of Mal and reached for the psychic. When Aabir touched her, she gasped.

"So much pain in your past, Deborah. So many scars. Much tragedy. But much bravery, too." Aabir's eyelids fluttered. "A bed and breakfast. The Rushmore Inn. I see misshapen, deformed people. They're after you. They want something from you. You're in a room. In bed. Someone is under the bed."

Deb's eyes got wide, and she tried to pull her hand back. But Aabir didn't let go.

"I see a mountain lion."

"Enough." Mal pulled the medium away, but then Aabir clasped his arm.

"The ghost who did this to your wife. He has a brother named Jimmy. Jimmy is the one who cut off your hand."

Mal tried to shake her off, but the woman's grip was like iron.

"Jimmy is here, in this house. He's followed you here."

Mal's sphincter clenched. She was relating the worst thing that ever happened to him. The cause of his nightmares.

Aabir's voice got low, so she sounded like a man.

"Maaaaaal.... I waaaaant your other hand..."

Mal was rooted there, terrified.

"Holy shit, bro!" Pang had some electronic gizmo pointed at Aabir. "The EMF is off the scale! I've never seen anything like this!"

"I WAAAANT YOOOOUUUUR HAAAAAAND!"

Mal shoved her away, and Aabir collapsed to the floor. Dr. Madison and Moni knelt next to her, and Pang was wide-eyed, snapping pictures with a digital camera.

"Will you fucking look at this!" Pan declared. He held out the viewfinder for Mal to see.

In the picture, Aabir was glowing like she was on fire.

Tom

Tom was on edge.

He still hadn't talked to Forenzi about Roy, and the whole examination room incident with Deb left a bad taste. Tom had interviewed enough victims to know Deb was one.

But what was she a victim of?

Everyone had moved into the great room. Aabir slumped in her lounge chair, looking like an inflatable float with half the air leaked out. Pang was hunched over a coffee table and typing something in his laptop, his face beaming. Mal and Deb were sitting on a sofa. Deb looked like a zombie, zoned out and slack. Mal was tapping his foot rapidly. Moni was near the front doors, whispering something to Wellington. Frank and Sara were on a loveseat, Frank's arm around her.

Despite Mal objecting, Dr. Madison had begun taking blood samples from everyone, going person to person, putting the vials into a metal case. He was also fitting everyone with a battery powered monitor, which recorded, among other things, electrical activity in the brain, heart activity, pulse, blood pressure, and calories burned. The device clipped to the belt, and worked wirelessly with ten electrode pads stuck to the skin in various locations, including the chest, wrists, neck, and temples.

"I'm scared, Frank," Sara said to him.

"I'm scared, too." Frank patted Sara's leg. "But keep remembering that we're *supposed* to be scared. That's the point of the experiment. All of this could be intentional, set up by Dr. Forenzi."

"Where is Dr. Forenzi?" Tom asked Dr. Madison as he was labeling a vial with marker.

"Hmm? In his lab, I suppose." The doctor seemed preoccupied with his task and didn't bother to face the cop.

"I need to talk to him."

"I'll tell him as soon as I finish up here."

"Now."

"I understand your urgency, Detective. Especially after what we all saw. But you have to understand, things like that happen in Butler House all the time. Dr. Forenzi has strict instructions not to be disturbed while he's in his laboratory. And even if I wanted to disturb him, the doors are steel and locked all the time. I've never even been in there. If he doesn't want to come out, no one can make him."

Tom wondered if he should push, but he still had all night to force the issue. Moni was right—he had no jurisdiction here. But he did have a gun, and a lot of questions, and by tomorrow he would be damn sure he got the answers he sought.

"These readings are mind-blowing." Pang was still staring at his laptop screen. "The electromagnetic field around Aabir surged like I was scanning a high tension power line. I wish I'd had my remote thermometer on. Did anyone notice a temperature change?"

No one answered.

"Okay okay okay." Belgium cleared his throat. "Besides the painting in the hallway with all of us in it, and what happened in the examination room, has anyone else witnessed anything unusual since arriving at Butler House?"

Sara spoke up. "In my room. A rocking chair. It was rocking by itself."

"Was there any explanation for it?" Belgium asked, obviously concerned.

"No. No window open. I wasn't anywhere near it. And when I say it was rocking, I don't mean a little bit. It seemed like someone was in it."

Belgium shivered. "Anyone else?"

"There was a cold spot in my room," Pang said. "Ten degrees cooler. Celsius, bro. But it went away before I could record it, so I don't have any proof."

"Tom?"

Tom shook his head.

"Mal?"

"What? No."

Deb mouthed something.

"What, hon?" Mal asked, putting his arm around her.

"Painting in our room." Deb's voice was scratchy, but audible. "Fell off the wall."

"Aabir," Belgium pressed, "have you noticed anything?"

Aabir remained quiet.

"Cornelius? Moni? Have you had had had any… um… encounters, since you're arrival?"

"Naw," Moni said.

"Neither have I," said the Brit.

"You told me you saw an orb," Pang countered.

Wellington shrugged. "I saw a flash of light in the hallway, while I was walking to the loo. You called it an orb, Mr. Pang, not I."

"What's an orb?" Belgium asked.

"Ghost lights," Pang said. "Also known as orbs, ignis fatuus, will-o'-the-wisp. One pervading theory is that hauntings are residual energy that lingers after a traumatic event. Another is that the energy leaks into our dimension from another one. Like in quantum theory, where a particle can be in more than one place at the same time. In this case, our world, and the afterlife."

"I thought you were a skeptic, Mr. Pang."

"I am, Mr. Wellington. But skepticism requires me to be aware of the hypothesis I try to debunk."

"There are reasonable, scientific explanations for everything that has happened so far," Wellington said.

"A ghost assaulted my wife, Mr. Wellington," Mal said, his chin out and his voice clipped.

"It could have been a man who said he was a ghost," Wellington said. "Or, perhaps, Mrs. Dieter might be mistaken in her account."

Mal stood up, his fist clenched. "Are you saying she's lying?"

"I'm not saying anything, Mr. Dieter. Only that I don't know. I haven't met anyone here before today, so I can't voice for anyone's honesty. But even if I trusted your wife was speaking what she believes to be the truth, couldn't her account of the events be colored by her past traumas?"

"So now she's not a liar. Now she's insane."

"I'm simply calling attention to the obvious. We have ample proof of liars in our society, as well as ample proof of mental dysfunction. But we don't have any proof of spirits. So if I'm being asked to dwell on what is more likely—either supernatural activity, or lies, hoaxes, and hallucinations—I think Occam's Razor bears me out. The simplest explanation is usually the correct one."

"Let's all of us take it down a notch," Tom said. Dr. Madison was attaching a sticky pad to his neck, and the conducting gel was cold. "But I think that anyone who wants to leave Butler House, should do so."

Moni snorted. "And give up a million bucks? You're on crack."

"Dr. Belgium?" Tom met his eyes. "Do you and Sara want to leave?"

They exchanged a look. "I believe we're staying."

"Mal and Deb?"

Mal faced his wife. "We should go, hon. We don't need this."

Deb shook her head.

"Deb..."

"I'm done running away," she rasped. "Go if you want. I'm staying."

Deb crossed her arms. Mal pursed his lips, and then he walked away, to the other side of the great room.

"Cornelius?" Tom asked.

He folded his arms across his vest. "Naturally, I'm staying. I don't believe we have anything to fear here, except our own overactive imaginations."

"That leaves you, Aabir. Do you want to stay, or go?"

The psychic's lips moved, but no sound came out.

"Can you speak up?"

"Paper," she whispered.

"Paper? Dr. Madison, can you give Aabir your clip board?"

"Certainly." The doctor placed it in front of the psychic, and put a black marker on top.

Her face still devoid of expression, Aabir began to write. Frank moved in for a closer look.

I IS JASPER

The words were in block letters, almost childish in their scrawl. They also took up most of the page, so Dr. Madison flipped to the next one.

I WORKS THE FIELDS AT
BUTLER HOUSE

"What's she doing?" Moni asked.

"Psychography," Pang said. "Also known as automatic writing. She's channeling a spirit and writing what it's telling her. Sounds like it's the ghost of Ol' Jasper, the slave that Colton Butler sewed two extra arms on. Shit, my EMF meter is going berserk!"

Tom remembered the Butler House website. The picture of the scarred, old slave with the extra arm.

THEY HURTS JASPER BAD

Dr. Madison flipped to a fresh page.

NOW JASPER GON' HURT DEM BACK

Frank realized he was holding the armchair of the loveseat so tightly his knuckles were white.

I... IS...

Aabir's eyes rolled up into the back of her head.

HERE

Aabir screamed, and collapsed onto the floor.

Then the lights went out.

The great room was very dark with the chandeliers out, but enough dusk was peeking in through the cracks in the shudders that Tom could still make out some shadows. A moment later, Pang's camcorder light went on. Tom followed suit, digging his tactical flashlight out of his pack.

"Cornelius, you're near the front doors." Tom pointed the beam in his direction. "Try the light switch there."

Wellington found the wall panel and flipped the switch, to no effect.

"Nothing. Might be the circuit breaker. Or the generator."

Tom waved the light across the group, taking a head count. He saw Deb and Mal, Moni, Frank and Sara, Pang, Aabir—"

"What's that sound?" Frank asked.

Everyone went quiet. Tom was acutely aware of how silent true silence actually was. Living in Chicago, silence was an anomaly. There were always sounds. Traffic, heat or air conditioning, birds, constant human noise from talking, yelling, playing music.

But this house was completely devoid of noise. The only thing Tom could liken it to was when he put on his ear muffs on the shooting range. Silence had its own sound; the steady, inaudible hum of consciousness, which made you realize how alone you really were in the universe.

And then, like a slap to the face, he heard it.

Something dragging across the wooden floor.

Like a claw. Or a—

"Machete," Tom whispered.

A machete like Ol' Jasper was supposed to carry.

Tom twisted his flashlight to widen the beam, and then did a slow pan across the great room, trying to locate the sound.

He saw empty chairs, the fireplace, an old piano, a wall, a hallway, a table, another hallway, another wall...

"I think it's near me," Wellington said in a metered tone.

Tom turned the beam on the author.

A few meters away from him was—

"Sweet Jesus Christ," Moni whispered.

It was a black man, muscular, shirtless, shuffling across the floor in a slow, steady gate, dragging a rusty-looking machete behind him.

At first, Tom thought it was Roy.

But Roy doesn't have four arms.

The two extra appendages sprouted from his back like angel wings, and hung, limply, over his shoulders.

"Well," Cornelius Wellington said, "I certainly do commend the make-up artist. That's quite a special effect. And the pure black eyes are a nice touch."

Ol' Jasper kept walking toward him.

Tom drew his Sig. "I'm a police officer. Drop your weapon and put your hands up."

"All four of his hands?" Wellington asked. Tom detected the bravado, but it seemed forced.

Ol' Jasper didn't stop.

"Halt right now, or I will shoot." Tom aimed his 9mm at the man's center mass, supporting his gun hand with the flashlight.

Wellington tried to smile, but it looked more like a wince. "Oh, let him come, Detective. I'll pull off one of those phony arms, and we'll expose this for the farce it is."

Ol' Jasper got within two meters.

"Last warning." Tom placed his finger in the trigger guard, and cocked the Sig with his thumb. "I will shoot you."

Ol' Jasper stopped an arm's length away from Wellington.

Then he slowly raised the machete.

"Oh my." Wellington giggled, but it sounded forced. "I'm so scared."

"Get away from him, Wellington."

"This is only a joke, Detective. I refuse to play along."

"Drop the weapon, now!" Tom ordered.

Ol' Jasper didn't drop it.

Time seemed to slow down. Tom had enough time to think it through, make a gut·decision, reverse the decision, then go with what his gut told him to do.

He squeezed the trigger twice, a double tap to the black man's chest.

He felt the gun buck in his hands.

He heard the shots.

He smelled the gunpowder.

He knew he'd hit the target, dead on.

But Ol' Jasper didn't even flinch.

Instead, he swung the machette with vicious force, connecting with the side of Wellington's neck.

Wellington went down like one of those buildings being demoed, collapsing in a heap right where he stood, his head flopping to the side as if on a hinge, a bright spray of arterial blood painting the front doors.

Chaos ensued.

Tom tuned out all the screaming from the others, tuned out the spectacle of Wellington's dying body flopping and twitching on the floor like a landed fish, and emptied his magazine into Ol' Jasper.

At least ten shots hit home.

Ol' Jasper stood there, unaffected.

Then he looked at Tom—

—smiled wide—

—and roaches came out of his mouth.

It was the scariest thing Tom had ever seen in his life.

He ejected the empty magazine, fished out a new one, and loaded it as he backed away. Tom's hands had begun to shake, and the beam flitted over Ol' Jasper, catching him sporadically, until Tom somehow lost him in the darkness.

"Everyone!" Tom yelled. "Follow me! Let's go!"

Tom hurried to the nearest hallway, alternating between lighting the way for people and trying to find Ol' Jasper. Pang with his camcorder brought up the rear.

"Keep moving!" Tom said, covering the rear and walking sideways. He followed the group down a left turn, and into a large room.

"Dr. Belgium?" he called, keeping his gun on the doorway. Not that shooting had helped, but Tom didn't have a better plan.

"Yes yes yes!"

"My fanny pack. I have some glow sticks. Pass them around."

He pointed the flashlight at his pack, and Belgium fished out a handful. Tom listened for the sound of a machete scraping the floor, but all he heard was cellophane wrappers being opened. Soon the room was bathed in soft, multicolored neon light. Greens and blues and pinks.

Tom took a quick look around, discovered they were in a massive library.

"Pang, Frank, get that desk, move it over here to block the door. Mal, you got your gun?"

"Left it in my room."

Shit. "Okay, do a head count."

Tom peeked his head down the hall. Still no Jasper.

"Everyone say your name," Mal said.

A bunch of people began talking at once.

"Okay, everyone shut up. Let's try this again. I'm here, Deb is here, Tom, Frank, and Pang are here. Moni?"

"Yeah. Here. I'm here."

"Sara?"

"Yes."

"Dr. Madison?"

No one answered.

"Dr. Madison, are you here?"

No answer.

"Did anyone see where he went?"

Sara, bathed in pink light, said, "I think he ran down the other hallway."

"How about Aabir?" Mal asked. "Aabir, are you here?"

"She was passed out on the table," Pang said.

Tom ground his teeth.

Shit. One dead, and two missing.

How quickly things all went to hell.

"Tom, move over."

Tom stepped aside, then helped Frank and Pang slide the heavy desk in front of the door.

"Are there any other doors in this room?"

General murmuring, and lights crisscrossing the space.

"I think that's the only one," Mal said.

Having only one entry point was a good thing. Easier to guard.

Having only one escape route was bad.

"Are there windows in this room?" Tom asked. "We need to find one, get out of here, and find the cars."

More scrambling around.

"Got a window!" Deb croaked. Her voice was getting stronger.

People rushed over.

"Bars," Moni said. "Thick ass metal bars."

Mal grunted. "They're set in concrete."

"Okay." Tom wasn't sure on what to do next. He knew the right thing to do was go and look for Dr. Madison and Aabir. But he didn't want to leave everyone alone.

Bullshit. Be honest. It isn't about them. It's about you. You're afraid to go back out there.

"Everyone look around. Find something you can use as a weapon."

"A weapon?" Pang giggled. "Why? Your gun didn't do much good with Ol' Jasper."

"Did you miss, Tom?" Sara asked.

"I don't think so."

"You shot a whole shitload of times," Moni said. "You sure you didn't panic and miss?"

"I'm sure," Tom said, but as soon as the words passed his lips he questioned them. He'd been less than five meters away, and had emptied an entire fourteen round magazine. He should have been able to hit that target with his eyes closed.

But could he have been so afraid he missed?

"Did you see those extra arms?" Pang's voice had an edge to it.

Tom ignored him. "Does everyone have something to defend themselves with?"

Grunts and grumbling.

"If not, find something fast. I'm..." Tom swallowed. "I'm going to go look for Madison and Aabir."

"Bad idea, Tommy boy," Moni said. "I saw that movie. As soon as the people split up, they start dying."

"They've already started dying," Pang said. "Did you see what happened to Wellington? His head was practically cut off!"

Tom swallowed again. "I have to go check. When I come back, I'll knock three times. Frank? Pang? Move the desk and put it back when I leave."

"I'm going with you," Moni said, stepping up next to him.

Tom shook his head. "You're staying here."

"I'm staying with the guy holding the gun. And you promised you wouldn't leave me."

Shit.

"Okay. You stay close, move when I tell you to. Got it?"

"Yeah."

"Pang, Frank, move the desk."

They shoved it back, Tom took a deep breath, held it, and opened the door, expecting Ol' Jasper to be standing right there.

But the doorway, and the hall, were clear.

Tom stepped out, Moni close enough to be his shadow. Behind them the door slammed shut, and Tom heard the scraping of the desk along the floor.

They began to make their way back toward the great room. Slowly. Cautiously. Tom waving the gun and flashlight in front of him in a steady, sweeping motion. Left to right to left to right.

"My nana believed in spirits," Moni whispered. "She told me some people were so wicked, the devil kicked them out of hell because he was afraid of them."

"Shh."

"I thought ghosts went through walls and shit. How could one hold a machete?"

"Be quiet."

The floorboards creaked under Tom's foot, and he winced at the sound.

"Why should I be quiet? Can ghosts hear us? Do they even have senses like we do? Maybe they can zone in on our life force or something like that."

Tom stopped. "And maybe," he whispered, "there are no such things as ghosts, and you're going to give away our position."

"Doesn't your flashlight and my pink glow stick give away our position, too?"

She had a point. Tom resumed creeping down the hall. He was coming to the left turn, a right angle corner he couldn't see around. He paused again, unsure of how to proceed.

"I wish I had a cross or a rosary or something," Moni said.

"That's for vampires."

"Did you hear about that vampire outbreak in Colorado? At some hospital? I read it in a tabloid. They said crosses didn't work."

"Can you please stop talking?"

"Do you believe in bigfoot?"

"Christ, Moni, can you please—"

That's when Tom smelled something.

BBQ?

He sniffed the air, trying to pinpoint where it was coming from.

Moni grabbed Tom's shoulder, startling him.

"Didn't that doctor guy talk about a ghost that smelled like burnt meat?"

Tom remembered. Sturgis Butler. A serial killer from the 1800s who killed prostitutes in satanic rituals. According to that website, he was caught and burned alive, laughing as he died.

Was the odor coming from around the corner?

Tom's heart rate, already above normal, got even faster. Against his better judgment he began to imagine Sturgis, his flesh burned black, his charred bones poking out through his crispy skin.

"Moni, let go of me," he said softly.

She did.

"I hear something, Tom."

Tom listened. He heard it, too. A shuffling sound. Not a scraping, like a machete being dragged. More like someone scuffing their shoes across the floor.

Tom flashed the light into the hallway behind him.

Empty.

The shuffling drew closer.

Tom gritted his teeth and did a quick peek around the corner.

Clear.

"Okay, we're going to run down the hallway. Keep up with me. And no matter what happens, keep silent. On three. One... two... three!"

Tom sprinted around the corner, barreling down the hallway as fast as he could, gun pointed ahead, flashlight bobbing and throwing crazy shadows. Right before he got to the great room he stopped, putting his back against the wall, sweeping his light ahead of him.

Moni stopped right behind him, again clutching his shoulder.

Tom didn't see anyone in the great room. But the charred pork smell had become overpowering. Like he'd stuck his nose over a meat smoker.

"Aabir," he said in a stage whisper. "Dr. Madison. Are you here?"

He focused the beam on the table where Aabir had been sitting. She was gone.

"I'm going to check the front door," Tom said. He was close to gagging from the stench. "If it's open, we'll go back and get the others, find the cars. Do you want to stay here?"

Moni squeezed him.

"Is that a yes?"

Moni squeezed again, so hard it hurt.

Tom laughed softly. "I'm glad you're finally taking this silence thing to heart."

He turned to look at her, and his smile froze when he saw it wasn't Moni grabbing him.

It was a man with a charred black face who smelled like burnt meat.

Frank

As a scientist, everything that had happened in the last half an hour ate away at Frank's rational side.

As a man who once lived through unimaginable horrors, it all seemed uncomfortably familiar.

Belgium locked eyes with Sara. He saw fear there. But determination, too. Frank couldn't imagine what it would be like to have a child taken away, especially after going through whatever hell she'd endured on Rock Island. This house had offered some hope to get Jack back, but after watching Wellington die, Frank reasoned it had been a false hope. Sara must have realized it as well.

They weren't brought here to be part of some fear experiment.

They were brought here to be slaughtered.

But why?

Frank knew national secrets, and could be considered a security leak. Perhaps the same could be said of the others. But the FBI could have shot Frank when he answered the door back at his apartment. Why all of this preparation if the goal was just to kill them all?

Unless...

"Maybe this is all a hoax," he said, trying the idea on for size.

"What do you mean?" Sara asked.

"Well, if this really is an experiment to study fear, we're behaving exactly as they they they want us to."

Mal came over, shaking his head in the pale green light of the glow stick he held. "That Cornelius Wellington was practically decapitated. And Tom shot Ol' Jasper at least ten times."

Belgium tapped his chin. "Are we sure?"

"That's what we saw," Pang chimed in.

"And we see magic all the time. Chris Angel levitating on the street. David Copperfield making the Statue of Liberty disappear."

"How about all the blood?" Mal asked.

Belgium shrugged. "Special effects. Movie props. Maybe Wellington is even in on it. It happened after the lights were out. How can we be sure what we saw?"

"That man, in the exam room." Deb's voice was still raspy and faint. "Franklin. He was real."

"Could he have been someone made up to look like Franklin? With make up? A good make-up artist can make Dustin Hoffman look a hundred years old, and Eddie Murphy look like a five hundred pound woman."

Deb seemed unconvinced. "He was going to drill my leg."

"But he stopped before he could. He scared you. And hurt hurt hurt you while drawing some blood. But what if all of that was scripted out? What if he wasn't a real threat?"

"So Tom is in on it too?" Sara asked.

Frank turned up his palms. "He certainly could could could be. I suppose any of us could be. We all just met today."

Mal rubbed his chin. "So this could still all be part of the experiment. They're just trying to scare us, but it's all a hoax."

"Shouldn't we consider that it's at least a possibility?"

"So Ol' Jasper was fake as well?" Sara asked. She looked so hopeful, Frank's heart fluttered.

"Dr. Forenzi said that Colton Butler was trying to sew extra limbs on slaves. Even with today's advancements in medical technology, that's impossible. Isn't it a more reasonable explanation to believe it's fake?"

Pang shook his head. "What about Aabir? She spiked on my EMF meter. And with my full spectrum camera, she looked like she was on fire."

Frank brushed away a drop of sweat from his forehead. "When you arrived, did you have your equipment with you the whole time?"

"Yes."

"How about when we were eating? Did you have it with you then?"

Another drip of sweat, and Frank wiped it off and looked at his hand.

It wasn't sweat. The smear was blackish in the glow lights.

Blood?

Was something above him dripping blood?

Frank looked up, but couldn't see the high ceiling. He raised his glow stick up over his head—

—and saw a man staring down at him, his back pressed to the ceiling.

A smiling man, his clothing soaked with blood.

Frank yelped, and jumped to the side just as the man dropped down, landing on the floor in a crouch, then rising to his full height. He shook like a dog, spraying blood everywhere.

"An... interesting... theory... Dr... Belgium..." the man said. There was something messed up about his voice.

It sounded like two or three people talking in unison. The sclera—the whites of his eyes—were black.

"It's Jebediah Butler," Pang squeaked, pointing his camcorder at him. "Floating on a pool of his own blood."

Frank didn't know what to do. He wasn't a fighter. And even if he was, would fighting work against a supernatural being?

"Tell... me... something..." Jebediah said with his freaky voice. His hand shot out, grabbing Frank by the wrist. Frank tried to pull away, but the grip was unbelievable. *"Am... I... a... hoax... or... a... real... threat?"*

Then he twisted.

Frank heard his own elbow snap, and stared in disbelief as his arm was suddenly bending the wrong way.

The pain hit a moment later, and it was unreal. Frank dropped to his knees, not sure if he should vomit or faint or both. He stared up into the grinning, bloody face of Jebediah, and realized he'd been horribly wrong.

This wasn't a trick.

They were all going to die here.

A chair splintered over Jebediah's shoulders, courtesy of Pang. The ghost backhanded the Asian man across the room. Then he turned his attention back to Frank.

"I... shall... keep... twisting... that... arm... until... it... comes... off... like... a... turkey... leg..."

And then a hand was in Jebediah's face.

A female hand, clutching a rosary.

Sara!

"Get away from him, you son of a bitch," she snarled.

Jebediah's eyes went wide. *"A... crucifix..."*

The ghost stuck out a black tongue—

—and began to lick it.

Long, wet, obscene strokes of the tongue, followed by quick ones. He moaned while doing so, as if in ecstasy, and then slurped the whole cross in his mouth and began to chew.

Then someone was pulling on Frank's good arm—Mal, dragging him to the door—a mad scramble to move the desk—and Frank was in the hallway being half-carried and half-yanked—and then through another door and stairs going down—down—down—and there was actual electric light there, dim but on just the same, then Frank was laid down on the ground and unable to think about anything other than the unrelenting, throbbing, unbearable pain before unconsciousness finally took him.

Forenzi

His patient was struggling to breath. Vitals were weak. The will to live gone.

"Fight, damn you," Forenzi said, shaking him. "You still have more to give."

The man stared blankly at him, then his puffy eyes closed.

Forenzi made a notation on the chart, then checked the monitors for the vital signs of his volunteers. They were elevated, as expected. Heart rate, blood pressure, brain activity. Every one of them was scared.

Which, of course, was the point. And the longer they remained scared, the better the results would be.

He once again lost himself in a familiar daydream. A world without fear. Which would ultimately lead to universal peace.

The ringing phone interrupted his thoughts.

"I'm working," he answered.

"There's been a death." It was Sykes.

Forenzi put his hand to his face and said, "What? A death? Who?"

"The skeptic. Wellington."

"How did this happen?" This was the worst possible thing that could have happened.

"There have been some complications," Sykes said.

Dear Lord, Forenzi thought. *What have I done?*

Tom

The thing's face was blackened, skin peeling off in strips, glistening with grease like a broiled pork chop.

Tom's mind flashed to the Butler House web site. Sturgis Butler, a serial killer from the 1800s who slayed prostitutes in satanic rituals. When he was caught by a mob they tied him to a tree and torched him, Sturgis supposedly laughing as he burned.

Deep set eyes bored into Tom, intelligent, malevolent, and he immediately spun away from the ghoul's grasp and fell backward, shooting as fast as he could pull the trigger.

Five shots fired.

Five shots hit.

But his attacker didn't even flinch.

Tom fell onto his ass, a shock of agony rippling up from his coccyx to the base of his skull. Ignoring the pain, Tom crab-walked backward, fast as he could, trying to get as much distance from the thing as possible.

Then he turned onto all fours, pressing the flashlight's off button as his fingers clenched it, and then scrambled onto his feet and sprinted for all he was worth toward the great room.

Eight strides later he ran into something—a chair—Tom hitting hard as a football tackle. He flipped, ass over elbows, and sprawled forward, his shoulder smacking into the wood floor.

Tom somehow managed to hold onto his Sig, but the flashlight bounced out of his grasp and went skittering off into the darkness.

He paused for a moment, trying to catch his breath, trying to hear any sounds of pursuit.

There was only silence.

Tom sniffed the air, but the scorched meat smell was gone.

"Aabir?" he called in a stage whisper. "Dr. Madison?"

No one responded.

Tom holstered his gun and began to crawl, sweeping his hands out in front of him, seeking the dropped flashlight. Remembering the light sticks in his pack, he fished one out, opened the package, and gave it a quick snap and shake. He was immediately bathed in a faint blue chemiluminescence. Tom spotted the flashlight, under the grand piano, and scurried over on his hands and knees, getting beneath the instrument's legs and snatching it up.

From the darkness, a scraping sound.

Ol' Jasper.

Tom shoved the light stick into his pants so it couldn't be seen, and then held his breath.

The scraping got closer.

Had he seen me? Does he know I'm hiding under the—

PLINK!

Something hit a key on the piano above him.

Tom's bladder clenched, and he fought not to wet himself.

As a Homicide cop, Tom was familiar with fear. Every time he served a warrant, kicked in a door, made an arrest, or pursued a suspect, he relied on his training and a shitload of good fortune to make sure he didn't get hurt.

But there wasn't any precedent for this. Ghosts? Demons? Undead zombies?

Whatever these things were, one of them killed Wellington, and bullets didn't do a damn thing to stop them.

All of Tom's experience, all of his training, was worthless when a hostile hundred and fifty year old slave with four arms wanted to hack your head off.

Tom waited.

He listened.

He sweated.

Every second that passed felt like a minute.

PLINK PLINK PLINK!

Tom shuddered, holding his knees so he didn't make noise.

Does it know I'm under here?

Is it playing with me?

Was Wellington unlucky to die so quickly?

Or was he the luckiest one here?

Tom realized, with chilling certainty, that if Roy had come to Butler House, he was dead.

And I'll be joining him soon.

Tom slowly removed the Mangus knife from his ankle sheath. He opened it with both hands, silently, grateful he kept the hinges oiled.

Whatever these things were, they had weight and mass. They were solid.

Bullets might not work.

But that didn't rule out stabbing it in the eyes.

Tom remained crouched. His muscles had begun to ache, to cramp. But he didn't adjust his position. If his legs fell asleep, he'd be compromised. But that was preferable to making a sound and giving away his position.

Time ticked by.

Tom heard a scraping sound, wondered if he was imagining it, but was able to confirm that it was real, and it was getting fainter as it moved away.

Tom stayed put.

He counted to a hundred.

Then two hundred.

Rubbing the on button of his flashlight, he knew he needed to take a look around.

After another count of two hundred.

A slow count.

Several minutes passed without any strange sounds, or weird smells. Tom flicked on his beam.

He didn't see some horrible disfigured face staring at him.

He didn't see any threat at all.

Tom made a slow sweep with the light, and the room appeared empty.

Wellington's body was gone.

Aabir was gone.

Dr. Madison was gone.

Fishing out his cell phone, he again searched for a signal that wasn't there. Then he unfolded his six-foot frame from underneath the piano, and practically cried in relief as his cramped muscles stretched and circulation returned.

Now I need to find the front door. If it's unlocked, I can grab the others and—

Then the edge of his light beam caught something. Movement, behind a love seat ten meters away. Tom turned the focus on the flashlight, amplifying it, and seeing—

Wellington?

The man was behind the loveseat, his head peeking out over the backrest, the rest of his body hidden. He looked pale and in shock. Eyes wide and vacant. Mouth hanging open. Jaw opening and closing, as if trying to speak.

"Cornelius!" Tom spoke as loudly as the conditions warranted. "I'm over here!"

Wellington's head turned toward Tom. The guy looked positively devastated. Tom had no idea how he was even alive, let alone still able to move. But the guy needed medical attention. Fast.

"I'm coming to you," Tom said.

Wellington nodded robotically, and then stuck out his tongue.

No—

That's not a tongue.

It's...

Two fingers.

Wellington has two fingers in his mouth.

As Tom was trying to comprehend why the man was eating human fingers, another possibility sprang, fully formed, into Tom's head.

Oh my god.

Wellington isn't chewing on fingers.

He's...

That's when the burned ghost of Sturgis Butler stood up from behind the love seat—

—wearing Wellington's severed head on his hand like a puppet.

Tom's muscles locked. His mind couldn't comprehend the horror of what he was seeing.

Sturgis continued to manipulate Wellington's skull as if it was a ventriloquist's dummy, making the jaw move.

And then he made it talk.

"Hello... Tom..."

The ghost's voice sounded like he was gargling motor oil.

"I've... got... my... eyes... on... you..."

Incredibly, Wellington's eyes began to bulge. Tom didn't understand how that could be possible—then they popped out and two black fingers wiggled through the empty sockets.

That was enough to get Tom to move. He sprinted across the great room, heading down a hallway, and then he slowed when he smelled something.

Smoke.

A cigarette? Moni?

He swept the hallway with his flashlight, finding a half-open door with a wisp of fumes coming out of it. Knife in hand, Tom cautiously approached the room.

"Moni? Is that you?"

Tom stopped before entering. He listened, and was answered with silence. Sniffing again, he realized it wasn't a cigarette. It was more like burning hair.

Tom gave the door a small push, and it squealed on its hinges, causing hackles to rise on his forearms. The room was brighter than the hallway, an orange glow from several candles.

Black candles. On a black stone slab, which was atop an old mortician's gurney. Next to the candles was a tarnished silver chalice with a lid on it.

It was a portable satanic altar.

Behind them, on the wall, an ornate wooden cross, over a meter tall. It had been turned upside-down. A naked figure of Jesus hung on the cross, painted in exquisite detail. His face was contorted in pain, and rivulets of blood ran from his crown of thorns and the spikes in his hands and feet. A bloody pentagram had been carved into his chest. Despite the obvious agony, the Christ figure had an obscene, blasphemous erection.

Tom wasn't religious, but he guessed he'd walked in on the unholy ritual of the black mass. Which wasn't something he wanted to take part in.

He was about to get the hell out of there when he noticed movement next to the altar.

Something under a black sheet.

Something human-shaped. Just sitting there.

Tom continued to stare. Maybe it hadn't moved. Maybe the shadows from the flickering candles just made it look like—

It moved again. A shudder.

Followed by a low moan.

Tom knew how important it was to act on instinct, and every fiber of his being told him to run away. His neck was gooseflesh. His hands were shaking. His tongue was so dry that it stuck to the roof of his mouth.

Tom did *not* want to see what was under that sheet.

But he had to.

It could be Moni. Or someone else who needed help.

So Tom took a slow step toward it, on the balls of his feet. Quietly, as if not to wake a sleeping baby. When he got within an arm's length, the thing under the sheet twitched.

What are you doing, Tom? Are you insane? Get out of here.

But he didn't get out of there. Instead, he pinched the sheet with the hand that held the knife.

Okay. Here we go...

He pulled, hard.

The sheet came off.

Aabir was kneeling there, staring up at him.

Her eyes were completely black.

It scared him so badly, he fell backward, onto his ass.

She smiled. Her teeth were black as well.

"Aabir, are you... are you okay?"

It was a ludicrous thing to say. The whites of her eyes were gone, and her teeth the color of coal. She was obviously in very deep shit.

So what should he do? Try to get her out of there?

"Aabir, can you hear me? Do you understand?"

Then Tom smelled it.

Burnt meat. Getting stronger. And footsteps, from the hall outside.

Tom quickly put Aabir's sheet back over her head, and then crawled beneath the stone altar, hiding behind the coverlet and killing his flashlight just as Sturgis walked in. Tom could see him through a break in the fabric.

The ghost approached the altar, and stopped there. Then he yanked off Aabir's sheet.

"Ready... for... the... sacraments..."

Aabir stared up at Sturgis and nodded. Then she turned her head and stared at Tom. Her eyes were so black they resembled holes in her head.

Don't look at me, Tom willed. *You'll give away where I am. Stop it. Please stop it.*

Then Sturgis placed his hand on her head, and she stared up at him again. He had a steak knife in his hand.

"Sanguis... satanas..."

Aabir opened her mouth and stuck out her black tongue. Sturgis jammed the knife into his palm and twisted it. Blood dribbled out, into Aabir's mouth.

Sturgis took his hands away, and Aabir once again stared at Tom. She licked her red lips.

"Corpus... satanas..."

Sturgis now had the silver chalice. Tom knew what it was. A ciborium. Used in Catholic Mass to hold Communion wafers. The priest carried it to share the Body of Christ to his Parrish.

But when Sturgis opened the ciborium, it wasn't filled with unleavened bread.

It was filled with cockroaches.

Sturgis snatched one, and held it in two fingers as it wiggled.

Aabir stuck out her tongue.

Tom squeezed his eyes shut. He could still hear the crunching. He felt his stomach flip-flop. Between the smell of burned meat, and the sound of eating bugs, he was very close to throwing up.

Then he felt a slight tickle on his nose.

His eyes sprang open and he saw Aabir holding the cup of roaches right in front of his face.

Tom knocked it away, then rolled backward, out from under the altar. His head hit the head of the upside-down Christ, and for a moment the world went wobbly. Then he slapped at a roach crawling on his cheek—

—and dropped his flashlight.

"I... took... good... care... of... your... partner... Roy..." Sturgis croaked in that otherworldly voice as he leaned over the altar. *"I... will... take... care... of... you... as... well..."*

Tom slashed out with his knife, cutting Sturgis across the chest. Then he got to his feet and ran.

Out of the room.

Down the hall.

Digging the light stick out of his pants just in time to see Ol' Jasper blocking his path.

Mal

Mal was having a hard time believing he was trapped in another psychotic nightmare fearing for his life.

Even more incredible was the sad fact that he'd volunteered for it.

After fleeing from the library, they'd somehow wound up underneath the house, in a labyrinthine maze of dirt floors and wooden support beams and low lighting supplied by old, bare, dim bulbs. Mal hadn't ever been in an underground mine, but he assumed this was what one looked like.

Frank Belgium was on the ground, unconscious, his arm bent in such a funky angle that it hurt Mal to look at it. Sara was kneeling next to him, an expression of shock on her face. The same look graced Deb, and Mal bet his face was damn near the same.

The only one who seemed to be handling this well was Pang, who was sitting on the stairs, digging through his bag of equipment, humming something softly to himself.

"We need to fix his arm," Sara said. She first looked at Deb, who didn't respond, and then to Mal.

"Sara..." He tried to keep his voice from cracking. "It will take a whole team of orthopedic surgeons hours on an operating table to fix that arm."

"It's bent the wrong way. We need to bend it back and put it in a sling before he wakes up."

"If we touch it, we could make it worse."

Sara barked out a semi-hysterical laugh. "Worse? Look at it, Mal!" She pointed at Belgium's arm, which looked like a swollen letter N. "How can that get any worse?"

Mal chewed the inside of his cheek. He wanted to run. Grab Deb, run up the stairs, make a dash for the front door, and get the fuck out of there. They'd just met Sara and Frank a few hours ago. They didn't owe them anything.

But that was the coward in Mal talking. The part he hated. The part that had taken over his life to the point where life wasn't good anymore. Maybe they could escape, but to what? More insomnia? More sleepless nights? More fighting with Deb because they were both so goddamn terrified all the time?

Why couldn't he just be brave?

That was the irony, wasn't it? The only time it was possible to be brave was when you were scared out of your mind.

"Please help him!" Sara cried.

Mal took a big breath. Blew it out. He took a last lingering look up the stairs, to potential freedom, and made his decision.

I'm done being this guy.

Time to be the man I want to be.

"Deb."

His wife didn't reply.

"Deb, can you help Sara hold Frank down?"

She used the wall to get down on all fours, then crawled to Frank.

"Both of you, put your bodies on top of his. Pang, can you come here?"

"Hmm?" he looked up from his tech stuff.

"They're going to hold Frank down. We're going to yank on his arm, try to get the bones aligned."

"Bro, if we pull on that arm, we might pull it right off."

"We have to try."

Pang shrugged, set down his bag, and came over.

Mal got on his butt and placed his feet against Belgium's ribcage. Pang sat behind Mal, straddling him like they were on a log flume ride. Mal grabbed Frank's misshapen wrist, and Pang grabbed Mal's arm with both hands.

"Now!"

Mal and Pang pulled, hard as they could, straightening out Frank's wrist.

There were popping and snapping sounds, followed by Frank waking up and screaming so loud it hurt Mal's ears.

When Mal released him, the screaming continued.

"It's okay, Frank. It's okay," Sara stroked his cheeks, trying to sooth him, but Frank was lost in a world of pain.

Worse, if he kept howling like that, he was going to attract some unwanted attention.

"Try to keep him quiet, Sara."

"Shhh, Frank. We have to keep it down."

"Anyone have a wallet? Give him something to bite on."

Deb patted down Frank's pants, found a leather billfold, and crammed it in his mouth. Frank clenched down on it, still screaming in his throat. Mal didn't know what to do. Knock him out? If only they could give him something.

Moni. She had that syringe filled with heroin.

"Did Moni have her purse when Deb was in the exam room?"

He tried to picture her when they were all in the hallway.

"No," Sara said. "She didn't have one."

"She's got some heroin in her room. And I've got a gun in my room."

Deb met his eyes. "What are you saying?"

"I guess I'm saying I'm going to go get some drugs and a gun."

"I'm going with you," his wife said.

"No."

"Mal—"

"It's *stairs* Deb."

Deb could do triathlons, but stairs were her nemesis.

"I got down here fine."

"Down isn't the same as up. You don't do well going up."

"I'm still coming."

There was no way in hell he was going to let Deb go back into the godforsaken house.

"You'll slow me down, Deb."

Mal saw a flash of anger.

"I'm coming, Mal."

"No, you're not. And if I have to wrestle your legs away from you and take them with me, I'll do it."

"You're being an asshole."

"I'm being the man you deserve, Deb. Because I don't deserve to have such a wonderful, strong, loving woman in my life." He smiled. "But that changes right now. I'm going to do this, and when I come back we're all going to get out of here. I love you, Deb. And I'll die before I let you go back up there with those… those *things*."

Deb's eyes got glassy. "Mal… we're a team."

"Always and forever, babe. But you have to let me swagger a little."

She nodded, tears on her cheeks, and Mal kissed her. Softly. Tenderly. With his heart as well as his lips.

Then he turned to the ghost hunter. "Pang!"

"I'm not going back into that house, bro."

"Stay here, make sure no one comes downstairs."

"I'm your man, bro."

"You got an extra flashlight?"

Pang reached into his front pocket and took out his keys. There was a tiny LED flashlight on the ring, which he took off and gave to Mal.

Mal took it, then looked at his wife. A terrible, powerful thought popped into his head.

Could this be the last time I ever see her?

He rushed to her once more, taking her in his arms, and kissed her again. But this time it wasn't soft or gentle. It was with all the passion, all the strength, of a man who loved a woman so much it practically consumed him.

When Mal broke this kiss he stared deep into her eyes and said with all the feeling he could muster. "I. Love. You."

"Then you'd better come back to me."

He winked. "You couldn't keep me away."

Then Mal headed up the stairs before he lost his resolve.

When he reached the top Mal put his ear to the door, listening for sounds from the hall. After twenty seconds of not hearing anything, he jammed the glow stick Tom had given him into the waist of his jeans, then snuck through the door. A quick press of the keychain light proved it was about as illuminating as a firefly, but the hallway seemed empty.

Mal moved quickly but carefully, heading for the great room. His original plan was to sprint up to the second floor and grab the drugs and gun. But when he saw the front doors, he realized he should check them to make sure they were open. His experience at the Rushmore Inn informed him that once the bad things started happening, it became increasingly difficult to leave. Though Mal readily admitted he suffered from paranoia—a paranoia he felt he'd earned—Butler House was beginning to feel more and more like the Rushmore. So it was with a sick, sinking feeling that he approached the exit, willing to bet everything he had that it would be locked.

Wellington's body had been moved, but the doors and floor were still splashed with his blood. Mal did a quick look around, making sure he was alone. Then—

—he stuck the key light in his teeth—

—put his hand on the door knob—

—turned and pulled—

—and it opened easily—

—revealing a shirtless man wearing a gas mask, holding a meat cleaver.

"Hee hee hee," the man giggled.

Mal backed away so quickly he slipped and fell. He tried to get up, but his feet couldn't get any traction on the bloody floor. At the same time, he couldn't look away from the Giggler, as Forenzi had called him during dinner.

A masked demon who would mutilate himself...

Which was when the Giggler raised his cleaver, and sliced a line down his scarred chest.

Mal stared, the fear so absolute he ceased to be a human being. Exactly like when he was strapped to the table at the Rushmore Inn. Mal lost his personality, his identity, and was reduced to an animal state. The evolutionary fear response, a chemical cocktail millions of years in the making, took over his body until every cell screamed fight or flight.

Acting on pure instinct, Mal chose flight, flopping onto his belly, getting his one hand underneath him, and then bicycling his feet until his toes found purchase on the hardwood floor.

And then he was off and running, beelining for the group of chairs and sofas in the middle of the great room.

Which was where he found Wellington's body.

The dead author had been stripped naked and was sitting in a chair, his severed head placed between his legs so he was giving himself oral sex. Stuck in his neck stump were a cluster of cattails, jutting out as if in a vase.

Mal kept running, trying to remember where the stairs were. He headed for the hall to the dining room and saw it had been blocked with a sofa. So he detoured and took another corridor.

He heard a high-pitched whining sound and realized he was the one making it. So ensnared in the throes of terror, he didn't even know where he was until the hallway he'd sprinted down abruptly ended at a closed door.

Confused, out of breath, panicked and sickened, Mal turned in a circle, trying to get his bearings. He began to backtrack, to get out of this dead-end, when he heard a *CRACK!* from the darkness ahead. Like someone slapping their hands together. Or...

Or a whip.

The ghost of the one-eyed slave master, Blackjack Reedy.

Mal spun back around, reaching for the doorknob, opening it and easing himself inside, then closing it behind him.

The room smelled of stale mildew. Mal used his tiny flashlight to look around, and even though the beam didn't penetrate very far, he realized he was in the laundry room.

He saw a large sink. Some rusty, metal wash basins. Clotheslines hanging on the walls. An old fashioned washing machine with rollers. A large pile of dirty clothes. Several washboards. A shelf full of antique detergent boxes.

But something about the room was... off. Though it didn't look like anyone had been in there in decades, Mal had the uneasy feeling he was being watched.

He got his breathing under control and listened.

The room was silent.

Mal took a few steps into the room, noticing a door on the other side. Maybe it was a closet. Or maybe it was an exit. Old houses often had a laundry room next to an outside door, to make it easier to haul wet clothing outside to dry in the sun.

Halfway into the room, Mal heard something.

A moan.

He stopped, mid-step.

Had it been a voice? The wind? Some other, harmless sound? His imagination?

Once again he played the flashlight beam around the room.

The sink, old and filthy.

Rusty basins.

The washing machine, its pulleys misaligned.

A pile of clothing with an old coat on top, its buttons glinting in the light.

The stack of washboards.

Shelves.

"Hello?" he whispered.

Immediately after speaking, Mal regretted it. Who was he talking to? And did he really want someone to answer?

Thankfully, no one replied.

Mal wasted no more time getting to the door at the end of the room. He grasped the ancient, metal door knob and turned.

Locked. He gave the door a sharp tug. It peppered him with dust, but held firm.

Squinting at the bronze doorplate, Mal saw an old-time keyhole.

Could there be a key around here?

He looked behind him, back at the shelves. If there was a key, that seemed like the place for it. Mal crept over, scanning row by row with the flashlight. On the third shelf, next to a disintegrating box of Borax soap chips, was a tarnished skeleton key.

Mal reached for it—

—and heard another moan.

He spun, again taking in the room.

But no one was there.

Basins, washboards, sink, washing machine, clothes. There wasn't anything else.

Then the pile of clothing blinked.

Mal was so shocked he jumped backward, into the shelves, old detergent snowing on him as the pile of clothing stood up—not a pile at all, but a figure in a dirty lab coat, what Mal assumed were glinting buttons had actually been its staring eyes.

Colton Butler.

Colton moaned again. He was clutching a leather medical bag in one hand, a curved surgical saw in the other, and he advanced toward Mal.

The fear was so absolute, it paralyzed Mal, pinning him to the spot. Colton raised the saw up.

"Time... to... operate..."

His voice was all messed up, like Jebediah's in the library, and so shocking it snapped Mal out of his catatonia and he lurched toward the locked door. Key and flashlight in the same hand, he was trembling too madly to fit it into the keyhole.

"Maaaaaaal..."

The voice was so close Mal didn't want to turn around, fearing that Colton was right behind him. He focused on opening the door, trying to block out everything else, putting 100% of his concentration into fitting the damn key into—

Colton hit Mal in the side of the neck with something, so hard Mal saw motes of light. Then there was a ripping sound, and a spike of pain like lemon juice on a paper cut, right across Mal's right shoulder blade.

The saw.

Mal pushed himself backward, knocking Colton away, reaching up and feeling the jagged cut in his neck.

He tried to saw my head off.

His hand now slick with blood, Mal jammed the keychain light in his teeth and went back to playing bullseye with the key.

"Maaaaaaaaaaaaaaaaaaaaaaaal..."

By some miracle, Mal got it in the keyhole. He twisted it, first one way, then the other, and when the bolt snicked free Mal yanked open the door and saw...

Stairs. Leading up.

He took them two at a time, breathing through his teeth as they clamped down on the flashlight, going up sixteen steps and then reaching...

A dead end.

There was no door. No room. No hallway. Just a wooden barricade.

"Maaaaaaaaaaaaaal..."

Below him, Mal heard feet begin to clomp up the steps.

Why have a stairway leading nowhere? What was the point? It made no sense.

He put his shoulder into it, pressing hard. Felt a slight bit of give.

Could this be some secret passage?

Mal held the keylight, looking for seams along the wall. On the right side, he found some old, rusty hinges.

Mal pushed again. No go.

"Maaaaaaaaaal....."

Colton was closer, already halfway up the stairs.

Mal ran his hands along the seam, looking for a switch, a release, a button. Anything that would open this sucker up.

"Maaaaaaaaaaaaaaaaaaaaaaal..."

Colton was practically on top of him. Mal's heart was hammering so hard he could hear the lub-dub in his eardrum. A wooden splinter jammed under his fingernail, and he dropped the flashlight. Mal opened his mouth to scream in pain and frustration when his fingers brushed against a latch.

"MAAAAAAAAAAAAAAAAAAAAAAAL!"

Colton's saw touched Mal's leg just as the passageway swung outward. Mal fell forward, pulling away, then kicking the secret door closed. He looked around, pulling the glow stick from his pants, and realized he'd gotten to the guest room hallway. But it looked different in the dark, and he wasn't sure which room was his.

The secret passage began to shake, and Mal got to his feet and ducked into the nearest bedroom. He quietly closed the door behind him, then took a minute to catch his breath. His neck throbbed, and he found a mirror on the wall and took a look.

In the green glow light, his blood appeared black. Mal probed the wound, wincing. It hurt, but wasn't deep. Stitches probably weren't required, but if he lived through this it would no doubt leave a jagged scar.

Squinting at his finger, he used his teeth to yank out a three inch splinter under his nail. He spat it out, and began to search the room.

The suitcase next to the bed wasn't his, and he didn't see any purses lying around. He checked the bureau drawers, and then the desk.

Nothing.

Mal crept to the door and put his ear to it. Then he opened it a crack, peering out. The coast seemed clear, and he quickly exited the room and entered the adjacent one.

Not his suitcase, but there was a purse on the desk. And inside...

Moni's syringe. He pulled the purse strap over his head and shoulder.

Okay, that's half the mission. Now to get my gun.

He remembered his room was next to Moni's, so all he had to do was sneak into it and—

The doorknob began to turn before Mal could touch it. He quickly stuck the light stick back in his jeans and looked around for a place to hide.

The bed.

Quickly dropping to all fours, Mal scooted under it just as the door opened.

"Maaaaaaaal... I... want... your... other... hand..."

Sara

Sara took off her sweater and tied a knot in the sleeves, trying to make a sling for Frank's arm. He'd been groaning since Mal left, biting his wallet, his eyes welling with tears. Fishing around in her purse, Sara found a pack of tissue. She gently wiped his eyes, and then mopped some of the sweat off of his forehead.

Frank let the wallet fall from his lips, and stared hard at her.

"I've... been hope hope hoping..." he said, the pain straining his voice.

"Hoping for what, Frank?"

"To see see see..."

"To see?"

"You... with your... shirt off."

He grinned, and Sara laughed. She didn't even remember what bra she had on until she looked. It was frilly, pink, Fredrick's of Hollywood. Somehow she'd had the foresight to wear her only good bra. If he'd seen some of her others, he probably wouldn't have been as impressed.

"When we get out of here," she whispered. "Maybe I'll even let you see me without the bra."

"I'd like that. Sara?"

"Yes, Frank?"

"I think think think my arm is broken."

"It's just a bad sprain," Sara said. "Mal is going to get you something for the pain. He'll be back soon."

"I'm scared, Sara."

"So am I, Frank."

She kissed his damp forehead, then opened her purse and stared at her last two tiny bottles of Southern Comfort.

Sara needed a drink. Badly. In fact, Sara may have never needed a drink more than she did right then. Her hopes for getting her son back had been torn from her. Seeing the first decent man she'd met in—well—*forever*—suffer like this was heartbreaking. And the very real possibility that she was going to die soon, and die horribly, made her adrenaline spike so hard her head hurt.

She pulled out the first bottle, twisting off the cap with practiced precision, and tilted it—

—into Frank's mouth.

He drank, then coughed. "Thanks."

"Got one more coming."

She opened the second, and he gulped it down.

"Got any any any orange juice?"

"Other purse."

She moved her thigh under his head as a pillow, and blotted away more sweat.

She didn't regret giving Frank the last of her booze.

In fact, in a strange sort of way, she felt liberated by it.

Sara looked over at Deb, who was sitting against the wall with her head in her hands, her fake legs spread out in front of her, looking strangely like skis. She seemed off in her own world. Sara then looked at Pang, and saw he had some new gizmo in his hand.

Pang glanced up at her. "I'd like to try an EVP recording."

"What is that?" Sara asked.

"Electronic Voice Phenomenon. I ask a question, and record the response. The human ear isn't as sensitive as a microphone. So answers could get picked up by the recorder that we wouldn't otherwise hear. Then we can hear them in playback, with the sound boosted up."

"Why do you want to do this?"

"Because maybe we can find out what these spirits want. I've investigated a lot of supposedly haunted houses. They've always had rational explanations or have been inconclusive. What's happening here, now—it's unprecedented. If we can prove that there is another plane of existence, and if we can get some answers from those who inhabit that plane, it will be the greatest scientific discovery of the century."

Sara thought it was a bad idea. "Deb?"

Deb didn't reply, apparently remaining a prisoner of her thoughts.

"Frank, what do you think?"

His eyelids fluttered. "I think it's a break, not a sprain. Sprains don't bend the wrong way."

"Look," Pang said, "you don't have to do anything. Just stay quiet. This isn't just for bad spirits. There may be some good ones around that can help us. But we won't get that help, unless we ask for it."

Sara sighed. She was used to life spiraling out of control despite anything she did. If Pang wanted to do this, Sara didn't see how she'd be able to stop him.

Pang stood, holding up a silver gadget with a red blinking light on it. Keeping it at arm's length from his face he said, "Are there any spirits here?"

Sara didn't hear a response, but she supposed that was the point. After ten seconds, Pang sat down and pressed a button. A moment later his recorded voice was heard, louder than he'd originally spoken.

"Are there any spirits here?"

They all listened to the white noise that followed. No ghosts responded to Pang's question.

Pang pressed another button and asked again, "Are there any spirits here?"

Sara found herself concentrating on the silence. The underground tunnel they were in had a slight echo to it, and the single bare bulb hanging from the wooden brace overhead didn't illuminate more than a few meters into the darkness.

Pang stopped the recording and hit play again.

"Are there any spirits here?"

He turned up the volume, until the recording became almost a hiss. Then he pressed stop.

"Did you guys hear that?" Pang said, the excitement in his voice apparent.

Sara shook her head.

"At the end. It sounded like whispering."

Pang played it again, the volume even higher. There was a faint murmuring sound, but Sara wouldn't have called it a voice.

"Someone said *yes* on the recording. Did anyone else hear it?"

"Apophenia," Frank said.

"What's that, bro?"

"Your mind is seeking a pattern in randomness. Like seeing Jesus's face in in in burned toast. You want to hear a voice, so you think you hear a voice."

"You still saying spirits don't exist? So what broke your arm, bro? Was that your mind seeking a pattern when that bleeding ghost dropped from the ceiling?"

"That," Frank said, "is harder to dispute. But your EVP recording is nonsense."

"Whatever, bro." Pang pressed the record button once more. "Are there any spirits here?"

The silence ticked past.

Pang played it back.

"Are there any spirits here?"

Sara listened hard, to see if the faint murmur returned. Then the recorder let out an ear-splitting screech and wailed:

"I'M COMING DOWN THE STAIRS!"

Everyone turned to look as Jebediah Butler, dripping blood, stepped off the dark staircase and into the dim light.

Fran

Fran set down the magazine in mid-sentence and glanced over at her sleeping men.

Duncan, fifteen years old, but still young enough that there were traces in his face of the little boy he once was. And Josh, caring, strong, as close to a soul mate as could ever exist.

She closed her eyes and thought about Butler House. Having survived Safe Haven, Fran could imagine all too well what was going on right now in South Carolina. There would be blood. And death. And unimaginable horror. They would need help.

Looking at her family, Fran knew there were things worth fighting, and dying, for.

For the hundredth time she questioned whether they were doing the right thing.

And for the hundredth time, she didn't know the answer.

Tom

Seeing Ol' Jasper in the hall ahead, Tom did a reversal and ran back the way he came, passing Sturgis as he stuck his head out of the satanic chapel. Without his flashlight, Tom was at the mercy of his glow stick, which didn't illuminate more than a few steps ahead of him. He bumped into a wall when the hall turned a corner, kept sprinting, and wound up in front of some double doors.

Tom tugged one open and saw he was in a large, open room. Tile floors. Ornate, crystal chandeliers. A row of chairs against one wall. A stage.

It was a ball room.

He drew his gun, keeping his knife in his left hand, and began to make his way across the dance floor. It was dark, quiet, eerie, and Tom was shaking so badly he felt he might fall over. He'd never been so frightened, and his mind kept flitting between the horror of what was happening and the horror of what he'd already gone through. He kept replaying the same terrifying scenes, over and over, and wanted to find someplace safe to hide and never come out again.

But people were counting on him. Good people. And fear be damned, Tom wasn't in the business of letting people down. Even if he was going to die of fright in the process.

Tom reached a doorway, cleared it, spinning as something lunged at him in the darkness.

He fired, his Sig kicking, and then jumped to the side as a black object hurtled past him. Keeping a bead, he stared as it jerked to a stop and swung from the ceiling.

A body bag.

But he quickly realized something was strange. Bodies had weight as well as mass, but this swung like it couldn't have weighed more than a few kilograms.

Tom reached for it carefully, and squeezed.

Fake. A prop, like they had in haunted houses around Halloween, where you paid ten bucks to have some teen in a mask jump out and say *boo!*

What was the point of that?

He followed the track on the ceiling—a metal rail that the body bag had been hanging from—and came to a breakfront.

Tom braced himself for something to pop out, and his expectations were met when a rubber zombie pushed through the cabinet doors, making a pneumatic hissing sound. Another phony prop, probably triggered by a motion sensor, like the body bag had been.

Though in a state of hyper-alertness, some rational thoughts still managed to gain traction in Tom's fear-addled brain. He felt like he was missing some key element. They'd all been summoned here, offered money to be part of an experiment. Forenzi, though certainly odd, seemed sincere enough. He'd told them the goal was to scare them, and he'd made good on his promise.

But had Forenzi's promise involved these silly Halloween gags? Was that his plan? And had something gone terribly wrong?

Tom was fighting for his life against an unknown enemy that apparently couldn't be harmed. He had shot two of his attackers, and also slashed Sturgis across the chest. But that didn't even slow them down.

Was there something supernatural going on? And if so, how did these dime-store attempts at scares mesh with what was happening elsewhere in Butler House?

Had the fake haunted house somehow become real?

He kept moving, and came upon a large, black crate in the center of the floor.

No, not a crate. A coffin. And not a real one. This was another Halloween prop, made of plywood. Tom approached, knowing exactly what was going to happen. The lid would open, and some fake monster—maybe a vampire or a mummy—was going to pop out.

Tom got within a meter of it, gun pointed forward, anticipating the obvious.

As predicted, the lid opened.

As predicted, a monster sat up in the coffin.

It wasn't a vampire or mummy. It was some bizarre, bloody mannequin with a gas mask on. There were many gashes on its bare chest, glistening with stage blood.

"Hee hee," went the prop.

Tom kept his Sig on it, then slowly walked past. It was creepier than the zombie in the breakfront, and the body bag on a conveyor track, but Tom was going to save his adrenaline for real threats, not fake ones.

"Hee hee hee."

Movement, in front of Tom. He held fire as another body bag swung past on a pulley track. He watched it swing past the empty coffin, and disappear into the darkness.

Tom pressed forward, and then his fear spiked. He spun again, staring at the coffin.

The gas masked prop was gone.

Tom looked side to side, sweeping with his Sig. That prop apparently wasn't a prop. Tom remembered Forenzi's dinner speech and realized it was—

"Hee hee hee hee."

The Giggler.

Now where the hell did it go?

Tom turned in a slow circle, ready to shoot anything that moved. He was so focused on what was around him that he wasn't paying attention to where he was walking, and suddenly he lost his footing and stepped into a hole, falling onto his ass.

He tried to pull his leg free, and his calf screamed at him. Tom holstered his gun and reached into the hole in the floor.

Spikes. Digging into his skin.

"Hee hee hee hee."

The Giggler walked out of the dark, into view. He was rubbing a large, bloody meat cleaver against his chest.

Tom drew his Sig and emptied his clip into the demon.

Nothing happened. The Giggler stood there, staring, swaying back and forth.

"Tom..."

Tom checked his other side, and saw a pink glow in the distance.

Moni. She had a pink light stick.

"Moni! Run!"

The pink light got closer.

"No, Moni! Get away! You need to get out of here!"

Moni slowly came into view. But it wasn't Moni.

It was Aabir, holding Moni's glow sick. Her eyes were completely black. She opened her mouth and roaches dropped out of it.

"Hee hee hee."

The Giggler had halved the distance between them. Tom realized he wasn't simply rubbing the meat cleaver against his bare skin. He was actually cutting himself, blood streaming out of the wounds he was making.

Tom blinked. His vision was getting blurry. His thoughts, fuzzy.

Drugged. Something in the spikes.

He stared back at Aabir. She was kneeling next to him. Tom held up his knife, pointed it at her, but he'd begun to see double.

He slashed at her, trying to keep her away, but everything started to fade.

Her hand shot out and she grabbed his wrist, easily prying the knife away.

Tom's eyes closed, but he forced them open.

Can't pass out. Not now...

Blackout.

And then he was in the throes of a full blown nightmare, unable to breath, drowning in some sort of slimy sea.

Tom's eyes popped open, panic making him shake. Aabir was on top of him. She had her mouth around his nose, her wet tongue sticking up his nostril.

He pushed her away, eyelids fluttering.

Must. Stay. Awake. Must...

Blackout.

Then Tom was choking, thrashing around, coughing and spitting—

—because his mouth was filled with cockroaches.

Tom looked up, and the Giggler was pinning down his shoulders, staring down at him. Aabir had her hands down Tom's pants, and she was jamming her fingers into his ass, feeling like she was tearing him apart.

"Hee hee hee."

Tom screamed.

He screamed louder and harder than he ever had in his life.

Then the Giggler pulled off his gas mask, and maggots rained down on Tom, squirming in his eyes, his nose, his mouth, as he continued to scream and scream until unconsciousness finally took him.

Mal

The dust under the bed got in Mal's eyes and the ragged gash on his neck, amplifying the pain.

He was so frightened he couldn't breathe.

Under the dust ruffle, Mal saw Colton's feet enter the bedroom. When he took a step, his old leather satchel clanged.

His bag of ghastly surgical instruments, still trying to conduct his insane experiments upon the living.

Mal let his breath out slow, then sucked dust into his nostrils—

Oh jesus I'm going to sneeze.

Mal clamped his hand over his mouth and nose, pinching his nostrils shut.

Please don't please don't please…

The urge to sneeze passed.

Colton continued to move toward the bed. His feet stopped less than half a meter from Mal's face.

He doesn't know I'm in here. If I keep absolutely still, he'll go away.

Mal kept absolutely still.

Then something tugged on Mal's foot.

Then he felt his pants cuff being raised up, baring his calf. He shook with effort as he fought not to scream.

What the hell is that?

It was small. Small and—

Hairy.

A rat? A rabid raccoon?

"*Maaaaaaaaaal,*" Colton droned.

The ghost dropped the medical equipment bag, which clanged inches from Mal's nose.

Then whatever was tugging on Mal's leg bit him.

The pain was immediate and excruciating, and Mal yelled and kicked out, hearing something screech, and then he was trying to paw through the dust and get out from under the bed. When he did, he stared up at Colton, standing over him.

"*I… want… your… hand…*"

Fast as a striking rattlesnake, Colton reached down and grabbed Mal's hand—

—pulling it off.

Mal clawed himself up to his feet and scampered past Colton, letting the ghost have his rubber prosthetic, rushing out of the room and down the hallway. He tugged out his light stick, flew down the staircase, found the route to the basement, and took more stairs down to the lower level where he'd left his wife and the others.

But they were no longer there.

Out of breath, scared shitless, and now in a state of full-on despair, Mal filled his lungs and cried out, "DEB!"

She didn't answer.

Mal began to jog, deeper into the underground bowels of Butler House, until he came to a V with tunnels leading off to the right and left.

"Deb!"

No reply.

Left or right, Mal? Which way to go?

Is she even down here?

He went right. The bare bulbs hanging from the overhead braces were dim and far apart, and Mal's light stick was getting weaker.

"Deb! Where are you?"

Mal heard his voice echo down the tunnel. But Deb's voice didn't echo back.

His neck hurt like crazy, but the bite on his leg was really starting to throb—bad enough that he'd begun to limp. He lifted his pants leg and took a quick look at it.

The bite was an oval, and some of the flesh was missing. Like he'd had a hunk gnawed out of him by a baby vampire.

He pulled his sock up over the wound, which was really all he could do with only one hand, and then the darkness was split by a sharp *CRACK!* and Mal felt his back scream at him.

Mal fell forward and turned over, because it hurt like he'd been set on fire. That's when he saw the figure with the eyepatch and the whip standing just a meter away.

Blackjack Reedy.

Frank

When Frank Belgium was in grade school, he got picked on a lot for being nerdy. Frank wasn't good at sports, was very good at science and math, and had a speech dysfluency where he'd often repeat a word three times. In sixth grade, he was challenged by a bully, and became a school legend for the fastest any kid had ever lost a fight. Eyewitness testimony was split on whether it took two or three seconds for Frank to go down, the result of a bloody nose.

It had been the most painful thing Frank had ever experienced, up until now.

His arm hurt a lot worse.

About ten to the eighth power worse.

They ran for their lives through the underground tunnels, away from Jebediah Butler, each step agonizing. Frank wasn't sure if it was his imagination or not, but he thought he could feel his broken bones grind together every time his foot hit the ground.

As in sixth grade, he felt no shame in crying. He was, however, able to refrain from the embarrassment of calling for his mother. But that was only because his mother was dead.

The alcohol Sara had given him lasted no more than fifty meters, before he stooped and puked it all over his shoes. Vomiting offered only a brief respite from the pain of jogging, because Sara was tugging him along before he was even able to finish.

They came to a fork in the tunnel, went left, and then went right at the next T junction, and left again, and then Frank lost track of where he was and just concentrated on praying for death.

Finally Sara pulled him into an actual room, unlike the mineshafts they'd been navigating. This had a concrete floor, and concrete walls, which were covered with crosses.

"We've found the Butler House crypt," Pang said.

That explained the concrete floor, walls, and crosses. Frank counted at least ten burial vaults, and then he had to stop to throw up again. When he finished, he sat on the floor and resumed crying.

Sara stayed with him, patting his back. He must have been the most pathetic, unsexy man on the planet right then, but she didn't leave his side.

"Did you see see see the movie *Titanic*?" he asked.

"Yes."

"Remember, after the ship sinks..."

"Bro, I haven't seen it yet," Pang interrupted. "You gotta spoiler alert that shit."

"After it sinks," Frank continued, "and Jack tells Rose that getting on the ship was the best thing that ever happened to him, because he got to meet her?"

Sara nodded.

"Well, Sara, meeting you may have been the best best best thing that has ever happened to me. But coming to Butler House was a really bad move."

"What's with the bells?" Deb asked.

Her voice was still raspy, but it had gotten a lot stronger. Frank had no idea what she meant until he saw her pointing at one of the vaults. Each had a tiny brass bell mounted in the corner.

"Safety coffins," Pang said. "In the 1800s, people had a huge fear of being buried alive. So they began interring people with a string that attached to a bell on the outside of the casket. If they were still alive, they could ring the bell and be rescued."

Frank filed that information tidbit under *didn't need to know* and then tried to will himself unconscious.

"At dinner," Sara said, "Dr. Forenzi said you actually met Satan. Did you really?"

"It's complicated. And I'm delirious with pain. But short answer, yes."

"And?"

Frank closed his eyes. "He wasn't very nice."

"When I..." Sara's voice trailed off.

"When you what?" Frank asked.

"When I was on... the island. It was bad. There was this guy. Lester Paks. He'd... filed down his teeth to points. I still have nightmares. Do you?"

"Yes."

"In order to survive, I had to kill. I don't regret it. I did what I had to, to save me and Jack. But sometimes I think about the afterlife. What happens to us after we die. We're being chased by spirits—"

"Alleged spirits, Sara. Nothing has been proven."

Pang laughed at that. "Nothing proven? Are you crazy, bro?"

"Frank, after meeting the devil, don't you believe in the afterlife?"

Frank thought about the question. He'd seen things that defied scientific explanation. But not having the answers didn't mean the answers had to be supernatural.

"I believe in the indomitable strength of the human will," he said. "I believe good can conquer evil. And, even though it has been a long time for me, I believe in love."

Sara didn't answer. But he knew what he said resonated with her, sure as he heard the soft, gentle tinkling of the wind chimes.

No, not wind chimes.

Bells.

Bells?

Frank's eyes opened in alarm, and he saw Sara with her jaw hanging open, eyes wide as saucers.

She was looking at the wall full of vaults. Frank followed her line of vision.

All of the bells were ringing by themselves.

"They were slaves, buried alive," Pang said, sitting up with his face buried in his hands. "Sealed in by Jebediah Butler for minor infractions. Through the holes for the bell strings, he fed them food and water. Some lasted for weeks before they died. He let their family members visit them. An object lesson, to keep them meek and afraid."

Deb had backed away from the ringing bells, her expression as horrified as Sara's.

"But when they died," Pang went on, "their spirits were released. They led the revolt that killed the Butlers. And now they roam Butler House, looking for people to possess."

Pang lifted up his head and smiled.

His eyes had turned completely black.

Deb screamed.

Sara screamed.

But both of their voices were drowned out by Frank, who screamed louder and shriller than both of them combined. Sara somehow found the courage to help Frank to his feet, and Deb added her hands to the effort as well. Then the trio was running out of the crypt, back into the tunnels.

"Which way?" Sara screeched.

Without Pang leading the way with the light in his camcorder, they couldn't tell which was the way they'd come.

Deb took the lead, Sara and Frank following her. But when they turned the corner, Deb was gone.

And then someone leapt out of the darkness, tackling Frank and Sara, pinning them to the ground.

Moni

A wooden crossbeam, old and weathered.

A dim lightbulb, hanging from brown wires.

Rusty iron shackles, bolted to the wall.

What Moni saw when she opened her eyes.

She blinked, yawned, tried to roll over.

Couldn't.

The memory came back, jolting.

She'd been following Tom through the hallway, trying to stick close, but he was moving so fast and it was so dark.

And then something grabbed her. Something big and strong.

Moni remembered the needle going in. Tried to fight for a bit. Tried to scream with a hand over her mouth.

And now...

Her hands and feet were tied to some sort of bed.

No, not a bed. Beds don't have thick metal cranks on them. Cranks meant to pull the ropes tighter until the human body stretched and broke in half.

Moni was on a rack. in a torture chamber, filled with all sorts of other horrible devices meant to inflict suffering.

Then she noticed the figure standing in the corner of the room. Staring quietly at her. Pale. Thin. Long, black hair.

It can't be. But it looks like...

"Luther Kite," Moni said, her voice cracking into a whimper.

"Hello, Moni." He was whispering to her. Soft. Gentle. *"It's so good to see you."*

Luther came to her, ran a finger across her cheek. He looked different then the last time she had seen him. Thinner. Frailer. Sharper cheekbones.

And his eyes were now completely black.

"Remember this?"

He held up a metal cylinder. On the bottom were six metal spikes, each half a centimeter long. On the top was a knob.

An artificial leech. When pressed into the skin and twisted, it shredded flesh.

"It's bleeding time, Moni."

Luther smiled, revealing black teeth.

Moni began to scream for help.

No help came.

Tom

Tom opened his eyes to the smell of burnt pork.

He was hanging from the rafters by his wrists, the rope tight and cutting off circulation to his hands. He was tall enough that he could touch the floor on his tiptoes, taking some of the weight off.

Tom spat, hacked, and spat again until he was sure he got all of the roach parts out of his mouth. Then he took in his surroundings.

The tiny room appeared to be carved out of dirt, with railroad ties bracing up the walls and ceiling. A root cellar, maybe. There was some low light, partly from a low wattage bulb on the overhead rafter, partly from a cast iron woodburning stove in the corner of the room, its chimney rising up into the ceiling.

Whatever drug he'd been given had left him foggy, but still very much afraid. His leg hurt from where he'd stepped in the spike hole, and his arms were cramped. Tom visually followed the length of the rope that bound him, and saw it was attached to a pulley and tied to one of the beams, near the doorway.

And standing in the doorway…

"Tom…"

Sturgis Butler, face and clothing burned, eyes black as oil, voice sounding like an echo chamber, walked slowly into the room. He stopped at the stove, opening the hinged door. Next to the stove, on a wall rack, were assorted pokers, pincers, and branding irons. Sturgis selected an iron, showed it to Tom, and stuck the end inside the fire.

The worst burn Tom ever had was when he was a child, stepping barefoot on a lit sparkler on the fourth of July. It had instantly seared into his skin and stuck there, requiring him to pull it out and also burn his fingers.

It had been bad.

A branding iron seemed a lot worse.

Sturgis left the iron in the fire and turned to Tom. He smiled, his teeth black as his eyes.

"I… see… your… fear…"

And then the realization of what was happening hit Tom like a slap. Not a full understanding, but enough for Tom to show some much-needed courage.

"Enough with all this bullshit," Tom said, punctuating his voice with forced bravado. "Let me talk to your boss."

Sara

On her back, stars dancing in her vision, Sara reached up to scratch out the eyes of whoever tackled her and Frank.

"Where's Deb?

Illuminated by a faint blue glow stick, Mal's face was frantic, eyes wild. His neck was bleeding, and he had bloody rips in his shirt.

Next to her on the ground, similarly sprawled out, Frank had begun crying again.

"Is Deb with you?" Mal demanded, raising his voice.

"Pang—Pang is possessed," Sara told him. "We all ran away. I don't know where your wife is. We were following her, then she was gone."

Mal helped Sara up, and then they both pried a sobbing Frank off the floor.

"Blackjack Reedy is behind me somewhere," Mal said. "He's got a whip."

Sara got a closer look at Mal's shirt, counting at least eight bloody gashes in it.

"Jebediah found us," she said. "We had to run. We can help you look for Deb. It's a maze down here."

"We'll find find find her," Frank moaned. Then he dropped over in a dead faint.

Mal looked at Frank, and then off into the distance. "How long ago did she go missing?"

"A few minutes."

Mal pulled the handbag off his shoulder. "The heroin. Take care of him. I have to find her."

Sara didn't want him to go, but she completely understood. "Thank you. Good luck."

"You, too."

He ran off. Sara opened the purse, found a plastic case with a big syringe in it. Somewhere, in the dark distance, she heard a whip crack.

Sara knelt down and gently slapped Frank's face. "Frank, you have to get up."

Frank moaned, but his eyes remained closed. Sara had no idea how much of the heroin to give him, or even how to properly administer a shot. She gave his shoulders a shake.

"Frank, it's Sara. I have some drugs for you. You have to get up."

"Just... leave me... here."

"I can help with the pain. How much am I supposed to give you?"

"I don't know."

"You're a doctor."

"Of molecular biology."

Sara wasn't sure how heroin worked. She'd seen enough movies to know it involved tying off an arm with something in order to find a vein. But did she inject him directly into his broken arm? Or could she shoot him up anywhere? She took the needle out of the case and did that thing where she held it point-up and flicked it with her finger to remove all the bubbles.

"That's too much," Frank said. "That would kill an elephant."

"So how much do I give you?"

"See those little lines on the barrel? Each one is ten milligrams. Start with that."

"Where do I inject you?"

"Straight into my eyeball," Frank said.

Sara stared at him.

"Kidding kidding kidding. Just jab it in my wrist. Intramuscular probably won't be be be as effective as a vein, but I'll take anything as long as it's quick."

He gave Sara his good arm. She held his hand.

A whip cracked again, much nearer.

Sara squinted at Frank's wrist, saw a blue vein, and slid the needle in on an angle. She pressed the plunger, giving him ten milligrams. Then she pulled the needle out, expectant.

"Well?" Sara asked.

The pain creases in Frank's face slowly relaxed, and the corner of his mouth turned up in a tiny smirk.

"You are so pretty," he said.

"Is it working?"

"Your breasts look like two big, beautiful scoops of ice cream in a bra."

Sara grinned. "Yeah. I think it's working."

She helped Frank up, and he put his good arm around her shoulders.

"Your lips are like a little red bowtie," Frank said.

"We need to move, Frank."

"Yeah. Move in with me. You and Jack. I have some money put away. We can get a good lawyer, get him back."

Another whip crack, so close it made Sara jump.

"Let's go!"

Sara began by helping Frank along, but then he let go of her and ran ahead. He turned down a corridor, and then began to jog backward while smiling at her.

"I feel great! Why don't they make heroin legal?"

"Frank! Watch—"

He ran backward into a wall, falling onto his face. When he got up, his makeshift tourniquet had come off.

"I'm okay," he said. "Doesn't hurt at all."

Frank shook his broken arm and it wiggled like a gummy worm, bending in all sorts of places it wasn't supposed to.

Then a pair of bloody arms wrapped around Frank from behind, grabbing him in a bear hug. Jebediah Butler. Sara ran to him, but was jerked off her feet as Blackjack Reedy's whip snaked around her neck, choking her until she passed out.

Deb

As soon as Deb realized Sara and Frank weren't behind her anymore, she stopped running.

"Deb!"

Sara's voice, echoing through the tunnels. But Deb couldn't pinpoint where it was coming from. She'd made two or three turns, and the faint echo seemed to be both in front of her and behind her at the same time.

"Sara!"

But even putting her lungs into it, Deb's voice didn't get any louder than speaking normally. Deb didn't know if it was something Franklin had done to her voice, or if it was psychosomatic because she'd been terrified out of her mind in that exam room. Whatever the case, she couldn't call for help.

She looked around. These underground tunnels seemed to go on forever. Deb could imagine herself, wandering around for hours, going in circles. A lesson from Girl Scouts came back to her. When lost, stay put. Let the rescuers come to you.

A wise idea. But while Sara and Frank might be looking for her, so were a legion of creepy mother fuckers.

Besides, she needed to find the stairs for when Mal came back.

Mal.

As crazy frightened as Deb was—and she was one scare away from curling up into a ball and sucking her thumb—the thought of her husband gave her strength. When he kissed her before he left, she saw the man she remembered. The one she hadn't seen in such a long time. Brave. Strong. Determined.

Deb swore she would be just as brave. She would fight and fight and fight until she saw him again. And when she did, there would be no more sleepless nights. No more bad dreams. No more constant paranoia.

Because together, they could conquer anything.

Deb ached to remind him of that. And it ate at her that she hadn't understood it before now.

She bent over, butt against a wooden support, and rubbed her thighs. As could be expected, her stumps ached. The prosthetics she wore weren't suited to running on dirt, and the constant balance adjustments she had to make were taking a toll on her muscles. It had been a long time since Deb had lost her legs, but she remembered with crystal clarity what it had been like. Obviously walking and running were sorely missed. But there were other, little things as well. Dipping her feet in a cool lake. Wiggling her toes. Feeling sand on the beach beneath her—

Deb sensed someone. Nearby.

She tried to peer into the darkness around her, but her eyes couldn't pierce it. The low watt bulbs strung up on the ceiling were few and far between, and the glow light Tom had given her was fading fast.

"Hello?" she croaked.

"Hello, Deb."

It wasn't Mal. Or Tom. Or Sara or Frank.

Deb knew that voice. From the examination room.

"It's so good to see ya again," Franklin said, walking out of the darkness. He still wore the plastic gloves he'd put on when he tried to take her blood earlier. But this time, he was holding a long, white stick that ended in forked prongs.

A cattle prod.

"This is quite a house, ain't it?" Franklin said. He pressed a button on the stick and the electrodes crackled, throwing a bright spark. "Reminds me of home. A home that you took away from me, Deb."

Deb backed away, but backing up in fake legs was even harder than navigating stairs. What she needed to do was turn around and sprint away. But she couldn't stop staring at him. Especially since, like Pang, Franklin's eyes had turned completely black.

"I owe you for that, lil' girl. Owe you lots."

He lashed out with the prod, and Deb dodged it but fell backward, arms pinwheeling, landing on her butt. She tried to crab away on all fours, but her prosthetics couldn't gain any purchase on the dirt ground.

"You look so a'scared right now." Franklin grinned. His teeth were also black. "Gettin' me all kinds of excited."

He zapped one of her artificial legs with the prod. Deb yelped at the sound.

"This here's a special kinda prod, called a *picana*. Make 'em down in South America. Those dictators love to interrogate rebels. Twenty thousand volts, low amps, so it won't kill. Supposed to be gawd-awful painful. Especially when applied to sensitive regions."

Deb backed against the wall, feeling like she was about to have a heart attack.

The feeling got worse when Franklin touched the prod to her thigh.

It was like being hit with a pick axe. A glowing hot pick axe. Her entire world was reduced to one infinite pinpoint of absolute agony.

"Yes indeedy," Franklin purred. "You 'n Mr. Picana are gonna get to know each other real intimately, lil' girl."

Forenzi

Dr. Emil Forenzi was extremely agitated, and more than a little frightened.

This was bad. Really bad. Once an experiment of this magnitude began to spiral out of control, it was time to pull the plug.

But he didn't know if he could stop this, even if he wanted to. So many unexpected variables had been introduced that stopping now could be catastrophic.

He sped through the steel doors of the clinic and peered into Gunter's habitat. But the monkey wasn't in his usual spot, hanging upside down from the tree. Forenzi moved closer to see if Gunter was hiding in the fake bushes.

He wasn't. The primate had either turned invisible, or someone let him out of his cage.

Or...

Forenzi checked the habitat's door latch, saw something thin and blood-stained sticking in the spring mechanism.

A bone. Probably from one of Gunter's unfortunate cellmates.

The Panamanian Night Monkey had learned to open his own lock.

Forenzi took a quick look around the lab, suddenly paranoid. While small, Gunter was a strong little animal, and he had a well-documented history of violence. He could also apparently utilize tools. If he got hold of a scalpel, it could become a very dangerous situation.

Trying to act nonchalant in case he was being watched, and he went to the closet where he kept the elbow-length Kevlar gloves, which would protect him from animal bites. He didn't like to handle Gunter without them, especially when the animal wasn't sedated. He was just about to put them on when the phone rang, making Forenzi jump.

"What is it?" he demanded, checking the ceiling to make sure Gunter wasn't hanging there, ready to drop on him.

"We have a problem. He figured it out."

Forenzi digested the words. It was, indeed, a problem. And the problems were piling up. How many set-backs could this project absorb before it imploded?

"Seal the perimeter," he said, setting the animal gloves down on a countertop. "I'll be right there."

Forenzi was halfway to the door when he stopped, turned, and went back for them.

Just in case Gunter was prowling the tunnels and in a bad mood.

Sara

The sharp stench of ammonia woke Sara up.

She was sitting down, immobile, legs, arms, neck, and chest all strapped down tight. The device was known as a restraint chair, and during her years working with troubled teens she'd seen them while visiting prisons and mental institutions. Supposedly a humane way to immobilize dangerous or violent inmates who posed a threat to themselves or others, Sara knew how often it was used for cruel and unusual punishment.

Sara looked around, saw she was in some sort of laboratory. White walls, bright lights, shiny tile floors, counters topped with medical equipment; beakers, Bunsen burners, glass bottles, scales, microscopes, storage racks. A far cry from the poorly lit, filthy underground tunnels she'd been chased through.

She also noticed that she had IVs in each arm, the tubes red with her blood and connected to a machine.

Could this be a hospital? Had she somehow been rescued, and they'd restrained her to make sure she was okay?

Another whiff of ammonia, and Sara gagged. Her forehead was strapped to a headboard, but she lowered her eyes and saw a male hand holding some smelling salts.

Someone was behind her.

"Who's there?"

The figure didn't reply. But the hand brushed up against her neck, and a finger drew itself across Sara's lips. Then it moved down her neck and squeezed her right breast.

This wasn't a hospital.

She hadn't been rescued.

Sara set her jaw, fighting not to cry out. She endured the groping, and then felt hot breath on her ear.

The horror she'd experienced on Rock Island had never gone away. Part of her had died that day, and she'd been coping with that loss ever since.

Meeting Frank, and daring to dream of a future that wasn't haunted by the past, had given her a small measure of hope that things might change.

But now, being molested in a restraint chair, Sara knew that life had no happy endings. It was failure and misery and torture and nightmares and cruelty. And the only escape from it was death.

Her tormenter walked around the chair to face her. Blackjack Reedy, his eye patch as black as his uncovered eye. Ghost? Demon? Psycho? It didn't matter, and Sara didn't care. She was frightened, but more than that, she was sick of living. Jack had been taken away, Frank was no doubt in a similar situation to hers, and now she was once again evil's plaything, suffering and dying for no reason at all.

She hocked up a good one and spat at the figure. "Do your worst, asshole."

He walked over to the counter, where, among all of the medical devices, was a common kitchen toaster. Next to it was a loaf of bread, the kind that came in a colorful plastic bag. He removed two slices, placed them in the toaster, and depressed the plunger.

"Where's Frank?" Sara said.

He didn't answer. Sara tested the restraints on her arms, legs, chest, flexing and stretching to see if there was any way to escape.

The toaster dinged.

Blackjack Reedy took the slices of toast, and knelt next to Sara's chair. He held them out to her. Sara began to wonder if he was mentally deficient. Like Lenny from *Of Mice and Men*.

"I don't want your toast. Let me go."

Blackjack held a piece out to her bound hand. Sara changed tactics. Forcing a smile, she said, "Thank you, I'd love some toast. Can you unstrap my hand so I can hold it?"

Blackjack pushed the toast under her palm. Quick as a mousetrap, he slapped the other piece on top of her fingers.

Then he smiled, and Sara saw that his teeth had been filed to points.

She screamed loud enough to wake the dead as Blackjack opened his terrible mouth and bent down to eat his sandwich.

Frank

Frank Belgium stared up at the ghost of Jebediah Butler, whose entire body was covered with blood, and said, "Need a Band-Aid?"

Belgium was strapped to a stainless steel gurney. It had gutters around the edges, which made Frank think it was a mortician's table.

The implications didn't bother Frank. At that moment, nothing at all bothered Frank. He decided, if he made it through the night, to pursue the glamorous and rewarding life of a heroin addict.

But living through the night was beginning to seem like a long shot.

Jebediah pushed a metal cart up to Frank, filled with all sorts of horrible-looking medical tools. Hammers and saws and blades and drills. Frank stared at a particularly rusty chisel and giggled.

"Can you sanitize those tools before you dissect me? I don't don't don't want to get an infection."

Jebediah loomed over Frank, squinting at him with his soulless black eyes.

"Aren't... you... afraid?"

"Friend, as far as scary things I've seen, you aren't even in the top five. Where's that Ol' Japser fellow? He's certainly handy." The pun delighted Frank, and he giggled again. "I also could have gone with *he's well-armed.*"

Jebediah picked up some sort of crusty mallet and brought it down on Frank's broken elbow. It stung, but the drug dulled most of the pain.

The ghost looked confused.

"You seem like a reasonable sort, Jebediah. So I'm going to offer you some advice. And I I I really think you should take it for what it's worth. Are you ready?"

Jebediah Butler gaped.

"I'm not going to say it unless you want to hear it."

"Tell... me..."

Dr. Frank Belgium looked the monster dead in the eyes and said, "Go fuck fuck fuck yourself."

Tom

Tom wiggled his fingers to keep the circulation going, but his hands and arms were becoming very numb due to being hung by them. He felt he'd bought himself a little bit of time, but had no idea how to get out of this situation. His hopelessness spiked every time he looked at the corner of the room, to the branding iron heating up in the wood burning stove, which the blackened figure of Sturgis kept fussing with.

When Dr. Forenzi finally entered the room, Tom was grateful for something else to focus on.

"Where's Roy Lewis?"

Forenzi clucked his tongue. "Out of all the things you can ask me, that's your first question? Where your partner is? He gave all he had to give. Like you soon will. How did you figure it out?"

Tom stretched on his tip toes to take some weight off his cramped arms. "Let me down and I'll tell you."

"I can assure you, Detective, you'll tell me anyway."

Forenzi went to the corner of the room and took a black covering off of a piece of medical equipment. It looked like a dialysis machine.

"It was Torble," Tom said, glancing at Sturgis Butler. "He said *I see your fear*. He said that same thing earlier today, at the prison."

Forenzi made a face and wagged a finger at Sturgis, née convicted serial killer Augustus Torble. "I didn't go through all the trouble of bringing you here to screw things up like that."

"And I don't get my kicks dressing up in a goddamn Halloween costume, spraying myself with liquid smoke to smell like a barbecue. Plus these goddamn contacts are killing me."

To drive home the point, Torble stuck his finger in his eye and pinched out the black lens.

"So everything was fake?" Tom asked. His curiosity was real, but he was more interested in keeping the doctor talking, hoping for a situation to save himself.

Forenzi nodded. The machine he'd uncovered was on a cart, and he was pushing it over to Tom. "Of course. The house is fully rigged. Trapped doors so people appear and disappear. Electromagnets to make chairs move or pictures fall."

He reached for Torble's neck and tore off a flap of latex make-up, holding it to his own throat. "*Voice... synthesizer. Hear... how... scary... I... sound...*"

"How about the painting of the house with all of our pictures on it?"

"Just painted yesterday. One of my men has some artistic talent. I doubt it has even dried yet."

"And the guns?" Tom asked. "Bullet proof vests?"

Forenzi took Tom's Sig from his holster and aimed at his chest. Just as Tom tried to twist away and began to yell, Forenzi fired twice.

It stung a bit, but Tom remained free of holes.

Forenzi tucked Tom's gun into his waistband. "When your luggage was brought in, your ammo was replaced. Soft wax bullets. There's an indistinguishable recoil, but they disintegrate before hitting the target."

Shit. Why hadn't Tom thought to check his ammo?

"What if I had the gun on me?" he asked. "How would you have switched?"

"The front doors to Butler House have an X-ray machine in them. You were scanned for weapons when you entered. If you were carrying a gun, you would have been the first one targeted, and your gun taken. My men are very good at what they do."

Forenzi had damn near thought of everything. A perfect ruse that fooled everyone, Tom included. "And Aabir?"

"One of us. Like Pang. They've played those parts before. Unlike the live roaches put into your mouth, theirs were rubber.

"What about Deb? In the exam room?"

"Franklin is real. I was able to secure his release from prison, as I did with our friend Torble here. In Deb's and Mal's case, we thought that touch of authenticity would help raise their metusamine levels. Franklin sprayed a chemical in Deb's throat—I call it traumesterone. It inflames the vocal chords so a person can't speak. Or scream for help, as the case may be."

It all made sense to Tom, except for the most important part.

"Why?" he asked.

Dr. Forenzi sucked in a breath, then let out a big, dramatic sigh. "I explained this at dinner. I need to frighten you to harvest the metusamine in your blood. The more you're frightened, the more you produce. And because you and the others have experienced high levels of fear in the past, it has altered your brain chemistry so your blood contains higher levels of metusamine than the general population. Much higher, in fact. And I require that neurotransmitter. In order to make anti-venom, you need real venom. The same applies to Serum 3, my anti-fear drug."

"So why kill Wellington? Or was that fake, too?"

"That was… unfortunate. I would have preferred terrifying him, then milking him for metusamine like you and the others. But that's the other half of the experiment. You're obviously aware of who is funding this research."

Tom thought back to the Butler House website, and who owned the property now. Unified Systems Association.

U.S.A.

"The government," Tom said. "The feds?"

Forenzi shook his head. "No. My men impersonated the FBI when they approach you and the others. This is a military operation. There have been two previous attempts to create the perfect soldier. I've studied the research of my contemporaries, Dr. Stubin in Wisconsin and Dr. Plincer in Michigan, and I've learned from their errors. Serum 3, my metusamine blocker, when given to soldiers, renders them fearless. It also has an unusual side-effect that the army has a keen interest in."

"It makes them homicidal," Tom guessed.

"How is it said in software parlance? *It isn't a glitch. It's a feature.* Besides making killing easier, it also gives them a much higher tolerance for pain, sharper instincts, and even boosts their stamina and strength, as Mr. Torble demonstrated for you in the prison visitation room. Wellington was an example of my drug working a bit too well, I'm afraid. But it is good practice for the soldiers. Many of them have adjusted quite well to the program. I daresay they've begun to enjoy it. Hunting humans in an old, dark house is good real-world practice."

Tom had previously dealt with megalomaniacs using science for evil, and Forenzi fit the bill. It never ended well.

"So why don't you just scare people, get what you need from their blood, and let them go?"

Another sigh. "We tried. That area of Butler House where you were caught, with the fake body bags and rubber props, it was set up to frighten people without harming them. But that didn't produce the levels of metusamine needed for my experiments. To get the higher concentrations, I had to induce *real* terror in my subjects. And after much trial and error, the type of fear that produced the best results was fear of the unknown. The stuff of childhood nightmares. Ghosts and demons and things that go bump in the night."

"But now I know this house isn't really haunted," Tom said. "So you can let me go."

Forenzi shook his head. "I still need to milk you. And I've discovered another way to induce fear. Sadly, it isn't as effective as ghosts, but it is more sustainable over a long period of time. The fear of pain. I'll be able to extract quite a bit of metusamine from you as Mr. Torble tortures you to death."

Torble was at the wood burning stove again, checking how the branding iron was heating up. And, as Forenzi predicted, Tom experienced a spike of pure, adrenaline-fueled fear.

"People know I'm here," Tom said.

"No, they don't. We've done this many times, Detective. My men are very good at tidying up loose ends. You were a loose end, searching for your missing partner. It is doubtful anyone will come looking for you with the same fervor. But if they do—your old boss Lieutenant Daniels, perhaps, or your girlfriend, Joan DeVilliers, in Hollywood—they'll be handled in the same way you've been."

"You do know you're insane, right?"

Forenzi laughed. "My dear Detective, I'm going to cure humanity of fear. Making any omelet requires breaking a few eggs. Take some comfort in the fact that your suffering will one day benefit all of mankind. But don't take too much comfort in it. I need you to be good and terrified for the little time you have left."

Forenzi pulled a length of tubing out of the machine, exposing the IV needle on the end.

"This machine is going to extract the metusamine from your blood, and then return it to you. I need to put these into your veins. If you fight me, I'm going to ask Mr. Torble to break both of your kneecaps."

"Isn't he going to do that anyway?"

"He might. But would you prefer that to happen immediately, or sometime later on?"

Tom could probably lash out and kick Forenzi, but that wouldn't help the situation. And if he were going to try that trick, it would be with Torble when the psycho came at him with the branding iron. So Tom nodded, letting Forenzi insert needles into each of his triceps. The machine clicked on with a mechanical whir, and Tom watched his blood travel out of his left arm, through the tube, through the metusamine extractor, and back into his right arm.

Forenzi regarded him. "I must say, Detective, I expected a bit more out of you. Your partner, Roy, fought with all he had. You seem to have given up rather quickly."

Tom stared the man down. "The price of freedom is eternal vigilance."

The doctor's brow wrinkled. "Who said that?"

"I did." Tom's lips twisted into a grin. "And I'll be coming for you, Forenzi."

"And my little dog, Toto, too?"

"No," Tom said. "Just you."

"Save your strength for Mr. Torble, Detective. He's been in prison for a long time, and has a lot of bottled up aggression he needs to let out."

"Lots of aggression," Torble said, smiling. He took the branding iron out of the fire, its end glowing orange, and Tom's metusamine production kicked into overdrive.

Mal

He'd managed to outrun Blackjack Reedy, but then Mal got lost in the labyrinth. One tunnel looked like the next, and Mal couldn't tell if he'd been going in circles, or was kilometers away from where he began.

Mal stopped jogging, sweaty, aching, terrified for his wife, and then he heard a sharp *crack* that he thought was Blackjack's whip. But it was quieter, and different somehow. Instead of running from it, he tried to follow the sound. Maybe it would lead him in some direction other than—

He turned the corner and froze, unable to comprehend what he was seeing.

It was Franklin. Just as Deb had insisted. Older, thinner, but undeniably the man who'd caused them both so much pain.

He was poking a long stick at someone Mal couldn't see, cackling as he did so, the stick making bright sparks to coincide with the cracking sound.

And then Mal heard a yelp. Soft. Hoarse.

But recognizable.

Deb.

He rounded the corner, and realized that Franklin was poking his wife with some sort of electric prod. Deb was crying, hysterical, feebly trying to slap the prod away with her back against the tunnel wall.

Mal froze.

It all came back to him. The helplessness. The fear. The feeling that all hope was gone, and there was nothing he could do to regain it.

That was the Rushmore Inn's legacy. It had rendered Mal useless. Forever weak. Forever afraid.

What a pale shadow of his former self he had become.

"Hey! Asshole!"

Mal wasn't sure who had spoken. He was about to turn around and look when a startling realization seized him.

That was me. I said that.

Franklin stopped tormenting Deb long enough to leer at Mal. "Well, lookee who came by. It's the coward who—"

Mal was on him in three steps, hitting him in the jaw so hard that Franklin spun around, the cattle prod flying. Then he had his fingers wrapped in the man's hair and Mal introduced the bastard to his knee, Franklin's nose exploding with all the juice of a squashed tomato.

Franklin howled, and Mal got behind him, still holding his hair, and bent his head back to expose his neck.

"Deb! Now!"

His wife didn't hesitate. Like a deadly ballet, she pivoted her hips, swinging her right prosthesis around in a reverse hook kick, connecting solidly with Franklin's adam's apple.

Mal released him and he slumped to his knees. He was no longer a threat. They'd all heard the man's windpipe crack.

Then Deb was in his arms, pressing her lips to his, her tear-soaked cheeks rubbing against his face.

"Don't you ever leave me again," she said.

"I won't."

"We're a team."

"The best team ever."

"I love you."

"I love you, too."

"We're going to get out of this, Mal."

"Goddamn right we are."

Another kiss, and then Deb squatted down and picked up the prod.

Franklin was turning an unnatural shade of blue, clawing at his neck in a futile effort to suck in air.

"You're suffocating," Deb told the dying man. "Point us to the exit, and I'll help you."

Mal was impressed by his wife's compassion. Apparently, so was Franklin, because he quickly pointed down the tunnel.

"Thanks," Deb said. Then she took off in that direction at a quick jog.

Mal ran after her. "What about helping him?"

"I did," Deb said between breaths. "I helped him get to hell faster. Besides, do you want him and six of his brothers to show up at our doorstep a year from now?"

She had a point.

Incredibly, after following the tunnel a hundred meters, they were back to the concrete stairs. Mal had taken so many twists and turns down there that it hadn't occurred to him to try a straight course.

Deb stormed the stairs like a champ, and then they were jogging down the hall and heading for the front door.

"Keep your eyes straight ahead," Mal warned her, wary of Wellington's headless corpse/cattail vase. "Focus on the door."

Mal positioned himself between Deb and the circle of chairs, and when they reached the front doors he paused. The last time he opened them, Mal had run into that giggling freak in the gas mask.

"Floor is slippery with blood," Deb said, placing a hand on Mal's shoulder.

"I'm opening the door. Get ready to run. Either outside, or back into the house if something bad is out there."

"Got it. What about the others?"

"Once we find the car, we'll drive until we get a cell phone signal, then call the police. We'll make them send the entire National Guard."

"Mal?"

Mal had his hand on the door knob, but he paused. "Yeah, babe?"

"Coming here… you were right. This wasn't my best idea."

He smiled. "Are you serious? I'm thinking we do this every weekend. We rent a car, you send some psycho to hell… it sure beats the hell out of therapy."

And the crazy thing was, it really did. There were no guarantees they'd live through the night, but Mal felt better than he had in months.

So it was quite a nasty shock when he opened the doors and found himself face-to-face with two people holding machineguns.

Moni

This guy was definitely *not* Luther Kite.

Kite had enjoyed making Moni suffer. It had been a turn-on for him. More than that, he'd considered it an intimate act, drawing it out while asking her mundane questions about her life. When he had finally broken her, he hadn't bothered to finish the job and kill her, leaving Moni in a state of shock so deep it took her weeks before she could speak again. It was almost as if allowing Moni to live had been a testament to his art.

This guy, with the black eyes, was going through the motions. And what he was doing hurt Moni, no doubt about it. Getting pierced with an antique medical device was fucking awful. But after a dozen lacerations his heart just didn't seem to be into it.

And surprisingly, Moni wasn't terrified. She was actually more angry than she was frightened. Like this was a bad BDSM session that wasn't working out.

In fact, the more she thought about it, the less she feared for her life and the more she got pissed off. This jackass didn't know what the hell he was doing.

And she was just the person to tell him that.

"You're pathetic," she said, using her dominatrix voice.

The wannabe Luther Kite stopped poking with the artificial leech and stared at her.

"You're a pathetic, worthless, sissy boy. Take off your pants right now."

He remained still, his expression confused.

"I told you to take off your pants!" she ordered.

As dommes went, Moni was good at her job. She had a deep, commanding voice that scared the crap out of guys, and she knew what the little perverts wanted. In a sick sort of way, Luther Kite had saved her life. After her ordeal with him she'd kicked heroin and stopped being a victim. No more street tricks. No more pimps. She took control of her life, and her clients paid her well to be a dominant man-hater.

"Take off your pants, and show Mistress Moni what you've got. Now!"

Incredibly, the freak began to unbutton his pants.

Just as Moni had suspected. He wasn't a top. He was a bottom.

"Show it to me."

He did. And with his dick out, he was a lot less frightening. Even though she was tied up, Moni felt the balance of power shifting from him to her.

"Get over here and put it in my mouth," she ordered.

Naturally, he complied. What guy wouldn't? And this was most certainly a guy, not a ghost. Not a demon. Not even a serial killer. Just a worthless little worm who wanted to hurt her, like so many men had before him.

But Moni had other plans.

As she worked her lips and tongue, she gave him just enough to make him want more.

"I can make it better," she said, deep and breathy. "But I need my hands free."

Without hesitating he undid the buckle on her right hand. Then Moni did something she'd been fantasizing about ever since she turned her first trick at sixteen years old.

She bit down, hard as she could.

It didn't come off as easy as she'd thought. Sort of like chewing through a tough steak. A tough, bloody steak, with lots of gristle. But she used her incisors, grinding and tearing, protecting her head with her hand as he screamed and beat at her with both fists.

And then her teeth met, and he fell away from her.

Moni spat his cock on the floor as he sprayed blood like fire hose. While he knelt down with his hands between his legs, wailing and trying to stop the hemorrhaging, Moni undid the other buckles holding her to the rack, pulled out the hefty metal bar used as a crank, and hit the son of a bitch hard enough on the back of the head to see brains come out the split.

They sort of looked like grits.

Wiping off her mouth and spitting several times, Moni got her shit together. She was free. For the moment she was safe. Now she needed to get the hell out of there.

Moni left the torture chamber, metal bar still in hand, and found herself in some sort of mine shaft. The floor was dirt. The walls braced with logs. Lights were bare bulbs, hanging from old rafters.

She spat again, hurrying down the tunnel, stopping when she heard talking.

"You, Jebediah Butler, are are are a jerktapus. That's a jerk multiplied by eight."

It sounded like Dr. Belgium. Moni snuck up to an open door, saw the doc was bound to a table. Some guy was standing next to him with a mallet. The mallet guy was covered, head to toe, with blood, but he didn't seem injured at all.

Another fake ass ghost.

The bloody guy hit Frank with the mallet, right on his arm, which was all twisted and swollen up to twice its normal size.

That son of a...

Moni rushed up to him, angry and pumped, and brained the bastard with the metal bar. He went down, and she kept hitting him, over and over.

"Looks like you invited the wrong goddamn dominatrix to your little party, bitch!"

His head was harder to crack open than the Luther Kite wannabe, but she kept at it until she got the desired results.

"Moni!" Frank said, smiling at her. "Your mouth is bleeding."

"I bit a guy's dick off."

"Great! That's great!"

She undid Frank's straps, wincing when she saw his arm. "Jesus, Doc. Doesn't that hurt?"

"I'm medicated," he slurred. "Tell me something... how hard is it to buy heroin?"

"It's all about who you know."

"Great great great!"

"Is that what you're on? Heroin?"

"Yes. I believe it's your stash. It's awesome."

He'd be singing a different tune when withdrawal kicked in, but Moni saw no reason to bring that up.

"I have to go and save Sara," Belgium said. "Want to come with?"

"Sure."

Frank picked up the mallet in his good hand, and then they were back to prowling the tunnels.

"Doc?" she asked.

"Yes yes yes?"

"We're not going to get our million bucks each, are we?"

"It's not looking too promising, Moni."

Moni frowned. The dozen or so lacerations on her body hurt like crazy, but the fact that she'd been played for a fool felt even worse.

"Doc?"

"Yes?"

"When we find everybody, let's burn this fucking place to the ground."

Josh

Fran had been on edge since they landed in Charlotte. While he and Duncan had slept most of the trip, his wife had trouble relaxing on planes. A twenty-two hour flight in coach was stressful enough to make even Gandhi want to shoot someone.

But unlike Gandhi, Fran already had done so. A perimeter guard, when they'd driven up to the Butler House gate, had drawn his sidearm and fired at them as they drove up. No warning. No provocation. While Josh was driving the rental van, Fran had used her night scope to put a tight grouping of three into the guard's chest from thirty meters.

Josh had expected an unwelcome reception, but nothing so blatant and aggressive. It only confirmed what he and Fran had suspected when they'd received the invitation; Butler House was a front for something very bad.

They pulled up to the house and parked in front, the element of surprise gone. Fran and Josh wore full body armor with chest trauma plates, and tactical ballistic helmets, as did Duncan. Woof had on a custom-made bulletproof dog sweater, which boasted a small saddle for Mathison. The capuchin didn't like to wear body armor because it restricted his movement, but he did don a plastic army helmet that belonged to an old GI Joe action figure, simply because he didn't like his family all dressing up without him.

"You got the wheel, son," Josh told Duncan, climbing out of the driver seat and holding the door open for him. "If we come out in a hurry with wounded, can you handle it?"

"Yeah, Dad."

Josh still beamed with pride every time his adopted son called him *Dad*.

"Keep the windows open. Listen to your surroundings." He placed a loaded 9mm on the seat next to him, and turned on Duncan's walkie-talkie. "Radio silence unless an emergency, but send two clicks every five minutes as the *all clear* signal."

Fran leaned into the driver side window and kissed her son on the helmet. "Aim for the center mass, Duncan. Shoot to kill. This isn't an exercise. It's the real deal."

"I know, Mom."

"Love you. We'll be back soon."

"Love you, too."

Josh did another check of his gear, then slung the AR-15 over his shoulder. He covered his wife as she rushed the front doors to Butler House and positioned herself on the right side of them. Then she covered him as he came up and took the left. Woof, with Mathison riding on his back like a jockey, heeled next to Josh.

Fran made the hand signal for "Ready?"

In a way, Josh had been ready for this moment since they'd survived the massacre at Safe Haven and had been forced to move out of the lower forty-eight. They'd been waiting, and training, for the day the bad guys finally came calling. After the phony FBI agents had shown up with their obvious bullshit invitation, the VanCamps had called a family meeting and voted. They could do nothing at all and wait for further developments. Or they could alert the media and spill everything, waiting for the inevitable repercussions. Or they could take the offensive.

In a unanimous vote, they decided to come to Butler House. If, as they suspected, another rogue military experiment was in progress, there would be innocent people in danger. Safe Haven had been a training exercise for psychotic killers, and Butler House smelled similar. The guard shooting at them when they arrived confirmed Josh's suspicion.

Bad shit was going down.

And the only way for bad shit to triumph was for good people to do nothing.

The VanCamps weren't the *do nothing* type. And Josh knew Duncan and Fran were just as sick of hiding from the past as he was. For years, they'd been waiting for the other shoe to drop. To end what a top secret, imminently evil branch of the military had begun.

So there they were, taking the fight to the enemy, ready to finish this once and for all.

Josh nodded to his wife, and they moved into position to open the front doors to Butler House.

But the front doors opened for them.

Weapons at the ready, fingers on their triggers, Josh and Fran covered the two people who had been trying to leave. One, a man missing his right hand, who had bloody tears in his filthy clothing and a gash on his neck. The other, a woman with artificial legs. They shared the same terrified expression.

"Don't move!" Fran barked.

They both froze, but the guy looked like he was about to try something.

"We're the good guys," Josh said, quickly trying to diffuse the situation. He had a feeling these people were victims, not the enemy.

"How do we know?" the man asked.

"We have a monkey and a dog," Josh said. "Woof, speak."

Woof barked and wagged his tail. Mathison waved.

"I was attacked by a monkey," the man said. "Under a bed."

"Not this monkey," Josh replied. "We just showed up. Right, Mathison?"

Mathison nodded, then crossed his heart.

There were a few seconds of uncertainty. Josh decided, if he had to act, he'd try to use non-lethal force.

Then the woman with the prosthetics said, "I'm Deb. This is my husband Mal." Her voice was raspy.

"You both got those invitations?" Fran asked.

Deb nodded.

"I'm Fran, and my husband Josh. Our son Duncan is in the car. We were invited, too."

The tension seemed to dissipate. Josh sensed that like was recognizing like. Deb and Mal had that look Josh knew all too well. That *I survived something awful* look.

"Things went bad," Mal said. "You have no idea what kind of hell is going on here."

"Actually," Fran said. "We do. And we're ready for it. How many people inside?"

"Two are dead," Mal told them. "One of us and one of them. Inside is a cop named Tom, a dancer named Moni, a psychic named Aabir, a biologist named Frank, a woman named Sara, and a ghost hunter named Pang."

Deb shook her head. "Pang is possessed."

"Possessed?" Josh asked.

"His eyes turned black and he freaked out."

"Chemical agent?"

"Spirits," Mal said. "There are at least five. A slave with four arms. A bleeding guy. A guy in a lab coat. A guy in a gas mask. And a guy with an eye patch and a whip. They're ghosts or demons or something. Guns don't work on them."

Josh let that go for the moment. He'd seen some crazy shit himself and would never automatically reject the unusual. "Anyone else inside?"

Mal nodded. "Two doctors, Forenzi and Madison. Don't know what side they're on. And some guards in gray suits. At least four."

"Some people may be down in the tunnels under the house," Deb said. "It's a maze down there."

"Woof can find them once he gets their scent," Fran said. "We couldn't find any blueprints of the house online, so we don't know the layout. We could use a tour, but if you two want to wait in the van with our son, we understand."

Deb and Mal exchanged a look.

"Cops would take at least an hour to get here," Deb said to her husband. "If we could even convince them to come."

"I'm in if you are. I'm done with running."

"Me too."

"We'll do it," Mal said. "But we want lights and weapons."

"Can you handle a firearm?" Josh asked.

"Guns don't work on these things. What else you got?"

He gave Mal his tactical flashlight and his asp; a steep baton that extended when you snapped your wrist out. Fran did the same with Deb, and also gave her a can of pepper spray.

"Lead the way," Josh said.

He sensed their reluctance to go back inside, but they did, which Josh admired.

"First guy died here." Mal pointed to the large amount of blood on the floor.

Fran crouched down, picked up something. "Rubber bug. Looks like a roach."

"Rubber?" Mal asked.

Fran leaned forward and found something else. Something shiny. She held it up. "Bullet casing. You said guns don't work?"

"The cop emptied his gun into the one with the four arms. Thing didn't even flinch."

Josh unclipped his spare Maglite and played the beam along the floor, following it up the wall. He walked over, running his fingernail along it, then holding his hand to his nose.

"Wax. Could the cop be in on this? Using wax bullets instead of real ones?"

"You mean he's been bullshitting us?" Mal asked. "He seemed legit, but I don't know for sure. We just met him."

"What's that?" Fran asked, sweeping her light over to the chairs in the center of the great room.

Mal made a face. "That's Wellington. Hon, don't look."

Mal put his arm around Deb, turning her away, while Josh and Fran went to investigate.

It was pretty awful.

"Looks like our hunch was right," Fran said.

Josh nodded. They'd both seen similar things in Safe Haven.

"We were too late for this one," he said. "Hopefully we won't be too late for the others."

Josh looked around the rest of the room. They'd spent several hours reading about Butler House, and Josh had prepared as much as possible. But now that he was inside, he couldn't get over how creepy it felt. If ghosts really did exist, this is where they'd hang out.

His radio clicked twice—Duncan's all clear signal. Woof got on the scent of something and then stood stock-still, growling low in his throat.

Everyone shined their lights—

—on a black man with four arms, dragging a machete.

"That's who killed Wellington!" Mal said, stepping in front of Deb and raising his asp.

"Freeze!" Fran ordered, raising her weapon.

The four-armed man kept advancing, heading for Deb and Mal.

Josh fired a warning shot, putting three rounds into the floor in front of the man's feet.

The supposed ghost stopped, dropped his machete, and then fell to one knee, pulling out a pistol from the back of his ratty pants.

Fran and Josh let loose. Their AR-15 rifles were loaded with 5.56 NATO cartridges and fired as quickly as they could pull the trigger.

The target took ten shots in the chest and didn't drop. Josh adjusted for the head shot, but Fran beat him to it, taking off the back of the ghost's head, dropping it where it stood.

"I guess bullets work," Mal said.

Josh approached first, sensing his wife flanking him. He kicked away the enemy's dropped weapon—a Colt 1911—and knelt next to him.

No pulse, obviously, but definitely made of flesh and blood and not ectoplasm. He touched one of the extra arms and it pulled off without too much effort.

Fake. Rubber and latex, glued on with spirit gum.

But he wasn't wearing body armor. The fact that he took ten hits and didn't go down scared the shit out of Josh. It was familiar, in a very bad way.

"He might have been enhanced somehow," Josh told Fran.

"Red-Ops?" He heard fear in his wife's voice.

"I don't know." Josh frowned, and his stomach clenched like a fist. "But if there are others, they're going to be damn hard to kill."

Sara

Sara stopped screaming.

The pain was beyond anything she could have ever imagined. Sara hadn't looked, but she guessed her little finger had been chewed down to the bone. It was so intense, so unremitting, that it almost drowned out every other thought in her head.

Almost.

Because part of her brain was still able to think clearly, to focus. This was the worst thing Sara had ever endured, but in the middle of it all a bit of clarity broke through the misery and Sara latched onto it.

I'm a survivor.

Sara had lost so much on Rock Island. So much of who she was. She'd been so devastated, so diminished, by the experience, it had resulted in her losing even more. Her son. The one thing she had left. Taken from her.

And she finally understood why.

All along, Sara had been drowning in self-pity. Wondering how all of these terrible things could have happened to her. Blaming the universe, and trying to numb the pain rather than deal with it.

Child services had been right to take Jack. She had been unfit. But even when that happened…

I'm a survivor.

She'd taken the hits, and she was still here.

She'd lost everything, and she was still here.

She'd tried to kill herself with booze, and she was still here.

And if this psychotic Lester Paks/Blackjack Reedy ghost demon bastard chewed her entire arm off, Sara knew she would still be here.

I'm a survivor.

I'll survive to straighten my life out.

I'll survive to get my son back.

I will survive.

In a sea of agony, Sara latched on to that little Zen lifeboat. All she had to do was get through this one more ordeal.

As he started on the second finger, Sara closed her eyes imagined the life she once had, and could have again. Her son. A house. A job. Maybe even Frank, because as gentle and funny as he was, Sara knew he was survivor too, and suffering be damned they'd both get through this and—

"Hey! Ugly pirate guy! I'll give you something something something to chew on!"

Frank!

Sara watched as Dr. Frank Belgium, his broken arm flopping uselessly at his side, ran into the room brandishing a gigantic wooden mallet and smashing a surprised Blackjack Reedy right in his face.

Blood and sharp teeth went flying. Blackjack went down. And then Moni was on top of him, hitting him over and over again with an iron bar until the monster stopped moving.

"Oh dear dear dear." Frank fumbled with the straps on her restraint chair, setting her free and then trying to examine the damage to her fingers.

Sara didn't care about her fingers. She threw her arms around Frank's neck, so overwhelmed with absolute joy that she started bawling.

"If you need need need some painkiller," he said, "heroin gets my highest endorsement."

"I don't need anything." Sara had never spoken truer words. "Except you."

"Well... that's... that's pretty terrific."

"You saved the girl, Doc." Moni said. "Kiss her already."

Sara offered her tilted chin, and Frank kissed her. There was a lot more heat this time, and for a brief, glorious moment, all the pain Sara felt just melted away until the only thing in the whole world was Frank's lips on hers.

"Okay," Moni said, interrupting the moment. "You guys gonna fuck, or are we getting the hell out of here?"

Frank pulled back enough to look at her, and he had a twinkle in his eye that told Sara he was weighing his options.

"We're going," Sara said, and she noted it was said with some reluctance.

"Okay. And you might want to put a bandage or something on your hand. It's gross."

Sara finally looked at the damage that had been done, and wondered why she was holding some raw hamburger.

That's not raw hamburger. That's my hand.

And she promptly passed out.

Duncan

Duncan VanCamp sat behind the wheel of the Dodge Caravan and wondered why he wasn't more scared.

Though he was just a kid when all the bad stuff happened in Safe Haven, he still thought about it a lot. And sometimes, when he was alone in his room at night, he was frightened enough to turn on his closet light.

But everything since then had been great. He loved Josh like he was his real dad. He loved living in Hawaii. He had cool friends. He'd even been seeing a few girls. When he went to the beach with Woof and Mathison, girls would flock around him like he was a celebrity. And these weren't like the girls in his freshman high school classes. These girls were older. One was even eighteen, and she kissed Duncan and they texted each other a lot, even though he told his buddies it wasn't serious because he was too young to get tied down.

But now here he was, thousands of miles away from home, helping his parents clean up the mess that began at Safe Haven.

He should have been freaked out. This wasn't kid stuff. This was real serious shit. People dying, government cover-ups, experimental military super commandos. But as Mom and Josh had told him too many times to count, *praemonitus praemunitus*; forewarned is forearmed.

In other words, if you're always prepared for anything, you can never be surprised.

So Duncan took judo classes, and learned to shoot and field strip various firearms, and was able to wake up from a dead sleep and get into the panic room in less than thirty seconds. He didn't find any of that strange. It was just part of his daily life.

He checked his watch, then reached for the walkie-talkie on the passenger seat next to the 9mm and tapped the talk button twice, giving his parents the *all clear* signal once again. The night, and the fields, and the house, was all pretty spooky.

But Duncan kept cool. He'd just seen Mom shoot some dude, and it didn't bug him at all. Dude shouldn't have shot first. Duh. You can't expect to act violent and not expect violence in retaliation.

Praemonitus praemunitus.

Duncan placed his hands on the steering wheel. The van was parked, the engine not running, but Duncan had already driven three times, even though he still hadn't gotten his permit, and he was pretty sure he knew what he was doing. He went through the start-up procedure, like Josh had taught him.

Put on his seatbelt. Done.

Check to make sure all of his mirrors were adjusted. Done.

Keys in the ignition, foot on the brake. Done.

Then Duncan pretended to start the van. In his mind he put it into drive and pulled onto the H2 Freeway in Mililani. He had Jenni, the eighteen-year-old he'd kissed, in the passenger seat. She was wearing a halter top, and her boobs were *huge*. If Duncan had a chance to kiss her again, he'd have to try to touch one and—

Something dark appeared in the passenger window.

Duncan turned and looked, but there wasn't anything there.

Weird. He would have sworn that—

The walkie-talkie that had been on the seat.

It was gone.

Duncan looked up, finding the interior light on the ceiling, switching it on. The radio wasn't on the floor. Could it have fallen between the seat and the door? If so, how?

He leaned over, trying to see, but the seatbelt only stretched so far. So he unbuckled it, opened the door, and walked to the front of the van. The moon was out, but not very bright. And there were no lights on in Butler House. Only the interior light of the van.

Then that winked off.

In Hawaii, even the darkest night was bright with stars, alive with sounds. This place was dark and dead. No frogs, no insects, no birds. The night was like a smothering blanket, covering Duncan's eyes and ears.

And he was afraid.

He hurried around to the passenger side, no longer caring about the radio, much more interested in getting that 9mm pistol Josh had left him in his hand. Duncan swung open the door, reaching for the seat.

The gun wasn't there.

He felt all the old fears come back and climb onto his shoulders, weighing him down, pinning him so he couldn't react.

Then he pushed all the fear away. This was being forewarned. Now what did he need to do to protect himself?

When he didn't check in, his parents would come back for him. That meant holding his position until they arrived.

Duncan immediately climbed into the van and crawled into the driver seat. He locked both doors, and rolled up the windows as he hit the overhead light again.

As soon as it went on, something lunged out of the backseat and attacked Duncan with a scalpel, driving it into the boy's shoulder.

Tom

Torble held the glowing branding iron in front of Tom's nose.

"This liquid smoke crap Forenzi insisted I spray all over my body, so I smell like Sturgis Butler burned at the stake, it's not right. I mean, it seems to scare people just fine. But the odor is off. As I told you in prison today, the real smell of searing flesh is much tastier."

Torble tore the buttons off Tom's shirt, exposing his bare chest. Just as he stepped back, Tom lashed out with his foot, trying to kick away the poker.

He missed. By a lot.

"Seriously?" Torble said, looking amused. "That was your big move? How long have you been planning that one?"

"A while," Tom admitted.

"That was pathetic, man. I mean, I'm actually embarrassed for you."

"It went better in my head."

"How so?"

"I kicked the poker, it went flying up into the air, and burned my rope off, freeing me."

Torble nodded. "That would have been pretty cinematic. But instead we'll have to settle for this."

When the branding iron touched Tom's chest, the sensation defied description. He'd been hurt before. Badly. Plus there were all the common, human pains everyone had to deal with. Toothaches. Back strains. Ear infections. Kidney stones. Kicked in the balls.

This was worse than all of that, happening all at once, confined to one small section of Tom's body, multiplied by ten.

It hurt like hell.

The next thing Tom knew, he was being slapped in the face. When he woke up, the pain was still there.

"You passed out," Torble said. "And you're crying. It's really disappointing, Tom. Aren't you supposed to be the hero? The one who rushes in to save the day?"

The branding iron was back in the stove. Tom was shivering all over, and the tears wouldn't stop.

"You smell that?" Torble took a big, exaggerated sniff. "That's you. Isn't it the most succulent scent? I confess, sometimes when I had a whore down here, the smell was so overpowering that I took a little nibble. I'll try to refrain from doing that with you, Detective. I wouldn't want to make you uncomfortable. But if I do have a moment of weakness, I hope you'll forgive me."

Tom kept looking at the stove.

"Don't worry, Tom. It'll be ready shortly. Iron holds its heat pretty well. If you're anxious, I can have two irons going at once, so one is always heating up. I've also got some pincers we can try. They snip out a bit of flesh while they're burning you."

Torble came over, gave Tom a gentle poke in his new burn.

"I believe that's going to leave a scar, Detective. That is, it would, if you lived long enough for it to heal. I have to say, you look really frightened right now."

Torble moved closer.

"Don't you have anything at all to say, Tom? No begging me to stop? No threats? Don't worry, you'll open up. You'll tell me all about your life. Try to get my sympathy. Try to distract me. By the end of the day, I'll know everything about you. Your hopes and dreams. Your fears. All the little secrets you're too embarrassed to even tell your lover. It's a bonding experience, Tom."

Then Torble stuck out his tongue and gave Tom's burn a slow lick.

"Sorry. Couldn't help myself. But it is delicious. You'll also be able to taste it for yourself, when I use the branding iron on your lips."

Torble went back to the stove, and Tom felt a scream welling up inside. A scream, if let out, would continue until his voice was gone.

"Mr. Torble, you're needed immediately."

Dr. Forenzi had come back into the room. He appeared agitated.

Torble's eyebrows furrowed. "What for?"

"We have some intruders, and they're causing some problems."

"How about all your super military killing machines? Why don't you get them to help?"

"Everyone is helping, Mr. Torble. Now please come with me."

Torble blew Tom a kiss, then followed Forenzi out of the room.

Tom let out a sob, and then considered his options. As far as he could tell, he only had one. Try and use his feet to pull one of his IV tubs out of the dialysis machine, and then hopefully bleed to death before Torble returned.

A pretty shitty option. And though it was preferable to being tortured to death with a branding iron, Tom wasn't quite ready to give up yet. Where there was time, there was hope. If there were even a slim chance he might get out of there alive, and see Joan again, he had to take that chance. Even if it meant days of unbearable agony.

What the fuck am I thinking?

Tom kicked out, grabbing the tube between his toes, yanking it free. Then he began to hyperventilate so his heart beat quicker, pumping blood out of his body at a faster rate. If he got lucky, he'd be in hypovolemic shock before Torble returned.

"Tom!"

He looked at the doorway, and saw Moni, Frank, and Sara.

"Oh my god," Moni cried. "You're bleeding all over!"

"Good thing you got here in time," Tom said. "Hurry up and cut me down."

No one had a knife, but Tom told them his original idea of burning the rope with the branding iron. Moni was able to untie his hands and remove his IVs, and Dr. Belgium offered him heroin.

Tom demurred. "I'm good, Frank. Where are the others?"

"We lost Deb. Mal went off to find her."

"Okay, we look for them, then get the hell out of here."

Much as he loathed it, Tom took the branding iron as a weapon, and they crept out into the hallway so search for survivors.

Fran

Woof took the lead, sniffing down the hallway with Mathison jockeying him, and Fran followed two steps behind. She'd mounted a flashlight on the rail of her AR-15, lighting the way as they pushed into the bowels of Butler House.

The house was creepy, that was for sure. Mal and Deb continued to contribute snippets as to what had gone down that night, and Fran was happy she'd missed that particular party. She also wondered what possessed these people, who seemed smart and capable, to come here in the first place.

Then again, Fran and her family had shown up as well. Better prepared, perhaps, and playing by a different set of rules. But Fran came here to exorcize her past demons same as the Dieters did. She just brought bigger guns.

Woof stopped, growling. The dog could track, but hadn't ever learned to point. That was okay, because Mathison did point, directly at a hallway door opening up.

Fran dropped to one knee, giving Josh a clear shot over her head.

A man stepped into the hall and faced them. Tall, thin, wearing a dirty white jacket and holding a leather bag and some sort of saw. Like the four-armed man in the great room, he also had eyes that were completely black.

"Colton Butler," Mal said.

Fran shivered, memories of Safe Haven pushing into her head, of the fear and helplessness, and then she returned to the here and now and sighted the target's head.

"Drop the weapon," she ordered. "We have real bullets."

Colton Butler rushed at them.

Fran wasn't sure who made the head shot, her or Josh, but the wannabe ghost went down in a pink mist of blood. When he hit the floor, the top of his skull gone, what was left of his brains spilled out like a tipped bowl of oatmeal.

Fran had experience trying to kill enhanced psychopaths. They didn't die easily. But that was so simple it was almost unfair.

"They can hear, right?" Fran asked.

"I think they're on a drug that eliminates fear," Deb said. "That's what they're making here."

Fran got up from her crouch. A drug that eliminated fear. On one hand, something like that could be a huge benefit to mankind. On the other, Fran didn't relish the idea of an entire army made up of kamikaze pilots and suicide bombers.

She changed her magazine, snapped her fingers, and Woof continued to sniff his way down the hall.

"Entrance to the tunnels is up ahead," Mal said.

Woof was already on it, scratching at the door and whining. Fran opened it, illuminating the stairwell.

"It's a maze down there," Mal told her. "We'll need a string to find our way back."

Fran hadn't packed a string, but she and Josh each had a sack of reusable road flares. She took one out, flipped the switch, and dropped the red light on the top stair.

"I got point, Woof."

The dog looked at her, wagging his tail, and Fran descended the stairs first. Rather than the expected basement, Fran found herself in a tunnel. She dropped another flare and whistled for Woof. Once again the beagle took the lead.

"Time?" Fran asked.

"Duncan is thirty seconds late," her husband answered. Fran listened to her walkie-talkie click three times—their signal for Duncan to respond.

There wasn't an answer.

"Duncan, come in," Fran said into the radio.

Her son didn't reply.

"I'm going," Josh said, turning around and breaking into a run.

"Mathison!" Fran said. "Find Duncan!"

The capuchin monkey hopped off Woof and scrambled up the stairs, faster than Josh could move.

"Duncan, are you there?" Fran said again.

Still no answer.

Fran's mind tortured her with nightmare scenarios. She and Josh had fought over whether to bring Duncan along or leave him in Hawaii. They'd ultimately decided to take him in case those fake feds came back. Fran figured she could better protect her son while she was with him, instead of him being home alone.

But now she regretted that decision more than she'd ever regretted anything. Could someone have taken her son? Could someone have hurt him?

Killed him?

"Duncan, it's Mom. Please answer me."

Then the radio exploded in Fran's hand, and three more bullets peppered her back and she fell to the ground.

Duncan

The scalpel poked at Duncan's bulletproof vest, four times in rapid succession, and then Duncan lashed out to swipe at his attacker and got stabbed in his palm.

He recoiled, batting at the blade blindly, and then something was in his lap, something Duncan recognized instinctively, and when he reached for it his hands locked around the waist of a monkey.

Mathison?

No. This primate was bigger by a half, its fur different, rougher. Duncan grabbed tight and pinned it to the steering wheel, hitting the van's horn. In the glow of the van's interior light, Duncan saw this was a much different animal than Mathison was. Besides being larger, it had huge, red eyes, almost like a lemur.

The monkey screeched, poking with the scalpel, digging it into Duncan's forearms.

Duncan managed to throw the little monster into the back seat, and then he fumbled for the door handle and tumbled out of the vehicle, landing on his back.

The monkey pounced on him, landing on Duncan's chest, bringing the scalpel up to the boy's bare throat.

There was a screech, loud and shrill and—

—coming from the front of the van.

Mathison!

The little capuchin stood there, wearing his silly little plastic GI Joe helmet, his teeth bared.

The monkey on Josh screeched a reply.

Mathison gave him the finger.

Josh's attacker hopped off and howled, stretching out its long arms, the scalpel glinting in the van's interior light.

Mathison calmly removed his helmet, and took out the C1ST miniature revolver holstered inside of it. The smallest handgun in the world.

The psychotic primate charged at Mathison.

Mathison stood his ground and fired five rounds of 2.34mm ammo, each shot hitting home.

His opponent spun, facing Duncan, who saw that Mathison had put rounds through both of its oversized eyes. The monkey flopped over, dead.

"Mathison!" Duncan yelled, overjoyed. In sign language, the boy told his friend, *"Thanks. I love you."*

Mathison put the revolver back under his helmet and signed back, *"Stupid simian. Brings a knife to a gun fight."*

Then he hurried over and gave Duncan a hug. Duncan hugged him back.

"Duncan!"

Josh ran up, gun at the ready. He stared at Josh and Mathison, and at the dead monkey.

"We're okay, Dad."

Josh spoke into his radio. "He's fine, Fran."

Mom didn't respond.

"Stay in the van, lock the doors," Josh told him. "Mathison, stay with him."

The monkey saluted, and Duncan's dad ran off, back toward Butler House. But before he reached the doors, two men in gray suits walked out and began shooting.

Tom

He had no idea where he was going, but Tom somehow had taken the lead, wandering through the endless underground tunnels without the slightest idea where he was going.

"That's new."

Sara pointed, with her good hand, to some steel doors.

Tom went through first, clenching the branding iron. It was a lab, lots of equipment on various counters, a table in the corner of the room, and standing next to the table—

Dr. Forenzi.

Tom set his jaw and raised the branding iron, beelining for the son of a bitch, when something he saw stopped him in mid-stride.

Strapped to the table. Shirtless. Bleeding. Hooked up to one of those dialysis machines.

Roy!

His friend had so many wounds he looked like he'd been pecked to death by dozens of birds. But he wasn't dead. He was breathing.

Forenzi quickly took a revolver from his coat pocket and pointed it at Roy's head.

"That's close enough, Detective. Drop the weapon."

Tom released his grip, letting it clatter on the tile floor.

"You and your friends have proven extremely resourceful," Forenzi said. "I'm impressed. But your little coup d'état has failed, I'm afraid. If you take one step closer I'm going to shoot your partner and—"

Moni ran straight at Forenzi, smacking him upside the head with her metal bar. Forenzi fell to the floor, and she continued to hit him until Tom pulled her off.

"Let him stand trial," Tom said. When he was sure she'd calmed down, he pocketed Forenzi's gun and went to Frank and Sara, who were doing their best to release Roy each using only one hand.

"Hey, buddy, can you hear me?"

Roy mumbled something, but he was completely out of it. He needed immediate medical attention. Tom helped them undo the straps binding his partner, and then they helped him off the table.

He couldn't even stand.

Tom looked around for a wheelchair or a gurney, and saw Moni in the corner of the lab, spilling chemicals onto the floor.

"What are you doing?"

Moni smiled, lighting a match. "I'm burning this fucking place to the ground."

"Moni! Don't—"

She dropped it, and there was a *WHOOSH!* of flame, spreading out across the floor.

"Everyone! Move!" Tom ordered. With Sara and Frank's help, they dragged Roy out of the lab and into the tunnels—

—where Torble was waiting with a gun.

Before Tom could draw, Torble fired, shooting Frank Belgium in the chest.

Tom fired back as Torble ran off into the darkness.

Frank was down on his back. Tom set down Roy and knelt next to Frank, ripping open his shirt.

The bullet hole was near his heart, gushing bubbles of blood.

Sara was crouching next to Frank, her good hand holding his. "Frank, oh Frank, oh god."

Frank stared at her. "It's okay. I don't don't don't feel anything."

Sara looked at Tom, her eyes imploring. "Don't let him die. Please."

"Hold your hand here," Tom said, placing it on Frank's wound. "Keep pressure on it. Moni?"

"Yeah?"

"My room. The first aid kit in my suitcase."

"I'm on it." Moni ran off.

There was another gunshot, from the opposite direction. The bullet pinged into the metal door, inches from Tom's head.

Torble.

"I've got to go after him," Tom said.

Sara shook her head. "Don't leave!"

"If I don't, he'll stay in the shadows and kill us all. I'll be right back. Keep an eye on my partner."

Then Tom ran after Torble, plunging headlong into the darkness.

Forenzi

Dr. Forenzi smelled smoke and opened his eyes.

Smoke had indeed filled the lab, and he was surrounded on all sides by fire.

His head hurt. So did his chest. But those pains paled next to the abject terror he felt by being trapped in a burning room. Everywhere he looked the flames stretched to the ceiling. There would be no escape.

Please. Don't let me burn. Not like this. Anything but this.

Forenzi had never been badly burned, but he saw the pain and fear it caused in his patients. Torture with fire was one of the most effective ways to harvest metusamine.

Now that he was surrounded by fire, about to be roasted alive, the irony wasn't lost on him.

But maybe I don't need to be afraid of it.

Next to him on the floor, like an answer to a prayer, was a syringe of Serum 3. Forenzi had never used it on himself, but now seemed like the perfect time.

He bared his forearm and expertly gave himself an injection of his life's work.

The effect was immediate and stunning.

His fear vanished instantly, to the point where Forenzi couldn't even remember what fear felt like. It was replaced by an overwhelming sense of well-being.

He stood up, chin raised, chest out. The flames closed in around him, but Forenzi didn't care one bit. Even as his coat caught fire, it didn't matter to him. Forenzi felt invincible.

But in short order, it did begin to hurt.

Quite a lot.

As he burned, Forenzi wasn't frightened at all, even when the pain became intolerable. And it occurred to him that being scared might actually be a good thing. Soldiers without fear would rush blindly into a firefight without taking the proper precautions. Nations without fear would hit that nuclear launch without considering the consequences.

"Maybe this wasn't my best idea." Forenzi thought as the flames ignited his hair.

Then his brain boiled and he didn't think about anything anymore.

Fran

She hit the dirt, falling onto her chest, bringing up her rifle and not bothering to check if the shots had penetrated her vest or not. Fran quickly sighted the targets, all armed with handguns. An Asian man with black eyes, a woman dressed as a gypsy, also with black eyes, and a guy in a gray suit.

None of them were even attempting to take cover. They walked up the hallway, guns extended, acting as if they were bulletproof.

They weren't. Fran took them out with three quick head shots.

"Clear!" she yelled to Mal and Deb, who had all fallen back.

Then she checked herself for damage. The Kevlar had stopped the rounds, but it still hurt like hell. Like someone had worked her over with a sledgehammer.

"Help! Help!"

Fran raised her weapon, saw a woman coming at her. She had at least a dozen bleeding wounds on her, and appeared unarmed.

"It's Moni," Deb said. "She's with us!"

Fran covered her anyway.

"Frank got shot," Moni said. "Sara is with him. There's also another man who needs help. I'm getting a first aid kit. Also, someone may have started a fire."

Moni ran past. Fran got off the ground and followed Woof as he led them down two turns and straight to the wounded. There was smoke, and it was quickly filling the tunnel.

Fran glanced at the man who was shot, and the other man, who looked like he'd been dropped in a blender on puree.

She didn't see how either of them were going to survive.

But she shouldered her rifle and helped just the same.

Moni

She wasn't quite sure where she was going, but she was in a damn big hurry to get there. It didn't help that the only light she had was the matches she'd found in the lab, and she had to stop constantly to light one to see where she was.

By some extreme stroke of luck, she found the stairs to the upper level, and less than a minute later she was opening the door to Tom's room.

Her match went out as soon as she entered. As Moni began to strike another one, she heard something that scared the shit out of her.

"Hee hee hee hee."

Lighting the match, Moni saw she was standing next to a bloody guy with a gas mask on, holding a huge meat cleaver.

"Hee hee," he said.

Moni cracked him upside the head with her iron bar, and when he fell she kept beating him until he stopped moving.

"What's so goddamn funny now, asshole?"

She lit one of the candles in the room and held it while she searched, finding Tom's suitcase open on the bed. The first aid kit was on top, and Moni grabbed it and ran out of the room—

—right into that psycho who shot Frank. The one who smelled like barbecue.

She swung the metal bar, but he ducked and came up behind her, getting Moni in a choke hold. He pressed the gun to her temple.

"Time to die, whore."

Tom

Torble ran as soon as he saw Tom coming, and after rounding a corner he ducked into a room. Tom followed, going in low, and saw he was in a root cellar.

An empty root cellar.

Torble had disappeared.

Tom looked around, but the room was completely empty. No place to hide. No exits. It didn't make any sense.

Then he recalled the Butler House website, which talked extensively about secret passages and hidden staircases. Walking to the far wall, he ran his hand across the brick until he found a seam. Tom pushed against it, and it swung on hinges, exposing an old, wooden ladder.

Tom looked up, unable to see where it led. He went up anyway, climbing in the dark, expecting Torble to shoot him at any moment. The smarter thing to do was to go back, meet with the others, and get the hell out. But Tom didn't want to spend the rest of his life looking over his shoulder, waiting for Torble to come calling. He wanted to finish this, today.

The ladder ended in a small, dark room the size of a closet. Tom found a latch, pushed it open, and then he saw he was on the second floor of Butler House, the only light coming from a candle—

—that Moni held. And behind Moni…

"Hello, Detective. What are you going to do now?"

Tom aimed at Torble's head.

"Don't you remember?" Tom said. "I'm the hero, rushing in to save the day."

"Don't be stupid. You're going to drop the gun, or I'll blow this whore's head off."

"I'm not a whore anymore," Moni said. "And I'm getting goddamn sick of all these goddamn psychos trying to hurt me."

Moni thrust the candle behind her, into Torble's face.

He cried out, letting her go.

She dropped to the floor.

Tom fired three times, two in his chest and one in his head.

Then he rushed over, pulling the gun out of Torble's dead hand.

"Not bad for a pig," Moni appraised. "I got your kit. Let's go save Frank."

They ran for the stairs as smoke began to fill Butler House.

Duncan

The men in gray walked out of the house and began shooting at Josh. He watched as his Dad was hit in both legs, watched as he fell to the ground, pinning his rifle underneath his body, unable to return fire.

The men kept shooting.

Duncan jumped into the van and didn't remember anything Josh taught him.

He didn't put on his seatbelt.

He didn't check his mirrors.

He didn't put his foot on the brake when he started the engine.

He just cranked it and mashed the gas pedal to the floor, the van spinning tires, and headed straight for those assholes shooting his father. They didn't even try to get out of the way as he ran them both over, splattering the hood and windshield with blood.

Then he hit the brakes, threw the van into park, and ran to Josh.

"Dad!"

"I'm okay," he said. "Just winged in the legs. Come here."

Duncan knelt down and hugged his father, hugged him so tight.

"Nice driving, son."

Duncan began to cry. "I forgot to wear my seatbelt."

Josh patted his back. "It's okay, buddy. It's okay. You did really, really good."

And they held each other until Mom and Woof appeared with a group of people, including two wounded. A moment later, two more people came out of Butler House, a man and a woman. The woman helped Mom use a first aid kit on Dad, bandaging his legs. The man put some sort of plastic disk on another guy's chest, the guy who had been either stabbed or shot.

"I hope hope hope heaven has heroin," the shot guy said.

Then everyone got into the van and Mom drove away. Duncan watched through the back window, petting Woof, Mathison perched on his shoulder, as Butler House burned, lighting up the night sky.

Epilogue

At Bon Secours-St. Francis Hospital in Charleston, South Carolina, Dr. Frank Belgium died on the operating table at 12:52 A.M. from a gunshot wound to the chest.

He was resuscitated at 12:53 A.M.

When he regained consciousness eight hours later, he asked the duty nurse for heroin. He repeated himself three times. He was administered morphine instead.

The woman who was admitted with him, Sara Randhurst, had eighty three stitches in her fingers, which she demanded be done in Frank's room because she refused to leave his side.

Both were expected to make a full recovery. As was Chicago Homicide Detective Roy Lewis, who was treated for shock, dehydration, and multiple burns, cuts, and contusions.

Josh VanCamp, also treated for GSWs, left the hospital after treatment against doctor's orders. He and his wife Fran called an immediate press conference, where they were joined by Mal and Deb Deiter. They all spoke at length about what had occurred at Butler House, and about what happened years ago in Safe Haven, Wisconsin.

Public outcry was universal. Full investigations were demanded.

Butler House burned for two full days, until almost nothing remained. What was left was bulldozed over by the state.

During the demolition, four construction workers reported seeing ghosts, and one was fatally injured when a piece of equipment malfunctioned, crushing him. When tested later, the equipment appeared to be in perfect working order.

FOUR WEEKS LATER

Hollywood, California

Tom

The sun beat down on Tom as he sprawled out on the chaise lounge, baking him almost as brown as Roy, who occupied the chaise to his right.

The Hotel Roosevelt was one of Joan's hang outs, and she'd pulled some strings and gotten them suites for practically free. Tom's Sam Adams was almost empty, and he was going to do rock, paper, scissors with Roy for who got the next round when a very pretty little blonde in a teeny little bikini came up to them.

"Ooh, how did you get all those scars?" she asked Roy.

"I'm a cop. I was tortured for a week by some maniacs dressed as ghosts. Shot me, too. You heard of Butler House?"

The swimsuit model's eyes got wide. "Oh my gosh! You were at Butler House?"

Roy nodded. "Lemme buy you a cocktail, I'll tell you all about it."

Roy took her hand and led her to the poolside tiki bar.

"He's adjusting well," Joan said. She was in the chaise on Tom's other side. Also in a bikini, also very pretty.

"Roy doesn't remember most of it. I think he's going to be okay."

"Are you?"

He reached out and held her hand. "I'm getting better every day."

Joan took a sip of lemonade. She had to visit a shoot later, so she wasn't drinking. "That hooker. Moni. She's a real trip. Killed three of those psychos by herself. Amazing woman."

"No kidding. And she's not a hooker. She's a dominatrix. No sex. Just figging."

"What's figging?"

"You don't want to know."

Joan whipped out her iPhone and Googled it. A moment later she made a face.

"Figging is sticking a ginger root up someone's butt. It is supposed to cause an intense burning sensation. Why would anyone willingly do that?"

"I said you didn't want to know. And thanks for finding a press agent for her."

"Are you kidding? I'm going to produce the movie. There's a bidding war now for her story. Up to seven figures."

Tom shook his head, amused as hell. So she finally got her million bucks. Go, Moni.

"Am I going to be a character in the flick?" Tom asked.

"Maybe."

"Who is going to play me?"

"We're talking to Nick Cage's people."

"Nicholas Cage? Really?

"No. But Jason Alexander is interested."

"George from *Seinfeld*?"

"He's got some serious drama chops."

Tom shrugged and drained his beer. The sun felt glorious, except for on the scar on his chest, which still hurt like hell a month later. Burns sucked.

"Mind if I ask you something?" Joan said. "Something personal?"

"Shoot."

"When you were being branded, did you ever want to give up?"

Tom turned to her. "Who? Me? Of course not."

"What kept you going?"

"Thoughts of you, of course. I realized I couldn't let him break me, because then I'd never see your face again."

"Really?"

"Really."

Joan leaned over and gave him a peck on the lips. "I call bullshit."

"As soon as Torble left, I kicked out the IV to try and bleed to death."

"That I believe."

"But I did think of you."

"I'm sure."

"I did. I swear."

Tom gave her a quick, but tender, peck on the cheek.

"So you really want to quit the force?" she asked.

"Yeah. Roy and I are thinking about opening up a fishing charter business."

"In California?"

"I heard they have an ocean somewhere close."

Joan ran a finger across his belly and grinned. "I think I could get used to having you around all the time."

"I could, too."

"And I remembered something. Something you asked me about. Last time I was at your place, I was watching you take a shower."

"Pervert."

"That was the night we drank all that wine. So I think it was me who wrote *I'm watching you* on your mirror."

Tom laughed. That was the last thing that had nagged him about the whole Butler House experience, and now it had been resolved. Case closed. Time to get on with life.

"You know what?" he said.

"What?"

"I think I'd like to watch you take a shower."

"Peeping Tom, huh?" She smiled and sat up. "Race you to our room. Loser washes the winner's back."

Joan won.

But Tom was the one who really did.

Pittsburgh, Pennsylvania

Frank

Dr. Frank Belgium was sitting in his easy chair, Jack on his lap. The boy was an absolute marvel. Cute. Smart. More fun than Frank ever could have imagined.

Even if he hadn't married his mother, he would have still wanted Jack around.

"Ma ma ma," Jack said.

"I think he wants you," Frank said to Sara. "He said mama."

Sara got up off the sofa and took Jack in her arms. "He didn't say mama. He said ma ma ma. He repeated his word three times."

"Hmm. Now where do you think he picked that up?"

"Where do you think?"

"Do I do do do that?"

"Yes you do do do."

They exchanged a smile. The moment was interrupted by the doorbell.

Frank moved to get up, but Sara told him to stay put.

"I'm not an invalid, dear. The doctor said I need the exercise."

He pulled himself out of the chair, wincing at the slight pain from his still-healing wound, and used his cane to make it to the front door.

Frank didn't like what he saw in the peephole. Two men in black suits. One holding a Secret Service badge.

"Who is it?" Sara asked.

"It's for me. I've got got got it." Frank opened the door a crack. "Can I help you?"

"Dr. Frank Belgium? The President sent us. Your country needs you."

"Tell the President I'm not interested."

"Please, sir. Can we have just one moment of your time?"

Frank was thrown by how polite they were. Asking, not demanding. Reserved, not threatening.

"I'm done with all this," he said. "I have a family now."

"Believe me, Dr. Belgium, your country recognizes the sacrifices you've made, and they are appreciated. But we truly need your help. Even if it is only on an advisory basis."

Frank sighed, then let them in. "Okay, but but but let's keep it in the hallway. I don't want you upsetting my wife or son."

He let them in, and one of them handed Frank a manila folder. Frank didn't want to take it. As if sensing his reluctance, the agent opened it and held a picture for Belgium to see.

It was of a cow. A very dead cow, almost stripped to the bone.

"I'm a very good scientist, gentlemen, but even I don't think I can help help help you save that cow."

"Here is a close-up of the lower right hand section of the picture, Dr. Belgium."

He held up a second photo, grainier, zooming in to the cow's ribcage.

Perched there, staring into the camera, was a tiny, red creature with bat wings and large horns.

"Do you recognize that, Dr. Belgium? We believe it is one of the demons that escaped from the facility you worked at. Project Samhain."

The biologist made a face, and the first thought that popped into his mind escaped his lips before he could stop it.

"Uh oh."

AUTHOR NOTE

For those interested in reading the backstories of the various characters in Haunted House, here is the chronological order of the works they appear in.

ORIGIN (Dr. Frank Belgium)

THE LIST (Tom Mankowski and Roy Lewis)

SERIAL KILLERS UNCUT (Moni Draper)

AFRAID (Josh, Fran, Duncan, Woof, and Mathias VanCamp)

TRAPPED (Sara Randhurst)

ENDURANCE (Mal and Deb Dieter)

Dr. Frank Belgium will return in SECOND COMING

Tom Mankowski, Roy Lewis, and Joan DeVillers will return in THE NINE

CAST OF CHARACTERS

Mal and Deb Dieter first appeared in the Jack Kilborn novel *Endurance*, which took place at the Rushmore Inn in West Virginia. Mal is a sports reporter. He's missing his hand. Deb is an athlete who competes regularly in the Paralympics and triathlons. She has prosthetic legs.

Roy Lewis and Tom Mankowski first appeared in the JA Konrath novel *The List*, which ended in Springfield, Illinois. They have made cameos in several novels in the Jack Daniels series (*Cherry Bomb*, *Shaken*, *Stirred*). They are both Homicide Detectives that work in Chicago.

Dr. Frank Belgium first appeared in the JA Konrath novel *Origin*, working for Project Samhain in New Mexico. He's a molecular biologist and has a speech dysfluency, where he sometimes repeats the same word three times.

Sara Randhurst first appeared in the Jack Kilborn novel *Trapped*, which took place on Rock Island in Lake Michigan. She's a former guidance counselor.

Fran, Josh, and Duncan VanCamp first appeared in the Jack Kilborn novel *Afraid*, which took place in Safe Haven, Wisconsin. They live in Hawaii with their pets, a basset hound named Woof and a capuchin monkey named Mathison. Josh and Fran live off a stipend. Duncan is fifteen years old, learning how to drive.

Moni Draper is a dancer and call girl who appeared in *Serial Killers Uncut* written by Jack Kilborn and Blake Crouch. She survived encounters with two serial killers, the Gingerbread Man (*Whiskey Sour*) and Luther Kite (*Stirred*).

ALSO BY JA KONRATH

Jack Daniels Thrillers

Whiskey Sour
Bloody Mary
Rusty Nail
Dirty Martini
Fuzzy Navel
Cherry Bomb
Shaken
Stirred
Shot of Tequila
Banana Hammock
Jack Daniels Stories (collected stories)
Serial Killers Uncut (with Blake Crouch)
Suckers (with Jeff Strand)
Planter's Punch (with Tom Schreck)
Floaters (with Henry Perez)
Truck Stop (short)
Flee (with Ann Voss Peterson)
Spree (with Ann Voss Peterson)
Three (with Ann Voss Peterson)
Babe on Board (short with Ann Voss Peterson)
With a Twist (short)
Street Music (short)

Other Books

Symbios (short,writing as Joe Kimball)
Timecaster (writing as Joe Kimball)
Timecaster Supersymettry (writing as Joe Kimball)
Wild Night is Calling (short with Ann Voss Peterson)
Shapeshifters Anonymous (short)
The Screaming (short)
Afraid (writing as Jack Kilborn)
Endurance (writing as Jack Kilborn)
Trapped (writing as Jack Kilborn)
Draculas (with Blake Crouch, Jeff Strand, and F. Paul Wilson)
Origin
The List
Disturb
65 Proof (short story omnibus)
Crime Stories (collected stories)
Horror Stories (collected stories)
Dumb Jokes & Vulgar Poems
A Newbie's Guide to Publishing
Be the Monkey (with Barry Eisler)

The interior design of this book was done
by Rob Siders at http://www.52Novels.com

The cover art was done
by Carl Graves at http://extendedimagery.com

Made in the USA
Lexington, KY
30 October 2013